B'ELANNA DOVE FOR THE FLOOR AND SLAPPED HER COMBADGE. "SECURITY TO—"

One of the Chiar flicked its baton in her direction. Instantly the device shifted from a simple baton into an alien weapon. Angry red energy flashed through the air and hit B'Elanna's shoulder before she could finish her sentence. She cried out and fell.

Tom shouted and lunged for the Chiar who had shot B'Elanna. It fired the pistol at him, and he barely twisted out of the way in time. Scrambling for balance, he reached for his combadge, but it was inexplicably gone.

B'Elanna lay motionless on the deck. As Tom turned to her, the other Chiar were converging on Seven. One of them flicked its baton into a boxy shape and spoke to it. Without the translator in his combadge, Tom couldn't understand the language, but he did catch the Federation phrase *beam away* among the alien words.

"No!" Without thinking, Tom vaulted into their midst.

The blue light shimmered, faded, and left B'Elanna Torres unconscious in the shuttlebay.

STAR TREK VOYAGER®

THE NANOTECH WAR

STEVEN PIZIKS

**Based upon Star Trek
created by Gene Roddenberry,
and Star Trek: Voyager
created by Rick Berman & Michael Piller
& Jeri Taylor**

POCKET BOOKS
New York   London   Toronto   Sydney   Singapore

This book is a work of fiction. Names, characters, places and incidents are products of the author's imagination or are used fictitiously. Any resemblance to actual events or locales or persons, living or dead, is entirely coincidental.

An *Original* Publication of POCKET BOOKS

POCKET BOOKS, a division of Simon & Schuster, Inc.
1230 Avenue of the Americas, New York, NY 10020

STAR TREK is a Registered Trademark of Paramount Pictures.

This book is published by Pocket Books, a division of Simon & Schuster, Inc., under exclusive license from Paramount Pictures.

ISBN: 0-7434-3646-6

First Pocket Books printing November 2002

10 9 8 7 6 5 4 3 2 1

POCKET and colophon are registered trademarks of Simon & Schuster, Inc.

For information regarding special discounts for bulk purchases, please contact Simon & Schuster Special Sales at 1-800-456-6798 or business@simonandschuster.com

Cover art by Cliff Nielsen

Printed in the U.S.A.

To my father

THE NANOTECH WAR

CHAPTER
1

CAPTAIN KATHRYN JANEWAY clung grimly to the arms of her captain's chair as the ship bucked and shuddered beneath her.

"How much longer?" she bellowed over the noise.

"About ten minutes!" Ensign Harry Kim yelled back from the science station. The bridge lights were dimmed, indicating an ongoing emergency.

"Shields at fifty-two percent," Tuvok reported from tactical. A nearby sensor panel exploded in a noisy shower of white sparks. The lieutenant commander's calm Vulcan features didn't even twitch. Janeway, however, had to work at keeping her own face schooled into a calm she didn't feel—this ion storm was one for the record books. Even Tom Paris's boyish face was grim as he bent over the navigation board in a desperate attempt to keep the ship at least halfway steady. To Janeway's left, First Officer Chakotay's fingers stabbed madly at his own boards. Though Janeway suspected he was doing nothing but monitor data, at least he could do something. All Janeway could do was watch and issue orders.

Janeway's chair dropped several centimeters as another barrage hit the ship and her morning coffee sloshed around her stomach.

"Janeway to engineering," she said. "B'Elanna, can we go to warp yet?"

"I wouldn't, Captain," came B'Elanna's voice over the intercom. *"We'd do some serious damage to the plasma manifolds, and the injectors are already misaligned. I'm trying to route more power to the inertial dampers, but it's a losing battle."*

"Shields at forty-six percent," Tuvok said.

Janeway clamped her teeth together.

The stars on the viewscreen leaped and squiggled into white worms as another ion onslaught hit the ship. Janeway was about to tell Tom to blank the screen when something flicked past. An alarm buzzed at Tuvok's station.

"What the hell was that?" Janeway demanded. The ship shook again.

"A ship," Chakotay interjected before Tuvok could reply. "It dropped out of warp and coasted past us."

"It is emitting a distress call," Tuvok said. "The ship is damaged. I am detecting only minimal shields."

"Mr. Paris, match course and trajectory," Janeway ordered. "Tuvok, can we extend our own shields around it?"

"Extending the shields would lower them to less

than thirty percent," Tuvok replied. "An inadvisable move at this juncture."

Another panel sparked, and a small cloud of acrid smoke exploded upward. The ensign staffing it jumped back with a yelp. Automatic fire-suppression units kicked in, filling the bridge with the chemical smell of extinguisher compound.

"I'm reading one life sign on the ship," Harry Kim said. He was operating the board with his left hand. His right was currently clutching the top of his console for balance. "It's a small ship, barely big enough for a—" His eyes widened. "Captain, the ion storm is eroding the shields around that ship's warp core. Breach in one minute."

"Extend those shields, Mr. Tuvok," Janeway snapped. "Lieutenant Torres, all power to the shields."

"Yes, Captain."

Tuvok's long fingers moved swiftly but unhurriedly over his panel. "Shields extended. They are now at twenty-eight percent."

Janeway shot a glance at the viewscreen. The ship was indeed small. It looked like a needle with an octagonal disk fastened to the back. Small protrusions stuck out from each corner of the disk, and Janeway, once a science officer, made an educated guess that they were either warp nacelles, thrusters, or both.

"The other ship's warp core is stabilizing," Harry said with genuine relief. At this range a warp core breach from even so small a ship would do far more damage than any ion storm. "The life sign is also remaining steady."

Voyager shook again. Janeway's knuckles were

white on the arms of her chair. The darkened bridge was lit solely by the red-alert emergency lights, and she could still smell fire-suppression compound.

And then it stopped. The floor settled down, and the chaos simply ended. Janeway's ears rang in the sudden silence on the bridge.

"We have passed through the storm," Tuvok reported.

Janeway stood up, wincing at the cramps in her fingers. She hadn't realized how tightly she'd been gripping her chair until she let go. "Stand down red alert," she said. "All stations, I want full damage reports. Open a hailing frequency."

The computer chimed once. "Open," Tuvok reported.

"Attention alien vessel," Janeway said. "This is Captain Kathryn Janeway of the Federation Starship *Voyager*. Can you respond?"

A static-strangled voice gargled from the speakers, and the viewscreen showed a fuzzy image. Tuvok's fingers danced over his panel. Voice and picture cleared a bit. The screen showed a creature approximately the size of a large St. Bernard. It had four legs and a long segmented neck with a flattened head perched atop it. The mouth was wide, the eyes spaced far apart. A pair of arms jutted from the place where the neck met the body and ended in six-fingered hands. Janeway blinked as Tuvok's ministrations brought the creature into clearer focus. Its body was covered in some sort of coating that shifted and scintillated like strings of tiny rainbow beads caught in a breeze. Janeway's mind tried to find a pattern to the movement and failed. It was simultaneously beautiful and unnerving.

The creature was working in a cloud of smoke. Wires and bits of equipment dangled from panels that gaped like open sores. Janeway winced in sympathy. Another wash of static distorted the image for a moment.

"*. . . your help,*" the creature said, voice still slightly garbled. "*I would otherwise have been destroyed.*"

"Is your ship heavily damaged?" Janeway rose and walked closer to the viewscreen.

"*Yes. Many of my systems are nonoperational. Who are you? I was unable to understand the first part of your broadcast.*"

Janeway repeated the information.

"*Federation starship?*" The creature ducked its head in what looked to Janeway like confused curiosity. "*You are a part of an intergalactic federation? Have you then been watching us?*"

"We are a member of a galactic federation, yes," Janeway said. "But we haven't been observing your civilization. Our presence here is coincidence. We were stranded in this quadrant several years ago, and we're trying to make our way home. The ion storm caught us just as it did you," she concluded. "My name is Captain Kathryn Janeway."

"*And my name is Zedrel Vu of the planet Chi.*" Zedrel's head leaned forward, as if to get a better look at Janeway and her crew. "*I . . . that is, perhaps it would be . . . I mean, I should say . . .*" Zedrel smacked broad lips in a sound Janeway took for exasperation or uncertainty, though she had nothing but instinct to base this on. "*I beg your pardon, Cap-*"

tain Kathryn Janeway. I am the first—" More static. *"—travel outside our own solar system and I was unaware that I would meet another species so—"* Static. *"—not trained as a diplomat."*

Uh-oh, Janeway thought. *Sounds like first contact.* She raised an eyebrow at Chakotay.

"His ship does have warp drive," the first officer reminded her, adding. "Or it did until a few minutes ago."

Janeway nodded. Her thoughts were running the same way. Starfleet's Prime Directive forbade contact with any species that was not already capable of warp travel, but the Chi had just barely passed that threshold. This *was,* however, still a first-contact situation, and such were always delicate. There was no way to know exactly how a given species would react to the new knowledge that other forms of life populated the galaxy. First-contact situations therefore made Janeway a little edgy.

"Do I understand, correctly, that this is your people's first warp ship?" Janeway asked carefully.

"It is," Zedrel replied. *"I—"* Static. *"—and built it myself. With the government's aid, of course. People already call it the Zedrel Drive."*

Janeway couldn't decide whether the remark was meant to be self-deprecating, boastful, or merely matter-of-fact, so she ignored it. "Do you need further assistance?" she said instead.

"I haven't fully assessed the damage yet," Zedrel admitted.

"The vessel's 'Zedrel Drive,' " Tuvok said with, possibly, a note of irony in his voice, "has been rendered inoperative by the ion storm, as have its thrusters. The ship appears to have spent only a fraction of a second at warp before the drive went offline, and it is uncertain whether the problem arose from the ion storm or faults in the engine design. Life support is functional. Communications are functional but starting to fail. The ship is completely unarmed."

"An excellent damage report, Mr. Tuvok," Janeway said. "Do you suppose you could also assemble one for *my* ship?"

"Of course, Captain," Tuvok replied, not seeming to notice the sarcasm.

Janeway turned back to the viewscreen. "Captain Zedrel—"

"I'm not really a captain," Zedrel interrupted, and a spurt of static disrupted the image. *"—an engineer."*

"Engineer Zedrel, then," Janeway continued, nonplussed. "Our ship has also been damaged by the storm. Once we've assessed the extent of it, may I contact you again and see what we can accomplish? Perhaps together we can ensure our mutual safety."

"A fine idea, Captain."

Janeway nodded. Was Zedrel staring at her? Perhaps that was the custom of his people. Unplanned first contacts were always complicated. With no background data there was no way to tell if you—or they—were being polite or abrupt, helpful or offensive. A word or phrase could lead to war, peace, or the accidental betrothal of your firstborn child. The best you could hope for was that everyone would understand you were trying to be polite. In this case, it looked as if *Voyager* was in some position of power, but there could be factors Janeway knew nothing about.

Zedrel's wide-spaced eyes continued to fix on Janeway, and the odd body covering glimmered and shifted.

"Good luck to you, then," she said. "We'll contact you soon. *Voyager* out."

The screen went blank, and Kathryn Janeway heaved a small sigh of relief.

"I can't give you more than warp one, and then only for short bursts," reported B'Elanna Torres. The bar on the collar of her uniform gleamed softly in the subdued light of the conference room. Although Torres was Janeway's chief engineer, the bar indicated her status as a provisional officer. A few tiny braids had been artfully woven into her shoulder-length brown hair.

Torres's husband, Lieutenant Tom Paris, sandy-haired and blue-eyed, sat to her left. Harry Kim kept his hands folded on the table next to Tuvok. Seven of Nine stood against one bulkhead like a statue, hands behind her back, features even more impassive than Tuvok's. Her severely styled blond hair and blue-gray eyes combined with the Borg implant over her left eye to make her expression seem even stonier. The Doctor drummed his fingers with a hint of holographic impatience.

"The impulse engines and life-support systems weren't even touched," Torres continued. "But the plasma injectors are a mess, and the—"

"Bottom line, B'Elanna," Janeway interrupted. "How long are we talking for repairs?"

"Without a shipyard or a station? Ten days if we're lucky. I'm betting on twelve. We also lost almost half our stock of dilithium."

"What?" Janeway said, still trying to take in the idea of spending ten days on repairs. "How?"

"When we extended the shields to protect the 'Zedrel Drive,' " Tuvok said, "enough ionic radiation penetrated cargo hold seven to irradiate the dilithium stored there. It has been rendered useless."

"We can continue recrystalizing what we have," Torres put in. "But having such a small stockpile makes me nervous."

Janeway puffed out her cheeks. "What else?"

"Sickbay is running perfectly," the Doctor said smugly. "I've successfully treated five cases of mild radiation poisoning and a dozen minor injuries related to the turbulence. Nothing serious."

"Long-range sensors were hit pretty hard," Harry said. "Short-range seem to be all right. There's still a lot of leftover radiation washing this sector, though, so I wouldn't count on using the transporters until it clears up."

"Not unless you want to arrive looking like one of Neelix's soufflés," Tom interjected wryly.

"The astrometrics lab has taken minor damage and requires repair," Seven said. "I assume, however, that you would prefer I assist in engineering."

Janeway got up to stand behind her chair. "You assume rightly. B'Elanna, how long would repairs take if we had the facilities of a shipyard or space station?"

Torres shrugged. "It would depend on the facilities. A full-blown shipyard could have us up and running in a few hours. A decent space station? I'd guess a couple of days, maybe three."

"Well, then, I think it's time we had another talk with Engineer Zedrel." Janeway headed for the door as the crew scrambled to their feet behind her.

Back on the bridge Chakotay looked up from his panel as the bridge crew relieved their substitutes and took their places. Torres and Seven both headed for the turbolift to engineering.

"How bad is it?" Chakotay asked. Without sitting down, Janeway gave a quick explanation, and he grimaced. "Could be worse."

"Could be better," Janeway said. "Mr. Tuvok, open a hailing frequency."

"Open."

"Engineer Zedrel, this is Captain Janeway."

Static crackled across the main screen again, and a distorted Zedrel shuddered into view. The odd body coating continued to shimmer and shift, though it had settled into varying shades of blue instead of the rainbow riot Janeway had seen earlier. *"Captain. I have just now completed my damage survey."*

"As have we." Judiciously, she explained their situation. "What's your status?"

"The ion storm destroyed most of my tool and repair programs," Zedrel reported. *"I am unable—"* Static. *"—than the most rudimentary work. The only systems that seem to be operational are life support and communication."* The picture fuzzed out for a moment, then came back into focus like a candle

that would soon gutter out. *". . . will probably fail soon as well. I will be stranded."*

Janeway raised her voice. "We can tow you back to your planet if you send us the coordinates."

"Gratitude, Captain. I am sure my people would also—" The screen fuzzed again. *". . . gratitude. Perhaps we—"* More static. *"—your repairs at our orbiting station."*

"That would be most kind," Janeway said, mentally filling in the gaps. "Perhaps you should send us the coordinates before your communications system fails completely."

". . . course, Captain."

"Got 'em," said Tom Paris at the helm just as Zedrel's image vanished entirely from the screen.

"Engineer Zedrel's communication system has gone off-line," Tuvok reported.

"We're about four hours away by impulse," Paris added. "B'Elanna will be happy—we don't even have to think about going to warp."

"Set a course, Mr. Paris," Chakotay ordered. "Tuvok, put a tractor beam on Zedrel's ship and let's get moving." He turned to Janeway. "What did Zedrel mean by 'tool and repair programs'? Do you think his ship is automated?"

"I was wondering the same thing." Janeway took her seat. "Zedrel is the only one on board. Doesn't that seem strange to you? You'd think these Chiar would send more than one person out to test something as important as their first warp drive."

On the viewscreen a green beam of light flashed out and caught Zedrel's needle-like ship. Chakotay shrugged. "Maybe they wanted to minimize the risk.

Something goes wrong, only one person is in trouble instead of an entire crew."

"But if something goes seriously wrong—as it certainly did—you'd want to have at least one more person to help with repairs, don't you think?"

"Perhaps," Chakotay said philosophically. "We can ask when we get to Chi."

CHAPTER

2

JANEWAY TOSSED THE PADD ASIDE. It clattered on her ready room desk, and she rubbed her face with a heavy sigh. The Federation prided itself on having regulations and guidelines to cover every first-contact situation a Starfleet captain might encounter. *First Contact with a Warp-Capable Species That the Federation Has Been Observing:* Section II, Subsection A. *First Contact (Accidental) with a Post-Industrial Species That Has Not Developed Warp Capability:* Section III, Subsection B. *First Contact with a Species That Previously Had No Concept of Alien Life and Therefore Wants to Destroy All Other Species:* Section XIII, Subsection D.

Janeway reached for her coffee mug. Unfortunately, Starfleet didn't seem to have any specific rules and regs for First Contact with a Species That Has Just Field-Tested Its First Warp Drive Somewhat Unsuccessfully Right Under the Nose of a Starfleet Vessel Which Is Lost In a Foreign Quadrant and Doesn't Intend to Stick Around Any Longer Than It Takes to Make Basic Repairs.

She would have to wing it.

Janeway sipped the bitter brew Neelix had conjured up for her from the galley. He called it "coffee," though it bore only a passing resemblance to the real thing. At first she had started drinking it so as not to hurt his feelings and to save on replicator rations, but over time it had begun to grow on her.

The padd lay quietly on her desk. Janeway grimaced and was reaching for it again when the door chime rang.

"Come in," she called.

The door hissed open to grant Chakotay entry. He was half a head taller than Janeway, with the chiseled features and facial tattoos of his heritage. His movements were relaxed and fluid as he approached her desk, a striking contrast to Janeway, who felt stiff as a board after her study.

"We're about ten minutes from Chi," Chakotay told her. "The residual ionic radiation has faded some, so the transporters are safe again. Any luck with the regs?"

Janeway shook her head. "Not really. I guess I'll have to make it up as I go."

"It seems like we do that a lot," Chakotay said with a wry smile.

"No disagreements there." Janeway stood up and stretched, wincing as her back and shoulders popped. "When we get back to the Alpha Quadrant, I'm going to spend the next decade in front of the review board, I just know it. Has Zedrel—or anyone else—tried to contact us?"

Chakotay shook his head. "Zedrel's communication system must still be down." He paused. "Is Zedrel a 'he' or a 'she,' do you think?"

Janeway laughed. "I've been wondering about that, too." She headed for the door. "For all we know, the Chiar have only one sex. Or a dozen."

"Zedrel strikes me as male," Chakotay said, following. "I can't put my finger on why."

"Just be prepared to adjust your perceptions when we learn more about them."

The bridge was calm, filled with the soft hum of the ship and beeps of panel displays. Various crewmen glanced at Janeway as she took her chair, Chakotay beside her. An engineer was working on the panel that had exploded during the ion storm. The viewscreen showed Zedrel's ship still bathed in the emerald light of the tractor beam.

"We're within sensor range of the planet Chi, Captain," Harry Kim said. "M-class planet, second from the sun. One moon—uninhabited—one space station, and several hundred satellites in orbit. And Captain—I'm detecting considerable dilithium deposits."

"Do they know we're coming?" Janeway asked.

Harry shook his head. "I don't know. We haven't been scanned that I can tell, but they may have sensors we can't detect."

"Put the station on screen."

The stars vanished, replaced by a blue octagonal disk, the same shape as Zedrel's ship, though much larger. A hemispherical hub was set on either side of the disk, and windows peppered many of the surfaces. It wasn't ring-shaped, which told Janeway that either the Chi had developed gravity generators or they didn't mind working in weightlessness. Spinning an octagonal space station to simulate gravity would be fraught with problems. As she watched, several smaller objects—ships, presumably,—coasted up to the station or drifted away from it. Ground-to-orbit shuttles, then, were common. Another bit of information for the mix.

It occurred to Janeway that this situation was very similar to the time when the Vulcans first contacted humans. Right after the legendary Zephram Cochran had tested his new ship, a passing Vulcan ship had spotted the warp trail and followed it back to Earth, sparking the eventual genesis of the Federation. Now Janeway was playing the part of the Vulcans. The humans had greeted the Vulcans with peace, friendliness, and, according to some historians, a fair amount of whisky. How would the Chiar greet *Voyager?*

May as well get this started, Janeway thought, and ordered Tuvok to open a hailing frequency. She schooled her features into neutrality and reminded herself that if she smiled, she should do it close-mouthed. Although humans saw smiling as a friendly gesture, some species regarded it as baring one's teeth.

"Attention, Chiar station," she said. "This is Captain Kathryn Janeway of the Federation Starship *Voyager.* We come with peaceful intent. Engineer Zedrel Vu encountered an ion storm that damaged his ship, though Zedrel himself is uninjured. We have offered him aid and are assisting his return to you. Please respond." Janeway paused and waited.

She didn't feel overly tense, but there was still a certain feeling of stress in the air.

"No response," Tuvok said after a few moments.

"Continue broadcasting that message on a multi-band carrier," she said. "Tom, slow to half impulse."

"Half impulse," Paris said, and tapped his console.

"Mr. Kim, scan the station for—"

"Captain," Tuvok interrupted, "I am receiving a transmission."

Janeway lifted a hand. "On screen, then."

Another Chiar appeared on the screen. This one was a bit larger than Zedrel and was flanked by two other Chiar whose faces were wrinkled and creased in what Janeway could only call consternation. The delicate shimmering substance covered all three of them just as it had covered Zedrel. A fourth Chiar head poked itself into the picture. Someone who wasn't visible spoke a sharp word, and the head hastily withdrew.

"Attention, Captain Kathryn Janeway of the Federation Starship Voyager," said the first Chiar. *"My name is Nashi Ki, Secretary of State and Chief Diplomat of the Goracar Alliance of Chi. I welcome you on behalf of the Chiar people and extend gratitude for your assistance. This is an historic moment for us. We were . . . we were not expecting so early to meet an alien . . . that is, another species in our explorations. Until now we had no proof that other life-forms existed. Your arrival is causing a stir."*

Janeway smiled without showing her teeth. "I can imagine, Secretary Ki."

"Secretary Nashi is my correct title, actually," Nashi said politely. *"And how properly should I address you?"*

"As Captain or Captain Janeway."

"Captain Janeway," Nashi repeated. *"Captain, I am frankly uncertain what sort of protocol to apply to this situation. In advance I hope you will forgive me and my people if I say or do anything that causes offense out of ignorance."*

Janeway relaxed slightly. "And I hope you and your people will do the same for us."

The two other Chiar, meanwhile, remained still and quiet, though colors continued to ripple across their bodies. They looked at Janeway with what seemed to be curiosity, but they didn't stare with the same intensity Zedrel had. Janeway decided not to ask who they were, opting instead to see if Nashi would introduce them instead.

"May I speak with Engineer Zedrel?" Nashi said. *"His family is relieved to hear he is uninjured, but they are understandably concerned still."*

Janeway awarded the Chiar silent points as a species—Nashi's first concern was for Zedrel's safety and not whether his warp drive had been successful. She quickly corrected that instinct. Just because one Chiar demonstrated compassion didn't mean that all, or even most, other Chiar had the same trait.

"Engineer Zedrel's communication system malfunctioned soon after we rescued him from the ion storm," Janeway said. "But as I said, he himself is uninjured."

"And the drive? Did it function? And from where do you come? Do you have a specific mission with Chi? Can we—" Nashi broke off with a chuffing noise. *"Apologies, Captain. I am supposed to be a*

diplomat, but my tongue seems to have run away from me."

Janeway leaned an elbow on the back of Paris's chair. As protocol dictated, Paris and the rest of the bridge remained silent and bent over their tasks, though Janeway caught them sneaking as many looks as they could at the Chiar. No matter how many alien species they came across, a new one was always fascinating.

"Perfectly understandable, Secretary," Janeway said cheerfully. "The short answer to your first question is that the Zedrel Drive was a qualified success."

The two Chiar in the background shook their heads like a pair of dogs shaking off bathwater. A sign of what? Mirth? Glee? Disappointment? Secretary Nashi's eyes widened. *"It works, then? Praise to the moon!"*

"It was a *qualified* success," Janeway said. "According to our readings, Engineer Zedrel stayed in warp for only a fraction of a second before both our ships were hit by an ion storm." She went on to describe the storm and the rescue. "As a result, Secretary," she concluded, "we find ourselves in a difficult position. Our ship also needs extensive repairs, and they will be difficult to complete in space before the next storm hits."

"Then you must use our station and its facilities," Nashi said promptly. *"It would only be proper after you rescued Zedrel. I insist, Captain."*

Janeway smiled again. "And we express our gratitude."

"There are, perhaps, other arrangements we can make, do you think?"

"Such as?" Janeway replied cautiously. Around

her, she could feel the rest of the crew come quietly alert.

"Trade," Nashi said, and the other two Chiar shook their heads again. *"There must be many things you have that would interest us and many things we have that would interest you."*

"I see." Less tense now, Janeway stood upright and put her hands behind her back. "We are actually running a bit short on dilithium, Secretary. Perhaps we could—"

"Why, the very thing!" Nashi interrupted. *"Captain, we must talk indeed!"*

"I should introduce you to our . . . trade ambassador, Neelix," Janeway said. "Would a few of you like to come aboard to negotiate? Or would you prefer to do so on your station?"

Nashi's eyes widened again. *"Come aboard your ship? Captain, I find you honor me."*

"I can make arrangements to transport you aboard as soon as we're within range, if you agree," Janeway said.

"Transport? You mean with a shuttle?"

"We have a more direct method," Janeway said. "A device that will bring you instantly from your station to our ship."

Nashi's head reared back slightly. *"I look forward to experiencing this device, Captain, when you are ready. Truly, this will be a day of history."*

"This is my first officer, Chakotay," Janeway continued. Chakotay, recognizing a cue, rose and came forward. "He will contact you once we're within transporter range and arrange for you and your entourage to come aboard."

Nashi's head bobbed once. *"Then I look forward to hearing from him."*

They exchanged formal farewells, and the screen blinked back to a view of the station again.

"That went well," Tom Paris said from his boards.

"Yes," Janeway agreed. "I'm almost suspicious. Commander Chakotay, once we're within transporter range, hail Secretary Nashi and bring him or her aboard. I'm going to look at a few more regulations. Mr. Tuvok, what is the status of Zedrel's ship?"

"Unchanged. The tractor beam is holding steady."

"Captain." Ensign Harry Kim raised a hand for her attention. "There's an . . . anomaly I think you'll want to look at."

There's always something. Janeway crossed the bridge and mounted the short flight of stairs that led up to the ops station. "What is it, Mr. Kim?"

Harry stepped aside to give her a better view of the console. "The planet has four continents. Sensors can't read one of them."

"Can't read?" Janeway bent over the boards. "What do you mean? Why not?"

"As far as I can tell, there's some kind of energy wave pulsing around the shore." Kim's fingers danced expertly across the panel, and the tiny screen conjured up an image of Chi. Like most M-class worlds, it had oceans of a gentle sapphirine blue. Three of the land masses showed various shades of brown and green. Preliminary readouts on atmospheric makeup, humidity, ozone levels, wind velocities, seismic activity, ocean depth, gravity, polar ice density, and other data scrolled beside the image. One irregular chunk of the planet was black. A pulse of light skimmed steadily and swiftly around the outer edge. Another readout indicated the pulse's frequency and strength.

"Microwave?" Janeway said in surprise.

"Confirmed," Tuvok said from his own station. "It appears to be some kind of microwave pulse emitted by a series of orbiting satellites."

"And it's interfering with sensor readings and transporter locks," Harry put in. "For all practical purposes, the fourth continent is invisible to us and the transporters."

"We could just look out the window," Paris said.

Kim ignored him and tapped the display again. The image backed away until the planet was a tiny dot. Curtains of energy that reminded Janeway of Terran northern lights coruscated across the screen. "I'm also reading higher-than-normal levels of background ionic radiation. Ion storms are definitely a regular event around here. My best guess says the next one will hit within eight days."

"That is two days earlier than Lieutenant Torres estimated completion of repairs," Tuvok said.

"And we won't be able to count on the transporters if ionic radiation levels increase," Janeway murmured. "Lovely. Mr. Tuvok, can that microwave pulse be used as a weapon against this ship?"

Tuvok checked his readings, his dark Vulcan features their usual impassive mask. "Doubtful, Captain. The pulse would not even be able to penetrate *Voyager*'s hull. Our shields will be sufficient."

Janeway gnawed her lower lip and continued to examine the ops station data. "So what are they keeping down there?"

"Perhaps," Chakotay said, "we should ask Nashi. Or maybe we should bring Zedrel aboard and ask him."

"I am reading something else of interest, Captain," Tuvok said from his own station. "It would appear the Chiar have a stockpile of rhometric weapons."

Janeway stared at him. "Rhometric? What kind of idiots would keep rhometric weapons on their own planet?" A volatile mix of compounds distinguished by a core of unstable dilithium, a rhometric reaction could render vast areas of land uninhabitable for generations.

"Indeed," Tuvok said. "In any case, the weapons readings are accompanied by a supply of chemical propellant, so I assume the weapons themselves are delivered by missile. They would pose little threat to *Voyager,* though if one got through our shields, it would irradiate a large part of the ship."

"What are the chances of that happening, Commander?" Chakotay said.

"Negligible," Tuvok replied. "Even a weak phaser blast would destroy the missile, and a simple shield would keep the radiation from affecting us. However, I felt it advisable to mention their presence."

"Noted," Janeway said as an alarm beeped softly on Tuvok's panel. She closed her eyes. "Now what, Mr. Tuvok?"

"It appears," Tuvok replied, "that Engineer Zedrel has managed to repair his communications array. I am detecting a faint audio signal being broadcast to the station."

"Can you read it?" Janeway asked, instantly suspicious.

In answer, the speakers came to life. The voices

were filled with static, but Janeway recognized Zedrel and Nashi.

". . . fascinating people, Secretary," Zedrel was saying. *"I would have found my way back never if it were not for them. They are clearly far more advanced than we."*

"We must be cautious, Engineer," Nashi admonished. *"It would be a lie to say they do not frighten me, even though they have done nothing aggressive. Thus far."*

"Secretary," Zedrel's voice was pleading, *"you must allow me to come on board with you. This is a dream for me—the chance to meet an alien species and see from the inside their ship! They are a captivating, fascinating people, and Captain Janeway seems to me trustworthy."*

"You are not a diplomat, Engineer," Nashi countered. *"She saved you, but she may have an ulterior motive. I myself found her a pleasant person, if very strange to look at"*— Chakotay raised an eyebrow at Janeway, who shrugged—*"but that means nothing. We must act with caution."*

"I still want to come aboard. I think I have earned it."

Nashi sighed. *"You have certainly paid enough, Engineer Zedrel. Very well. I will ask their Commander Chakotay if this can be arranged."* Nashi paused. *"I am glad Captain Janeway referred to Chakotay as 'he.' Janeway immediately struck me as female, but this Chakotay was a mystery."*

Tom Paris coughed wildly, and Harry Kim put a hand to his own mouth. Chakotay sighed.

"Monitor the rest of the conversation yourself, Mr.

Tuvok," Janeway said. "Let me know if anything else of interest turns up. I have more regulations to read." She strode for her ready room, fighting to supress a smile.

Commander Chakotay was striding for the transporter room when he almost ran into Seven of Nine as she emerged from a side corridor. She was staring down at a padd instead of watching where she was going. He caught her by the shoulders just before they would have collided, and her gaze snapped upward. Chakotay found himself trying to puzzle out whether her eyes were more blue or gray.

Gray, he decided.

"My apologies, Commander," Seven said. "I was not paying attention."

"No harm done," Chakotay replied. He realized he was still holding her shoulders. He quickly dropped his hands. "What are you working on? Must be pretty intense," he said to cover his consternation.

Seven tilted the padd closer to her chest, though Chakotay was hardly adept at reading upside-down. "It is a new holodeck program."

They fell into step together, though Seven was careful not to let the padd display tip into Chakotay's field of view. He was seized with a wild impulse to snatch it away.

"What's it about?" he asked.

Seven blanked the padd screen. "It is unimportant."

"It had your attention so riveted that you almost knocked me flat," Chakotay teased. "Come on—what's it about?"

Seven gave him a long look. "It is an educational program."

"Who for? Naomi?"

"It is for me." Seven reactivated the padd and tapped at it as they walked. She kept her gaze down, as if she were . . . embarrassed? Chakotay had never thought of Seven as someone who got embarrassed. Probably it was simple uncertainty.

"If it makes you uncomfortable to tell me about it," he said, "don't feel you have to—"

"It does not," Seven said, still looking at the padd. "It is just something I did not feel you would . . . take an interest in."

"Try me," he said. "If it's boring, I'll let my face go all slack and disinterested so you'll know."

That actually elicited a small smile from her. "You are as persistent as Mr. Neelix."

"Did you tell *him* what it was?"

"No, though he was most insistent."

Chakotay laughed. "Fine, don't tell me, either. Keep it a secret. My feelings won't be hurt."

"Good." She continued to work.

"Uh, Seven? That was sarcasm."

She looked at him. "So your feelings *will* be hurt if I don't tell you."

"Maybe a little," he said airily. Then he made a mental pause. That sounded like something Tom Paris would have said.

It was disconcerting.

". . . comply."

He blinked. "What?"

"If my reticence would hurt your feelings," Seven said, "then I must comply. The holodeck program is meant to help me . . . recapture my childhood."

Chakotay shook his head. "I don't understand."

"Every human has a childhood," Seven explained. "But I did not. I was assimilated by the Borg at age six, years before my childhood would have come to an end. I am aware that my background sometimes makes it . . . difficult to interact with people, and I have lately come to wonder if part of that is because—"

"—you had a deprived childhood?" Chakotay interjected.

"An interesting way to put it," she said, and frowned. "But, yes. I have been observing Naomi Wildman as well as teaching her." Naomi Wildman was the daughter of Ensign Wildman and the only child on the ship. "She has a certain . . . exuberance that I have come to admire, and I suspect that certain human behaviors stem from recalling this childish—"

"Childlike," Chakotay corrected amiably.

"Childlike behavior," Seven finished. "Tom Paris, for example."

Chakotay laughed again. "Want some help with it?"

"I had considered asking Naomi Wildman to join me," Seven admitted. "But I ultimately decided that it might compromise our teacher-student relationship."

"I meant me, Seven," Chakotay said.

Seven stopped. "But you are not a child."

"No," Chakotay was forced to admit. "But I do remember what it was like. I might be able to give you a few pointers the holodeck computer might miss."

"I would appreciate that," Seven said. "I have holodeck two reserved for nineteen hundred hours. Please be on time." And she walked away.

Chakotay blinked, and realized he was standing outside the door to transporter room one.

Seven of Nine kept her face an impassive mask as she walked up the corridor. This was a new feeling, and she wasn't sure what it meant. She found it oddly pleasing that Chakotay had asked to join her in what she had intended as a private holoprogram. Pleasure, of course, was nothing new. It was pleasing to sing a new aria with the Doctor. It was pleasing to focus the astrometric sensors on a rare type of nebula and recover new data. It was even pleasing to sample certain of Neelix's recipes in the mess hall, especially when he had created something new just for her. But this was pleasing in a different way. She couldn't quite explain how it was different, and that bothered her.

As she continued her way to the turbolift, she found herself thinking more and more about her conversation with Commander Chakotay. It felt as if she could still feel his hands on her shoulders when he stopped her from colliding with him, and this, too, was pleasing. Everything was pleasing.

Perhaps she would have to find a different word.

The turbolift opened and Seven ordered it to take her to engineering. Now that *Voyager* had arrived at Chi, the Captain would go through a certain amount of diplomatic maneuvering before the ship would be allowed to dock with the Chiar space station, even though the Chiar had agreed to it. There would be first meetings, speeches, and tours of the ship. A waste of time, in Seven's estimation. It would be so much simpler and make more sense for Janeway to tell the Chiar that *Voyager* required repairs, and since Janeway and the crew had saved their Engineer Zedrel, the Chiar owed a debt of obligation. Experience, however, had taught Seven that this approach rarely worked for the Federation. They were unwilling to take the steps necessary to ensure efficient compliance from the lesser civilizations.

Decks fled rapidly by as the turbolift dropped toward engineering. After the diplomacy, Lieutenant Torres and the rest of the engineers would have to take stock of the station's facilities before beginning repairs. Seven was sure she could find efficient ways to facilitate the process, though once again experience had taught her that it would take a certain amount of (inefficient) diplomacy of her own to make Torres understand that her ideas were superior.

Chakotay had known Torres longer than anyone else on the ship. Perhaps she would ask him about it.

Commander Chakotay stood at the base of the transporter pad. He had already caught Bethany Marija, former Maquis and now transporter technician, hiding a smile as she stood at the controls. For a dreadful moment he thought he had said or done something to let slip his recent thoughts about Seven. Then he realized it was probably that Nashi's remarks about Chakotay's gender were making the rounds. *Voyager*'s grapevine was operating with its usual efficiency, no doubt due in large part to Tom Paris.

Tuvok, who was standing behind him, was oblivious to Marija's amusement. "Do you have both sets of coordinates, Crewman?" he asked.

"Yes, sir," Marija said. "Zedrel is on his ship, and the secretary is waiting with two other Chiar on the station. I can bring all four of them here at the same time."

"Energize," Chakotay said.

The soft metallic hum of the transporter swelled, and four columns of blue light shimmered on the platform. Then an alarm blared on Marija's boards. The light columns instantly vanished, and the transporter powered down.

"What happened?" Chakotay demanded, turning around. Marija was scanning her panel, fingers flicking quickly at the sensors. Her expression registered puzzled surprise.

"Sensors detected nanites, Commander," she said. "Trillions of them."

"Nanites?" Chakotay's stomach turned over, and he immediately came around to Marija's side of the controls. "Where? In Nashi's body?"

"Yes, sir. And in the bodies of Zedrel and the others." Marija pointed to the monitor that was reporting the alarm. "According to this, nanites make up almost a fifth of their mass. The transporters automatically classified the Chiar as a threat and aborted the transport."

"A sensible precaution." Tuvok murmured.

Chakotay silently concurred. Microscopic Borg nanoprobes, similar to nanites, had been designed to assimilate people and technology into the Borg Collective—and destroy a person's own identity in the process. As a result, the Borg were one of the most feared and hated forces in known space. The fact that the Chiar used nanites in quantities that would stagger even the Borg . . . The very thought sent ice running down Chakotay's back.

Chakotay's combadge beeped. *"Commander, what's going on down there?"* asked Janeway's voice. *"I've got Secretary Nashi on the screen in my ready room."*

He tapped his badge in response and explained what Marija had told him. There was brief silence.

"I see," Janeway said slowly. *"Janeway out."*

"Crewman Marija," Tuvok said, "did any nanites manage to slip through during transport?"

Bethany Marija checked her display again, and Chakotay glanced sharply at Tuvok. Had he heard a bit of strain in the Vulcan's usually steady voice? Then Chakotay remembered that Tuvok, along with Janeway and Torres, had once infiltrated the Borg by allowing themselves to be assimilated. Tuvok's neural suppressant, however, hadn't functioned as well as planned.

"The transport was aborted before anything arrived, Commander," Marija was saying. "Internal sensors aren't detecting any nanites."

To the untrained eye, Tuvok's expression didn't change. Over the last several years, however, Chakotay had learned to read some of the tiny subtleties in the Vulcan's face and thought he detected relief.

"In that case," Chakotay said, "we'll have to wait and see what the captain decides."

CHAPTER
3

CAPTAIN KATHRYN JANEWAY clenched her toes beneath her ready-room desk so she wouldn't tap her fingers on the console. Although she doubted the Chiar would notice a nervous habit in humans, there was no point in taking the risk.

Secretary Nashi's wide eyes blinked at her from the viewscreen, and Janeway found herself perversely wishing the universal translator worked on body language as well as the spoken word. True, the Chiar would also be able to read Janeway's gestures, but right now she would have given a lot to have even a hint of what Nashi was thinking.

"Our people view the . . . excessive use of nanites with great caution," Janeway explained. "That was why the transport failed."

"Excessive use?" Nashi said, apparently bewildered. *"Captain, among my people I am in this*

32

arena considered quite moderate." She held out one arm, and the shimmering colors swirled and danced.

"Is that a coating of nanites on your skin?" Janeway asked in what she hoped was a neutral voice.

"In a way," Nashi said. *"My nanites are a part of me. Literally."*

"Literally? I don't understand."

"I don't know how familiar you are with nanotechnology, Captain. It would be difficult to explain."

Janeway leaned forward slightly in her chair. "Let's assume I know next to nothing but have a good background in robotics."

"Very well. Nanites are tiny robots, and some are so small they can actually operate within individual cells. All Chiar have them. They are integrated with our nervous systems."

"I'm with you so far," Janeway said.

"When I want something done, this desire creates a very specific chemical change in my brain cells—I would imagine a similar thing happens in your own brain, Captain—and my nanites read and decode those chemical changes. They then do what I want done."

"And what is it that you might want done, Secretary?" Janeway asked.

A wave of purple shifted across Nashi's body. *"Dozens of things. The nanites keep us free of disease, and they heal damage more quickly than our bodies could do on their own. They change the molecular composition of my outer coating into—"*

Janeway leaned further forward. "What do you mean by 'outer coating'?"

Nashi held up a shimmering rainbow arm. *"As I*

said, this is not my skin, Captain. Nor is it all nanites. It is also partly a special composition, a series of polymers that reacts well to small molecular shifts. My nanites can change it into whatever is appropriate for my situation—thick for cold weather, thin for warm, and so on. It can even serve as crude armor, if necessary."

Janeway cocked her head, fascinated despite herself. To her knowledge, not even the Borg used nanotechnology this extensively. "What else do you use them for?"

"We use them to alter these." Nashi held up a short, thick rod.

"And this is . . . ?"

"A universal tool," Nashi explained. *"It's a synthesis of several materials. If I need a particular tool, my nanites rearrange the materials into what I need. Like this."* Nashi shook the rod once. It flicked and changed into a multiheaded tool Janeway didn't recognize. *"The tool also contains an energy cell so we can form power tools. Provided we have the proper program, that is."*

"Proper program," Janeway echoed faintly.

"Of course," Nashi responded, seemingly a bit surprised. *"Even an engineer couldn't visualize a tool or component perfectly down to the last micrometer. We upload programs to our nanites so that if I think 'span wrench' or 'warm clothes,' my nanites know what to build. Each object is a separate program, you see."*

Light dawned on Janeway. "Did Engineer Zedrel use nanites to repair and maintain his ship, then?"

"Of course. We would hardly send him out on such a mission with nanites not programmed to han-

dle repairs. The programs were expensive, of course, but well worth it. Fortunately Engineer Zedrel comes from a wealthy family, so he could supplement the governmental allocations."

"And his tool and repair programs were damaged in the ion storm," Janeway said, half to herself. "That's why he couldn't repair his own ship and why he was the only one on board."

"Yes," Nashi said. Her head bobbed sideways on her segmented neck. *"Captain, are you telling me your people do not have this technology in any form? I find this very hard to believe."*

Janeway shook her head, then realized that Nashi may not recognize the gesture. "We don't use it," she admitted. "But as I said, my people treat nanotechnology with extreme caution. There was an . . . incident involving nanites on another of our ships, one called the *Enterprise*. And then there are the Borg."

"The Borg?" Nashi echoed.

"An alien species that uses nanoprobes to . . . alter other species and change them and their technology into other Borg."

Nashi's outer coating went white, then black. *"That is . . . that is disgusting! Are these Borg nearby?"*

"Not that we know of," Janeway reassured her. *Though they have a way of popping up when you're not expecting them.* "At any rate, Secretary, I must be frank. I can't allow your nanites on board my ship. This isn't meant to be offensive—it's a security measure. I'm sure you understand."

Nashi cocked her head. *"Of course, Captain. And I will keep my promise of offering you our fa-*

*cilities in repairing your ship. We will simply evac-
uate all nanites from your docking area on the station."*

"Thank you, Secretary."

"Engineer Zedrel will indeed be disappointed,"
Nashi went on wistfully. *"He—and I, for that matter—were greatly looking forward to seeing your
wonderful ship."*

Janeway leaned back in her seat, careful not to
narrow her eyes. Nashi didn't appear offended, but
Janeway had the feeling she was suddenly treading
on thin ice with the Chi. And she needed their goodwill. *Voyager* had to be repaired before the next ion
storm pulsed through the sector or the ship might
well be torn from stem to stern. Torres and Janeway
both were nervous about the reduction of *Voyager*'s
dilithium stores, and Neelix constantly needed more
food supplies. Not to mention how diplomatically
nerve-racking it would be having the ship docked at
a station full of people who were coldly polite at
best. Janeway decided to listen to her instincts.

"We might still be able to arrange something, Secretary," Janeway said, and tapped her combadge.
"Janeway to engineering."

"Go ahead," came Torres's voice.

"B'Elanna, would it be possible to set up a mobile
containment field for the Chiar so they could visit
the ship without their nanites . . . um, interacting
with the ship's systems?"

Brief pause. *"Maybe after an hour's work. It
would involve mounting a shield generator on a
gravity sled and recalibrating the emitter so that—"*

"That's fine, Lieutenant," Janeway interrupted.

"I'll send Mr. Paris over to pick the Chiar up in the *Delta Flyer* when you have it ready. Janeway out."

The wistfulness vanished from Nashi's voice. *"Wonderful, Captain. Your generosity continues to astound."*

"You're welcome, Secretary." Janeway paused a moment before continuing. "There is one other small matter I wanted to ask you about, if I may."

"What would that be?"

"Our sensors have detected the presence of a stockpile of rhometric weapons. Secretary, we consider these weapons very dangerous, and we treat them with extreme caution."

Nashi waved a hand. *"An ancient weapon system developed long ago. We have never used them, for obvious reasons."*

"And they haven't been dismantled?" Janeway said.

"We considered it," Nashi said, *"and then decided it would be safer simply to program a series of nanites to oversee them and ensure they are kept from detonating. As it turns out, their development ultimately led to the discovery of how to use dilithium in a warp core. But I assure you, Captain, that your ship is quite safe."*

"Our ship is shielded from them, in any case," Janeway said. "I just thought I would mention them. I'll contact you again when everything is prepared for your transport, Secretary."

"I look forward to it." Nashi's head scooped down and up once before the screen blanked out.

"Uh-oh." Tom Paris pointed over B'Elanna's shoulder and down at the *Delta Flyer*'s engineering console. "What's that?"

B'Elanna looked down, instantly worried. "What's what?"

Tom took advantage of her relaxed guard to kiss her loudly on the cheek. Laughing, B'Elanna shoved him away. "Will you knock it off? We still haven't completed preflight."

"What's the point in being married if you can't steal a kiss once in a while?" Tom said, pretending to sulk.

"Now, now," came Neelix's reedy voice from the sensor boards. "If you stole that kiss, Lieutenant, it's my job as morale officer to insist you give it back."

B'Elanna rolled brown eyes. "He can have it." She paused. "For now."

Tom strolled nonchalantly up to the pilot's chair and put his hands on the controls. Per his own design, the *Delta Flyer* used a pair of joysticks for flight control instead of a flat board. Tom loved it. Tapping a console was all well and good, but moving a joystick and feeling the *Flyer's* instant response—now, that was *real* flying. The *Flyer* itself was quite a bit larger than a standard Starfleet shuttlecraft, but it was faster and more maneuverable. Certainly more fun to fly.

The trio finished the preflight, and B'Elanna went aft to make double-sure the newly modified shield generator was properly secured. Tom glanced over his shoulder to watch her go. He had always noticed how beautiful she was but it had taken him a long time to appreciate how compellingly perceptive and resourceful she was. To be honest, it hadn't been love at first sight. B'Elanna Torres had looked at Tom Paris as a failure and a traitor to the Maquis. She had barely given him the time of day. Not that he had wanted it from her. She was arrogant, headstrong, and stubborn, and she usually bulldozed straight over anyone who got in her way. But the Delta Quadrant had changed them both. B'Elanna had mellowed considerably, and Tom—well, Tom had to admit that he had grown up. A little, anyway.

"Preflight completed, Lieutenant," Neelix said. "Ready for takeoff."

Tom hit the engines, and the *Flyer* almost delicately lifted off the shuttlebay floor and slid smoothly toward the force field that separated the bay from open space. Neelix tapped his controls, and the field shut off just in time to let the shuttle through. Stars sprinkled themselves across the *Flyer*'s windows, and *Voyager* slid quietly beneath them as Tom brought the shuttle around. Ahead lay the octagonal station and the blue-green planet beyond.

"Paris to *Voyager*," he said. "We're clear of the ship and are heading for the Chiar station. We should arrive there in less than five minutes."

"Acknowledged," came Chakotay's voice. *"They're expecting you. And, Mr. Paris, you will be pleased to hear that I made it clear to the secretary that you are male. She sounded intrigued."*

"Watch it, Paris," growled B'Elanna, who had reentered the bridge at that moment.

"Maybe we can set her up with Neelix," Tom said. The space station loomed ahead of them, and a docking port had already irised open.

"I'm never averse to feminine company," Neelix said. He ran a hand through long yellow hair and gave his mutton-chop whiskers a quick finger brushing. His amber eyes were merry in a strangely speckled face, and he had donned a tunic made of brightly colored squares.

"Even feminine company with four legs and a seriously weird neck?" Paris asked.

"You never know, Lieutenant," Neelix replied airily. "You never know."

There was a muffled *thump* as Tom docked the *Flyer* at the station. B'Elanna moved back to the airlock and the portable shield generator. When Tom and Neelix joined her, she was fiddling with the controls. The generator, about the size and shape of a soccer ball, sat on a small gravity sled which hovered at waist level. In addition to creating the force field, it also recycled air so B'Elanna and the Chiar wouldn't suffocate inside the airtight field.

"I've set the airlock systems to erect a force field in front of us and behind us," B'Elanna explained. "When the Chiar board, I'll bring down the one over the hatchway. You bring them into range of the portable generator here"—she flicked a hand at it—"and I'll bring down the field that's behind us. As long as the Chiar stay within two meters of the portable generator, they'll be fine. Both of you will need to stand outside the radius. Otherwise you'll be trapped inside with me and the Chiar."

"Got it," Tom said, and Neelix opened the airlock.

Six Chiar stood in the bay on the other side. Their segmented necks brought them only to the level of Tom's shoulder, and he noticed Neelix slump a bit, subtly bringing his own head a little closer to their height. Tom wondered if he should imitate Neelix or just stand and smile. He decided on the latter.

"Secretary Nashi," Neelix said brightly, stepping

toward the lead Chiar. There was a slight flicker in the air as B'Elanna deactivated the first shield.

The smell nearly smashed Tom flat. He took a surprised, involuntary step backward and coughed once. The smell was pungent and instantly pervasive, as if the force field had been holding back a cloud of ammonia. Even Neelix, an experienced mediator and ambassador, looked startled.

The six Chiar, including Secretary Nashi, were clearly the source of the smell. Tom smothered another cough and felt his eyes begin to water. The smell wasn't necessarily bad, just *strong,* so strong that it forced all five senses to rally together for sheer survival. It was like having a gallon of mixed cologne and sweat thrown into his face. Tom shot a glance at B'Elanna and saw she was similarly affected, though she was struggling not to show it.

"I greet you," said Secretary Nashi formally. Tom could only stare through teary eyes.

Neelix was the first to recover. "It is a great pleasure to meet you, Secretary. I am Mr. Neelix, Ambassador for the Federation Starship *Voyager.* Captain Janeway sends her greetings and asked me to say she's looking forward to your visit."

"Thank you, Ambassador," Nashi replied gravely. "I look forward to it as well. These are my assistants Madam Tell and Master Ree." She didn't introduce the other three Chiar, who stayed to the rear of the group. Their outer coating was a matte solid in clear contrast to the rainbows that danced across the bodies of the others. They wore what looked like some type of saddlebag slung over their backs.

Neelix introduced Tom and B'Elanna and gestured the Chiar on board the shuttle. B'Elanna, covertly wiping tears from her eyes, worked the generator controls, activating the containment field, deactivating the second airlock field, and cycling shut the hatchway while Neelix kept up bright, gentle chatter. The procedure was done so smoothly that Tom barely noticed the fields going up and down. Once the containment field was in place, the smell cut back sharply. B'Elanna shot Tom a sick look. He spread his hands helplessly and chewed a lower lip. She was trapped in there with that overpowering stench.

"We'll stop at Zedrel's ship to pick him up on the way back," Neelix was saying as if nothing were wrong. "We thought it best to bring you aboard first, Secretary." The words *because you outrank Zedrel and we don't want to step on your toes* went unsaid. "The passenger bay is over here."

Neelix ushered the group down a short flight of steps to the belowdeck. Tom hung back out of range of the generator. He didn't want to get too close and have the field shock him for his trouble. The smell outside the field was almost gone now. Nashi, Tell, and Ree, meanwhile, threw quick glances in many directions, obviously fascinated with the shuttle but not wanting to be blatant about it. They ignored the other three Chiar and B'Elanna completely. At first Tom wondered if this was intended to be a slight, and he felt his temper rise. Then he realized it was probably because B'Elanna was there to ensure the Chiar nanites didn't "infect" the ship, something the Chair could see as an insult. Best just to ignore the entire affair, much like someone ignored a body-guard.

Inside the field, B'Elanna took a series of shallow breaths, and Tom licked dry lips. There had to be something he could do to help her. After a moment it came to him. While Neelix was guiding the group slowly to the passenger area, Tom dashed back to the *Flyer*'s little sickbay and activated the communications system. A second later the Doctor blinked into life on screen, with *Voyager*'s sickbay in view behind him.

"Mr. Paris," he said in his dry voice. "What can I do for you?"

Tom quickly explained the situation. The Doctor raised an eyebrow. "Is it that bad?"

"You have no idea, Doc."

"Very well. I'm sending you a formula for a neuro-synaptic inhibitor that should deaden B'Elanna's sense of smell. And yours and Neelix's too, for that matter." The Doctor's shoulders moved as his hands, off-screen, worked his own panel. The *Flyer*'s computer blinked confirmation, and the tiny replicator glowed to life. When the light faded, it left three ampules behind. "The first one is for humans. The second should work for a Talaxian. The third is for a human-Klingon hybrid. It will shut down the olfactory bulb in your brain for approximately an hour. I should warn you that as a side effect, you won't have much taste left." He paused. "In your case, I doubt anyone will notice."

"Thanks, Doc. Warn the captain, will you? And you might want to whip up a batch of this stuff for the rest of the crew."

"They won't smell anything through a force field, but your point is well taken. I'll see you at your next duty shift."

Tom blanked the screen.

With the swift ease of many hours spent in sickbay as chief medic, Tom racked each ampule into a hypospray, pressed the first to his own neck, and thumbed the release. The last shreds of Chiar scent vanished. He sighed in utter relief, then went back up to the pilot's chair. There was no way to innoculate B'Elanna right now, and the best thing he could do for her was get her back to *Voyager* as fast as possible. Neelix's conversational voice floated up from belowdecks as Tom took the controls.

The next leg of the trip took them to Zedrel's ship, still hovering in *Voyager*'s shadow. Tom docked with it, then went down to the airlock. He realized to his chagrin that someone should have suggested the Chiar wait by the airlock instead of going to the passenger bay, since now the entire group of aliens had to troop up from below so B'Elanna could overlap the force fields. From the chagrined look on Neelix's face as he emerged from below, it apparently was only now occurring to him as well.

"Right this way, Secretary," he was saying, "and you can congratulate Engineer Zedrel in person on his successful warp drive test."

Well, Tom thought, *leave it to Neelix to cook up a diplomatic excuse for bringing them back up.*

The Chiar followed Neelix, B'Elanna still trailing behind with the generator. She looked distinctly green. The Chiar crossed the threshold of the airlock, but B'Elanna did not follow. Instead, she hit another control, and a force field went up behind the Chiar, effectively sealing them out of the *Delta Flyer* and leaving B'Elanna inside. She slapped a pad and the portable field collapsed. She took a deep breath of what was, to her, much cleaner air, though Tom smelled nothing. Neelix stiffened as the leftover Chiar scent hit him.

The airlock opened and Engineer Zedrel stepped into the group of Chiar, who greeted him with enthusiasm and made congratulatory noises. The three silent Chiar hung back, saddlebags firmly in place.

"I can't do this, Tom," B'Elanna murmured. "That smell! They don't seem to notice anything, but my god! How am I going to spend ten minutes in that field with them, let alone the time it'll take them to tour the ship?"

In answer, Tom pressed the hypospray against her neck. She gasped, then inhaled appreciatively.

"Present from the Doc," Tom said out of the corner of his mouth. He slipped her the hypospray. "Dose lasts an hour."

"You're an angel," B'Elanna said without moving her lips. "Paybacks will be heaven."

Tom winked at her, then stepped up behind Neelix, who was still watching the Chiar. He clapped a friendly hand on the Talaxian's shoulder and used the motion to cover the hypospray. Neelix shot Tom a grateful look, palmed the proffered hypospray, and turned back to the Chiar with a smile.

The rest of the trip was routine. Neelix and B'Elanna guided the Chiar aboard the *Flyer*—Zedrel peppered Tom with questions about the shuttle's warp drive until Neelix rescued him—and Tom piloted them safely back to *Voyager*'s echoing shuttle-bay. Janeway, Chakotay, Tuvok, and Seven of Nine were waiting for them. For a moment Tom wondered why Janeway had brought Seven down, then realized it was probably because the former Borg drone was the ship's resident expert on nanotechnology. The captain would want her present in case something went wrong.

Neelix made formal introductions while B'Elanna made silent adjustments to the field generator. Her expression was untroubled, and Tom was relieved. Watching her suffer even a little was surprisingly painful. He watched his wife's skillful hands with admiration and wondered if she felt the same way when she watched him pilot a ship.

"And who are the others?" Janeway asked, nod-ding at the three Chiar Nashi had failed to introduce. Their outer coatings were still dull solid colors, and they continued to keep their heads lower than Nashi, Tell, and Ree did.

Nashi looked surprised at Janeway's question. "Servants, Captain. No one worth mentioning."

Tom blinked.

"Ah" was Janeway's only comment.

"This is truly a marvelous ship, Captain," Nashi continued as they all headed for the shuttlebay doors. "Zedrel's vessel must seem terribly primitive to you."

Zedrel's neck folded, dropping his head, and his eyes narrowed. Madam Tell and Master Ree didn't react.

That was rude, Tom thought.

"Zedrel's ship is no small accomplishment, Secre-tary," Janeway replied, neatly sidestepping the potential diplomatic tangle. "It's the first step toward great adventure and exploration for your people."

"And toward trade," Nashi said. The shuttlebay doors closed behind the group, leaving them in the corridor. Nashi held a hand out behind her. One of the servants instantly opened a saddlebag, plucked out a red, leafy plant stem, and placed it in Nashi's hand. One by one she stripped the leaves from it and munched on them with no sign of self-consciousness whatsoever. Tom's first impression was that it was another sign of rudeness, and he had to remind himself that this form of snacking in public was probably normal for the Chiar. For all he knew, they were wondering why none of *Voyager*'s crew had similar snacks with them. Even as Tom watched, Master Ree held out his hand, and another of the servants handed him a stem, though this one was more purple, with larger leaves.

"What sort of goods are your people interested in trading for?" Neelix asked solicitously.

"Computer programs," Nashi replied promptly.

"Programs?" Tuvok echoed with the slight tilt to his head that Tom had, over the years, taken as an indication of curiosity.

"I mentioned to the captain that our nanites need to be programmed for what we need," Nashi said. "Most of the time such programs are rented, rather than bought. After all, why pay to own a program for a tool you'll only need once when you can pay a smaller fee, build the tool, and let the program erase itself? But in your case, we would buy outright. Your computer programs would have immense value to us. Communications, engineering, food recipes—all of them. The fact that the programs come from an alien world would enhance their worth as collector's items, even if they didn't work well for us. Why, Captain, you could retire on the profits from the sale of your holonovels alone."

"Holonovels?" Janeway said, shooting a glance at Neelix.

Neelix shifted uneasily. "I may have mentioned one or two things about holodecks and holograms while we were en route."

"I see," Janeway said in a neutral voice.

"We would also trade for any assistance your people can give us with our own warp drive," Nashi concluded.

Janeway nodded. "I will, of course, have to discuss this possibility with my staff. The Federation has regulations which I cannot violate."

"Of course, Captain."

"Meanwhile," she continued, "Ambassador Neelix and Seven of Nine will be happy to give you a tour of the ship."

Zedrel, who had been shifting impatiently from foot to foot to foot, shook his head doglike in the Chiar gesture of emphatic agreement. "Please," he said.

Neelix and Seven led the little group away. B'Elanna went along to tend the force-field generator, and Tom Paris watched her go before returning to his duty station.

"Whenever something sounds too good to be true," said Kathryn Janeway, "it means we're missing something."

"I agree," said Chakotay.

"The human desire to seek wisdom in banal maxims never ceases to intrigue me," Tuvok put in, "but in this case I must also agree."

Janeway refreshed her coffee cup from the insulated decanter and sipped thoughtfully. Outside the readyroom windows, she could see both the octagonal Chiar space station and the blue-green planet Chi. The coloring reminded her strongly of Earth, and a familiar thread of homesickness trickled down her spine.

"They're willing to trade programs for dilithium and probably for supplies," Janeway said. "We'd essentially be getting something for nothing."

"I don't think *they* see it that way," Chakotay said. He was sitting on the couch, tapping large fingers on his knees. Tuvok was standing next to him.

"First things first, though." Janeway set the mug down on her desk. "Would this kind of trade be a violation of the Prime Directive?"

"My instincts say it wouldn't be," Chakotay said. "The Chiar have built a fairly elaborate space station and they have warp drive."

"The Chiar," Tuvok pointed out, "have only had warp drive for a few hours. Certain of our programs and designs could potentially damage their culture or unbalance some political situation we know nothing about. We do not even know if Secretary Nashi represents all of Chi or merely a single government. Furthermore, aiding them in repairing their warp drive would indeed be a flagrant Prime Directive violation."

"Not technically," Chakotay argued. "Once a race has developed warp technology, it's eligible for Federation membership and the Prime Directive no longer applies. There isn't any mention of a minimum time requirement. However," he continued, holding up a finger to forestall Tuvok's next comment, "giving the Chiar everything they've asked for may not violate the letter of the Directive, but it would certainly violate the spirit."

Janeway gnawed her lower lip in thought. "We'll take a middle road here. I'll tell Neelix we can trade for harmless programs like Tom's holonovels or Neelix's recipes."

"Some might consider trading the latter an act of war," Tuvok said dryly.

"Seven and the Doctor have recorded several operas together," Chakotay said. "The Chiar might find them intriguing."

"As for their warp drive," Janeway continued, "we won't repair it or correct any design flaws, but we can certainly follow Zedrel on his next test flight in case he gets into trouble again."

"I'll tell Neelix," Chakotay said.

"Now," Janeway said, "what about this smell the Doctor and Mr. Paris reported? I didn't notice anything, but the force field would prevent that."

Chakotay shrugged. "There are worse problems. Anyone who ends up interacting with them directly will need to take the Doctor's inoculation. We won't be able to taste Neelix's cuisine afterward, but sacrifices must be made."

"I like his cooking," Janeway said. "He's gotten much better with practice."

Tuvok raised an eyebrow. "He could hardly have gotten worse."

* * *

"Computer," Neelix said, "end program." The black-and-white bridge of Captain Proton's ship, with its 1950s-style levers, dials, and gauges, vanished, leaving behind the bare grid of the holodeck.

"Wonderful!" Master Ree exclaimed. "I really could never have imagined solid holograms. We have intangible ones, of course, and I think we could easily adapt this—a holonovel, you called it?—to something we could use. It reminds me of the games I used to play when I was a child. Why, my cousin and I—he had a stilt house and I was so jealous—we used to play games of raiders and pirates, though we did not actually play in space, so I suppose this is not quite the same as—"

Seven of Nine's features did not flicker in annoyance, though she felt an urge to put her hand over Master Ree's mouth. The majority of his speech was irrelevant chatter, a waste of time. She felt the same way about this tour. What did it matter what *Voyager* looked like? It was highly unlikely Captain Janeway would give these creatures anything of true value. Why were they being shown what they could not have? It was an inefficient use of time, time she could spend on her own holodeck program.

"Yes, well," Neelix said, interrupting Ree's vocal musings, "perhaps we can continue?"

"To engineering?" Zedrel asked hopefully.

Neelix made a slight bow. "Of course. Right this way."

The Talaxian guided the entourage to the holodeck exit. The big doors hummed open and clanged shut. In the corridor Neelix took the lead a bare pace ahead of Nashi and Zedrel. Master Ree and Madam Tell, who hadn't spoken a word, followed with the three servant Chiar behind them. B'Elanna Torres came next with the little gravity sled. She kept most of her attention on the generator, which made tiny beeping noises as she continually made adjustments and recalibrations. It was a challenge Seven herself would have been hard-pressed to meet, though she would never have admitted it. Force fields weren't meant to glide across hard surfaces, nor change shape to pass through corridors and doorways, and the process seemed to be taking up most of Torres's concentration. Like the servant Chiar, Torres hadn't spoken, and the Chiar seemed content to ignore her.

Seven brought up the rear of the group. The Borg implants in her left eye allowed her to scan visually for stray nanites, and she held an open tricorder in one hand. To her regret, the mobile shield prevented her from studying, or even detecting, the Chiar nanites. It would have been interesting to compare Chiar technology with Borg, though she was certain the Chiar would fail to measure up to Borg standards. She wondered what Commander Chakotay thought of the Chiar, then suppressed herself. There were other matters to occupy her mind, and she didn't need the distraction.

It took some shuffling to fit everyone into the turbolift, but they managed. Seven noticed Zedrel was staring at her. She cocked her head. Seven had not encountered this species before, but something in his expression felt . . . distasteful to her. A servant Chiar handed Madam Ree a leafy stem, and she ate it with delicacy. Zedrel continued to stare.

"Is there something you require?" Seven asked.

Zedrel looked away and his shimmering outer covering took on a blue tinge.

"I think Engineer Zedrel is fascinated by you . . . what is the term? *Humans?*" Master Ree said.

"Engineering," Neelix said, and the turbolift started to move.

"The term you are looking for is *humanoid,*" Seven said stiffly. "It refers to any species with my basic shape. The term *human* is only applied to people of my specific species. Mr. Neelix, for example, is humanoid but not human. He is Talaxian."

Zedrel chuffed. "I apologize if I was rude."

"Not at all," Seven replied. "Encountering a new species always provokes curiosity. I am . . . accustomed to it."

Zedrel ducked his head, but Seven still remembered the look on his face from before.

"Do you encounter many other species?" Nashi asked.

"Oh, my, yes," Neelix said. "Sometimes it seems like we run into a new one every week." He paused. "Secretary, the captain tells me a section of your world has been . . . er, cordoned off by a microwave pulse."

Nashi's head bobbed once up and down. "It is. How did you know this?"

"We have sensors," Seven said. "What is the function of this pulse? Please," she added as an afterthought. This was, after all, supposed to be a diplomatic discourse.

"The continent is called Ushek," Nashi replied. "The Ushekti went to war against us."

"Us?" Neelix asked. The turbolift changed direction.

"The Goracar Alliance," Nashi explained. "It consists of the two northern continents on Chi. Ushek and Sherek, in the south, declared war on the Alliance. We won. Sherek is now a protectorate of the Alliance. These three"—she gestured at the trio of Chiar with solid-color outer coatings, they continued to stare at the floor—"are Sherekti."

"And Ushek?" Neelix probed.

"Ushek refused to surrender," Nashi said. "We were therefore forced to set up the pulse. Nanites are such a part of our daily lives that losing them is akin to losing both arms and both legs, so the Ushekti remain imprisoned on their continent."

Neelix blinked rapidly. "I don't follow."

"Microwaves," Seven explained, "can destroy nanites."

"I thought your people didn't use nanotechnology," Zedrel said.

"The Federation does not," Seven agreed. "I, however, was raised among the Borg, and I have retained the use of my nanoprobes."

Nashi drew back in alarm. "Captain Janeway mentioned the Borg."

"You have nothing to fear," Seven said matter-of-factly. "I am no longer part of the Collective and will not assimilate you or your people."

The turbolift doors popped open before Nashi could reply, and Neelix led the group into engineering. The circular room and the catwalks above it buzzed with activity as the crew set about repairing the damage from the ion storm. Although the Chiar had promised the use of their space station, Torres hadn't seen any reason to sit idle and had ordered the crew to continue their work. The two-story blue column that made up the warp core pulsed and hummed. The Chiar raised their heads high, trying to see in all directions at once. Seven, however, noticed that Zedrel seemed intently focused on the technology and the people operating it.

"This is engineering, the heart of the ship," Neelix said. "Er, perhaps Lieutenant Torres, our chief engineer, would care to explain what we're looking at?"

Torres made one more adjustment, then looked up from the generator. "As long as we don't move from this spot, I'll be happy to."

Zedrel stared at her. So did the rest of the Chiar. "You're the chief engineer?" he blurted.

"Does that surprise you?"

"I thought you were—" Zedrel muffled a yelp as Nashi trod on one of his front feet.

"My apologies, Chief Engineer," Nashi said loudly. "My own engineer seems to have forgotten his manners."

"You thought I was a what?" Torres demanded.

Seven raised an eyebrow.

"You conducted yourself silently, as a thrall," Zedrel said. "I was going to ask, in fact, if you were for sale."

Torres drew herself up, and Neelix hastened to intervene. "An easy mistake to make," he said with a small chuckle. "I'm sure the lieutenant is not offended. No hard feelings, B'Elanna?"

Torres gave Neelix a hard look. "No," she said at last.

"You do not keep thralls?" Master Ree asked, gesturing at the three Chiar servants, who Seven now realized must be slaves, though the Chiar obviously called them thralls. Madam Tell took another leaf stem.

"No, we don't," Torres said a bit curtly.

"How does your economy survive?" Ree said, aghast.

"Master Ree," Nashi interrupted firmly. "I believe Chief Engineer B'Elanna Torres was about to give us a tour of engineering. Engineer Zedrel will doubtless have many questions."

"Of course, of course," Ree muttered. Madam Tell placed a hand on his flank. She still hadn't spoken. If silence was one mark of a thrall, Seven thought, then Madam Tell must also be occasionally mistaken for one. This particular Chiar spoke even less often than a Borg drone.

"We're standing in front of the warp core," Torres said. "It uses dilithium to facilitate a reaction between matter and antimatter that powers our warp drive."

"Just like mine," Zedrel breathed. "Only so much larger. Tell me, Chief Engineer—"

"Lieutenant," Torres corrected.

"Lieutenant," Zedrel repeated. "How do you overcome the ratio magnification factor? Every time I try to expand my dilithium matrix, it threatens to collapse."

Torres shook her head. "I'm afraid I can't get more specific until I have permission from the captain."

"But—" Another tiny yelp as Nashi stepped on his foot again.

Torres launched into a general lecture about the ship's operations, one Seven had heard her deliver to visiting dignitaries a dozen times before. She scanned the area with implant and tricorder. No stray nanites.

Neelix sidled up to her. "Did you hear that?" he said quietly. "These people keep slaves."

"What of it?" Seven said, still intent on her tricorder.

"That's monstrous," Neelix said, looking shocked. "Buying and selling people is something I thought I'd left behind with the Kazon. The Chiar seemed so pleasant, despite the smell. I would never have thought of them as slave owners."

Seven closed the tricorder. "Many cultures trade in slaves. It is usually inefficient, but so are many aspects of non-Borg society. Besides, one could argue that even Starfleet keeps slaves."

"Now, really, Seven, how can you say—"

"When crewmen enlist, they must serve Starfleet for a certain period of time," Seven said calmly while Torres continued her lecture to the rapt Chiar. "They are given the most undesirable tasks and must obey all orders from those higher in the chain of command, which, in the beginning, is everyone. If they disobey these orders, they are punished with extra work or confinement. If an officer wishes to transfer them to another division or ship, they have no choice but to go. In return, they are given food, clothing, a bed in a shared barrack, and a small living allowance. How is this different from slavery?"

"But they enlist voluntarily," Neelix objected. "No one forces them. And once their service time is ended, they can leave."

"Many cultures allow people to sell themselves

into slavery and earn their way back out," Seven said. "Perhaps the Chiar are the same."

Neelix looked as if he wanted to argue further, but Torres's lecture came to a close at that moment. "And now I think Neelix will want to take you to meet with Captain Janeway to begin trade negotiations."

"I was just about to say that very thing," Neelix said brightly. "Right this way, if you would, ladies and gentlemen."

With a small sigh, Seven of Nine took out her tricorder and hoped the captain wouldn't require her to stand through hours of negotiations. On their way to the turbolift, she twice caught Zedrel staring at her and at B'Elanna Torres.

CHAPTER

4

CHAKOTAY HURRIED DOWN THE CORRIDOR toward holodeck two. It was almost 1900 hours, and he didn't want to keep Seven waiting. That, he decided, would be rude. Besides, she had made a point about his being on time.

And admit it, he thought. *You're looking forward to seeing her.*

Well, why shouldn't he? Seven was intelligent, articulate, and interesting. She was a good friend, and he was hoping to be able to help her with a project that sounded kind of fun. Just because he was looking forward to seeing her didn't mean he was necessarily nursing a romantic interest in her. He wasn't. He was going to spend some time with a friend on the holodeck. There was no reason to overanalyze.

Seven was waiting for him at the holodeck entrance. "You are three minutes early," she said with a hint of approval.

"So are you," he said. "I was actually wondering if we'd be able to keep this appointment. *Voyager* needs extensive repairs, and I didn't know if B'Elanna would let you out of engineering."

"After the Chiar delegation left," Seven said, "I consulted with Lieutenant Torres. I presented her with several proposals that would make the docking and repair procedures more efficient. However, she wanted to study them. So I have a certain amount of free time."

"Generous of her," Chakotay said, suppressing a small grin. He would have to ask B'Elanna later about Seven's efficient "proposals" and see if B'Elanna had used Seven's holodeck time as an excuse to get her out of engineering so the chief engineer herself could handle the docking procedures and repair schedules without further input.

Seven only nodded and tapped the holodeck controls. "I have completed the basic program and it is ready to run."

They entered the holodeck and allowed the doors to hum shut behind them. The blank grids on the walls and floor glowed faintly, waiting for the computer's command to create matter and energy and manipulate both with invisible tractor beams. Seven and Chakotay stood in the middle, the latter waiting expectantly.

"Computer," Seven said, "load program Seven of Nine delta six."

The walls vanished. Chakotay found himself standing on a playground. Swings, slides, jungle gyms, forts, and other timeless play equipment were scattered all about a park with plenty of trees and picnic tables. The park trees supported a series of treehouses connected by swings, ropes, and walkways. Beyond the playground was a thick woodland. Perhaps two dozen human children of varying ages stood frozen about the park.

"Looks nice," Chakotay said. "Are we anyplace in particular?"

"I have vague memories of a place similar to this from a time before my parents left Earth," Seven said. "I have combined that with a certain amount of research. The Doctor, for example, gave me access to his pediatric files."

"Impressive," Chakotay said.

"There is one final touch," Seven continued. "But it is only noticeable once the program begins." She raised her voice. "Computer, run program."

And the park . . . changed. The play equipment loomed abruptly larger. The trees were taller, the treehouses farther up, the woods farther away. Before Chakotay could react to this, the children sprang to life. Shouts and squeals filled the air. Four kids off to Chakotay's left played with a hoverball. It swooped and dodged just above the ground as the children tried to hit it with hands and feet. Another group played freeze tag. Two boys ran across one of the treehouse walkways overhead, making the boards clatter and sway. One of them slipped and fell through the ropes holding the walkway up. A force field sprang to life and shoved him back to safety. He laughed and continued running.

Chakotay looked down at his hands. They were

smaller than they should be. His body was different, too—shorter and stockier. He was . . . a child?

"What did you do?" he half-asked, half-demanded, and was startled to notice the pitch of his voice was being modulated—it sounded like a young boy's.

"It is primarily a matter of perspective," Seven explained. She was also a good deal shorter, with a little-girl build. Her eyes were larger, and her straw-colored hair was pulled back into a pair of ponytails. Her Borg implants were gone. "I wanted me—us—to be eight or nine years of age, but the holodeck is unable to make a real person larger or smaller. We haven't actually changed except for some minor cosmetic alterations accomplished by holographic overlay."

"We didn't shrink," Chakotay said in realization. "The playground—and the children—grew."

"Correct."

Chakotay looked around. "So what do you want to do?"

"Hey!" A dark-haired girl ran up to them a bit breathlessly. "Joe and Nina have to go home. You two want to play freeze tag?"

"Seven?" Chakotay turned to her.

Seven had shrunk back a little. "I am . . . unschooled in this game."

"What?" the girl said.

"I do not know how to play."

"It's easy," she said. "Hectora's It. If she tags you, you have to freeze in place like a statue until someone who isn't frozen touches you. If Hectora can get everyone frozen, she wins."

" 'It'?" Seven asked.

"The antagonist, Seven," Chakotay supplied.

"What is the purpose of this game?" Seven said.

"To have fun," Chakotay said. "That's why you're here, right?"

"Your name is Seven?" the girl said. "That's a funny name."

"I'm telling," Chakotay said instantly.

The girl flushed. "I didn't mean it like that. I meant that it's different. Kind of neat. My name's Tenna."

"I'm Chakotay. Are you playing or not, Seven?"

Seven licked her lips. Chakotay could almost see what was going through her head. Although she had spent considerable time creating the program, it had been a simple abstract, data to manipulate and move. Now came the reality, and it was more than Seven had anticipated. The realistic appearance of the holodeck could do that sometimes. He wondered if she was going to back out and if he'd be able to talk her into continuing.

"Actually," Seven said softly, "I would prefer to be called Annika."

With a grin, Chakotay grabbed her hand and towed her toward the group of children. The freeze tag game began. Chakotay ran and dodged and shouted with the rest of the children. Shortly, however, he called a time out.

"Sev—Annika," he said. "I think I should explain a few things to you."

"Oh?" Seven was barely breathing hard despite the exertion. Chakotay was sweating.

"The real purpose of freeze tag is less to win the game and more to run around and yell a lot," he said. "That means if someone is frozen, you're supposed to try to unfreeze them yourself. Trying to assemble a strike force to 'free the prisoner' is . . . a different game."

Seven looked nonplussed. "I see."

"And while dodging is a perfectly acceptable way to avoid being tagged by It, using a karate sweep to bring her feet out from under her before she touches you is definitely cheating."

"This playground is equipped with multiple safety features. She was unharmed. Besides, it is more efficient."

"You're a *kid*," Chakotay said in exasperation. "Kids don't worry about efficiency."

"I did."

"But you didn't have a real childhood, remember? That's why you're here." He scratched his nose in thought. "Look, the next time you want to do something, ask yourself this: What would Naomi do?"

"Naomi Wildman."

Chakotay nodded. "You've interacted with her a great deal. Think of how she might react in these situations."

"Hey!" Tenna called. "Are you guys going to play or not?"

"They love each other!" shouted Tenna's brother Mel. He began to chant. "Annika and Chakotay sittin' in a tree K-I-S-S-I-N-G—"

"What is the purpose of that?" Seven said, staring.

"First comes love—"

"It's a very old children's rhyme," Chakotay said under his breath.

"—then comes marriage—"

"Shut up, Mel!" Tenna said, shoving him. "Time in! I'm It!"

The children squealed and scattered. Tenna ran straight for Chakotay and Seven, who split up and dodged. Chakotay kept an eye on Seven, who now seemed to enter more into the spirit of the game. Her faced was flushed and she was actually smiling as she dodged around Tenna and slapped the hand of a girl who had been frozen. Chakotay smiled, too.

As the game progressed, Chakotay noticed Mel was giving Seven a hard time. Several times he bumped against her, and once when she was frozen, he pretended not to notice and didn't unfreeze her, even though she was right in front of him. Finally he caught and pulled one of Seven's ponytails while she was running. The move caught her by surprise, and she fell flat on her back. By the time she got to her feet, Mel had dodged away laughing. Angered, Chakotay ran over to her.

"Are you all right?" he asked, helping her up.

"I am unhurt," she replied. "But I do not understand Mel's behavior."

The words popped out before Chakotay could stop them. "Do you want me to beat him up for you?"

She gave him an odd look. "No. He is only a child."

"So are you, Seven," Chakotay pointed out.

"Why would he do these things?" Seven asked again.

"He's a bully. Low self-esteem makes him try to hurt other people so he can feel strong. Either that or he likes you."

"He likes me?" Seven echoed.

Chakotay grinned. "Boys who like a certain girl sometimes show their affection by bullying her or performing other strange acts to get her attention.

They haven't learned how to express attraction yet, so they resort to improper methods."

Seven looked dubious. "Do human females—girls—respond positively to this?"

Chakotay thought back to Marjala Azul. She had been, in his eleven-year-old eyes, the most beautiful girl in the entire world—shining black braids, wide brown eyes, fingers that tapped interesting rhythms on her desk when she was trying to concentrate. He couldn't keep his eyes off her. So he made her life miserable. The problem for Marjala ended after Chakotay's teacher called home. After that, Chakotay stayed well away from Marjala Azul.

"No," he said to Seven. "They don't. Eventually the boys learn how to approach the girls, and things balance out."

"Why do the girls not approach the boys?" Seven asked.

"Simple." Chakotay grinned. "Boys have cooties."

And before she could ask the obvious question, he dashed back into the game.

A while later things wound down. The group broke up to slurp water from the drinking fountain and find other games. Seven ended up with Chakotay again.

"I am confused about certain phrases the children use," she said as they walked towards the water fountain. "Can you explain?"

"Which phrases?" he asked.

"I understand the concept of being It," Seven said, "but what does *I'm telling* mean, and why does it elicit such a negative response?"

Chakotay laughed. "It means you're going to tell an adult what the other kid did, usually in the hopes that the adult will mete out some kind of punishment while you watch."

"But the phrase is sometimes used even when the offense is a small one," Seven said, "and hardly worth the trouble."

"One of the mysteries of childhood, Annika." Chakotay reached the fountain and took a long, cold drink. He had to stand on tiptoe to reach the water. It was a distinctly strange sensation and brought back echoes of his own childhood. For a moment he was back on the tiny playground behind his school, back on the colony where he grew up. Seven's recreation was nothing like the tropical forests of his homeworld, but straining to reach the drinking fountain brought some of it back anyway.

"And I still do not fully understand the concepts of tagbacks, time in, and time out."

"Tagbacks are usually illegal in these games," Chakotay explained seriously. He stood aside to let her drink. Her ponytails shone gold in the holodeck sunlight. "If It tags you, you have to give the former It a chance to get away before you tag him again for fairness. *No tagbacks. Time out* pauses the game to resolve a dispute or if someone is injured. *Time in* resumes the game."

Seven wiped water from her mouth. The gesture was definitely a child's. "Who enforces these rules?"

Chakotay shrugged. "Peer pressure. An idea of what should be fair. The occasional adult."

"I had no idea being a child was so complicated," Seven muttered.

"I suppose when you grow up with it all, you

learn as you go and it isn't so hard. What do you want to do next?"

They explored the overhead treehouses and briefly joined in a let's-pretend game of space pirates. During the latter game, Mel ran up, sprayed a mouthful of water into Seven's face. While she was thus blinded, he pushed her down.

"You smell," he said. "I had to give you a shower." And he ran away. Chakotay considered going after him, then decided not to. Seven got to her feet, her little girl's face filled with anger.

"I wish to hit him," she said. "Hard."

"Maybe you should," Chakotay said. "Sometimes that's the only way to get a bully off your back."

Seven didn't respond, but instead strode toward Mel, her hands balled up into fists. At that moment the computer chimed. "Warning! Holodeck reservation time will elapse in five minutes." Seven hesitated.

"Scaredy, scaredy," Mel chanted. "You're a scaredy!"

"Computer, freeze program," Seven ordered, and the entire scene froze. "Delete character Mel."

"Computer, belay that order," Chakotay interjected. Mel flashed transparent, then became solid again.

"What are you doing?" Seven demanded. "It is my program. If I wish to delete—"

"I think it would be a mistake," Chakotay said.

"He is a bully," Seven said. Her face was flushed and angry. "The purpose of this program was to become a child again and have fun. He is interfering."

"Seven, part of growing up is learning how to deal with people like Mel. There are plenty of adults who act the same way, you know. If you want to delete him, that's your decision, but I think you'll be undercutting what you've set out to do—experience a slice of normal childhood."

"Warning!" the computer said. "Holodeck reservation time will elapse in four minutes."

"We should go," Chakotay said.

"Computer," Seven said, "save program and exit."

The playground and the children vanished. All that was left was the echoing silence of the holodeck. Chakotay and Seven had been restored to their normal sizes and appearances, though both of them were hot and sweating. Seven turned to Chakotay and for an absurd moment he thought she was going to kiss him.

"Thank you for the advice, Commander," she said in a clipped voice. "I will take it under advisement."

She was still angry. "Perhaps we could do this again?" he said tentatively. "I had fun."

"Parts of it were fun," Seven admitted. "Other parts were not." She turned toward the door.

As Chakotay watched her exit the holodeck, he realized she hadn't said whether she wanted him along for the next playground visit. He also felt as if he was partially responsible for her anger. Was she mad at him? The prospect was more unpleasant than he thought it should be.

Tom Paris held up his dress uniform and sighed.

"Put it on," B'Elanna ordered. She stood in front of the mirror, reweaving the tiny braids in her hair. Should she do more? No, no point. The Chiar would never notice. "Hurry up. We have to leave soon."

"It's going to be boring," Tom said. He yanked his shirt—more blue silk—over his head and sat on the bed to pull off his boots. B'Elanna kept weaving, but kept a covert eye on her husband in the mirror as she worked. She liked watching him. It didn't really matter what he was doing—changing his clothes, combing his hair, realigning a shield grid—it was all good. His chest muscles bunched interestingly as he removed his boots. B'Elanna noted with annoyance that she had misbraided the strands. With an irate grunt, she unwove the braid and started over, making herself pay closer attention. As a result, it surprised her when a pair of lean arms encircled her from behind and a pair of blue eyes met her brown ones in the mirror.

"What are you looking at?" she said.

"Only the most beautiful wife in the galaxy," he said.

She snorted and went back to braiding. With a mischievous grin, Tom planted a kiss on the back of her neck that sent shivers down her spine.

"Not now," she said. "We'll be late."

"Not if you stop braiding and just let your hair fall free," he murmured. He ran his fingers through the stuff in question. "I like it that way anyway."

"You're only stalling because you don't want to go to the welcome banquet," she said, but the protest was halfhearted. She reached back to touch him. "Hey! You aren't—"

"Nope." And that was all either of them said for quite some time.

Afterward, they were just heading for the door when their combadges beeped.

"Lieutenants Torres and Paris," Janeway said. *"Will you be joining us? We're waiting in transporter room two."*

B'Elanna glared at Tom. He met her gaze with an unabashed grin. She rolled her eyes and slapped her badge. "We're on our way, Captain."

"Sorry, Captain," Tom put in, tapping his own combadge. "We thought it was transporter room one."

"Oh, she'll believe that," B'Elanna said once the comlink was closed. "A word to the computer will tell her we were in our quarters."

"I'm counting on our dear captain's good manners to prevent her from checking," Tom said.

B'Elanna strode off down the hallway, trying to rein in her annoyance. Tom sometimes had that affect on her, holding the power to convince her to go against her better judgment. She didn't like it, especially when it earned her a rebuke from Captain Janeway. What had she been thinking?

"You're in a mood," Tom said, hurrying to keep up with her. "What's wrong?"

She almost snapped at him but managed to bite back the words. It wasn't really him she was angry at. "I'm sorry," she said. "I've just got a lot on my mind, and you're a handy target."

"Just be sure you fire a warning shot so I can raise my shields," he replied amiably. "What's going on?"

"The repairs, dealing with the Chiar, having to figure out docking procedures, putting antinanite protocols in place without offending our hosts, and adapting Chiar technology to meet our needs." B'Elanna sighed in exasperation. "And then Seven comes in with an enormous list of procedures she's drawn up to make everything 'more efficient,' and she wants me to put them in place without even reviewing them, but I *have* to review them, of course, which takes even more time, and thank god she had the holodeck reserved or I would have never gotten rid of her but don't get me wrong, she's learned a lot about being more polite and not stepping on people's toes and she's practically indispensable around here but every once in a while she backslides and comes across as Miss Efficient again and it's always when we're under a tight deadline and it drives me insane and now we have to go to a waste-of-time banquet where we won't even be able to taste the food when I *really* need to be down in engineering."

Tom blinked. "Wow. Pretty difficult schedule."

"Welcome to life as a chief engineer," B'Elanna growled. "But thanks for listening."

"Part of the job description. Section one, subsection seven, paragraph three a: Spouse shall let partner vent at him or her as necessary."

B'Elanna laughed in spite of herself and squeezed his hand. They reached the transporter room and found Janeway, Chakotay, Kim, and Tuvok all in dress uniforms. The Doctor stood to one side with a hypospray. He inoculated both Tom and B'Elanna the moment they cleared the door.

"This dose should last the duration of the banquet," he said without preamble. "You won't be able to smell the Chiar. I've already scanned samples of the food, and everything the Chiar eat appears quite edible for the crew."

"Even if it all tastes like cardboard," Kim said.

"I trust you will keep such remarks to yourself while we are with the Chiar," Tuvok said from the transporter pad, and Kim flushed.

"You know Harry," Tom said. "The soul of tact."

"Aren't you coming, Doctor?" B'Elanna asked as she and Tom mounted the steps. He shook his head.

"We aren't sure how the Chiar would react to a holographic CMO who can't eat their food," he explained. "And I don't want to risk their nanites getting into my mobile emitter. Have fun."

"Energize," Janeway said, and the transporter pad faded in a shower of blue light. A moment later the group was standing in the middle of what looked like a giant greenhouse. The building was the size of a soccer field. Potted plants of varying heights, breadths, and colors were scattered thickly over a white tile floor or rested on low shelves. Crystal-clear windows showed a breathtaking mountain view on one side and a lush, multicolored forest on the other. Chiar and *Voyager* crewmen mingled together among the plants. The room echoed with conversation. A little under half of the fifty or so Chiar swirled with color, some in eye-twisting patterns. The remainder of the Chiar population was matte solid—thralls—and each one was paired with a colored Chiar or with one of the crew. Secretary Nashi, Master Tell, and Madam Ree were standing in front of the area cleared for the transport.

"Captain Janeway," Nashi said with a quick head duck. "It is good to have you here."

"We're honored to be invited," Janeway replied with brief nods to Tell and Ree. "I assume Mr. Neelix made introductions as the others transported down. This is the rest of my crew, though you already know Lieutenants Torres and Paris."

B'Elanna made polite noises at the secretary and let her gaze wander about the greenhouse while

Janeway introduced Tuvok and Kim. The place didn't look like a banquet hall. Maybe now that the captain was here, everyone would be herded into the dining room.

At that moment she saw one of the thralls pluck a handful of leaves and hand it to a Chiar engaged in conversation with Neelix. The Chiar accepted the leaves without looking at the thrall who offered them and delicately munched them down. The thrall assigned to Neelix handed him a red fruit from a different bush. Neelix took the proffered food, looked as if he was about to thank the thrall, then apparently thought the better of it and ate the fruit without glancing at its source. B'Elanna frowned, remembering the thralls who handed leaves to the Chiar aboard *Voyager* during the tour. The Chiar seemed to be herbivores who browsed continuously rather than eating set meals, but they couldn't feed themselves? Perhaps it was a status symbol. In any case, the very idea of thralls still put B'Elanna off.

"Please mingle and eat," Nashi said. "There are a great many people here who wish to meet you."

"Representatives from other governments?" Janeway hazarded.

Nashi drummed her front feet on the ground in a quick pattern B'Elanna took to be a negative. "The Goracar Alliance is the primary government on Chi. It started as an emergency alliance when the Ushekti and Sherekti from the south declared war on the two northern continents. The Alliance remained stable finally after the war ended, so it was never dissolved. Sherek is our protectorate, of course, and Ushek has unfortunately become a prison."

"We are seeking ways to integrate the Ushekti into the world government, but it is complicated," Master Ree put in. "We try to help them, but they resist. They would rather live in poverty than allow us to help them reconstruct."

"I see," Janeway said in a neutral voice.

"But enough politics," Nashi said. "Come and meet our people. As I said, they are anxious to meet our visitors."

The custom seemed to be to spread out and mingle in groups no larger than three or four. B'Elanna and Tom ended up going in different directions, and as B'Elanna entered the party proper, a thrall Chiar fell into step behind her. A moment later it handed forward a small bunch of purple leaves. B'Elanna accepted them self-consciously.

"Thank you," she said to the thrall.

The thrall lowered its head and hunched forward. It didn't answer.

"There is no need to offer gratitude to a thrall," said another Chiar. "They offer *you* gratitude by serving you."

"Gratitude in return for what?" B'Elanna asked without thinking whether it might be a rude question.

"We give them their lives—a better one than they had before—and they give us service," replied the Chiar, who also had a thrall in tow. "My name is Benjir, and I govern this province."

"Lieutenant B'Elanna Torres. I'm the chief engineer on *Voyager*."

Benjir ducked his head. "It is . . . far more than an honor to meet you and offer gratitude for your help to Engineer Zedrel."

"You're welcome." B'Elanna realized she was still holding the purple leaves. Trying to look as if she ate them every day, she pushed a couple into her mouth and chewed. It was like eating lettuce, though there was no flavor beyond a trace of sweetness. Benjir's slave plucked a speckled green fruit from a nearby bush and handed it to him. To B'Elanna's amazement, the empty twig on the bush swelled with a new bud that burst into a pink blossom. A few moments later the petals fell and the center of the flower grew round and hard with another fruit. It swelled and ripened even as B'Elanna watched.

"Impressive," she said, indicating the plant. "I've never seen anything quite like it. How does it work?"

Benjir ducked his head. "Your pardon, Lieutenant, but I am no horticulturist. I do know that the plants are genetically engineered and overseen by nanites. The regrowth process would be quite impossible without them. Tell me, what is the name of your home planet?"

"Depends," B'Elanna said. "I grew up on Kessik IV. My father came from Earth—some people call it Terra—and my mother came from Q'onoS. I lived there for a while, too."

"I am fascinated," Benjir chuffed. "Your people grow up on many different planets?"

"Some do." B'Elanna ate another leaf. "Other people stay on one planet all their lives."

"I hope we can one day accomplish a similar society, and soon. We must, in fact."

There was a decidedly wistful note in his voice. B'Elanna ignored a proffered fruit and cocked her head. "Is there some kind of problem?"

Benjir hesitated. "I hate to mention our problems

to honored guests, but I believe already you may know, since Secretary Nashi has said you have powerful sensors."

"Know what?"

"Our planet is terribly overpopulated. This forest is one of the few left on Chi and is reserved for governmental use. Every place but the deserts and high mountains is dense with people. Without constant maximization of crops by our nanites, famines would be widespread. Resources were strained further by the war with the Sherek-Ushekti. We are hoping the Zedrel Drive will allow us to find and colonize other worlds and to relieve the burden on our planet."

The fruit disappeared and another handful of leaves came into B'Elanna's range of vision. She accepted them. "Well, you have what appears to be a functioning warp drive and a plentiful supply of dilithium, and the shuttles that go up to the space station and back tell me you can build spaceworthy vessels. With all that going for you, it shouldn't take long to build a decent colony ship once Zedrel gets the bugs worked out of his warp drive."

"We hope so, though shielding seems to be our biggest trouble. How do you handle it?"

"Shielding?" B'Elanna echoed. "I'm not sure I understand."

"The radiation storms out in space are harsh," Benjir explained. "We are barely able to shield our station with thick walls and our best shields. Our world, of course, is protected by ozone. Zedrel thought his shields were strong enough, too, but he was obviously wrong. How does your ship withstand the storms?"

"It doesn't," B'Elanna replied bluntly. "Storms of that magnitude are so rare, you can go a lifetime in space without ever hitting one so large."

"They are for space not normal?"

B'Elanna shook her head. "Not even remotely. They seem to be common in this sector, but once you get clear of it, there shouldn't be any trouble."

"I must get you to talk to my spouse," Benjir chuffed in excitement. "She will be—ah! Over here, Trin." He signaled to a Chiar whose outer coating shone like mother-of-pearl. "Her communication program hasn't been functioning well lately, so pardon my use of gross gestures."

"You can communicate with each other through your nanites?" B'Elanna asked.

"Over short distances, yes," Benjir said. Trin approached, thrall behind her, and Benjir made introductions. "Trin is an astronomy educator," he concluded. "She'll want to hear about this."

"Do you have spouses among your own people?" Trin asked.

"Oh, yes," B'Elanna said. "Mine is around here somewhere, probably getting into trouble."

"Isn't that just the way of spouses?" Trin said with an ironic head duck and an affectionate pat to her husband's flank. "How many do you have?"

"Uh, spouses? Only one, and that's plenty for me."

"We rarely have more than one as well," Trin said, "though the Sherekti sometimes form multiple groups."

"Trin, you will want to hear about the radiation storms," Benjir interjected. "The lieutenant tells me—"

Every window in the greenhouse shattered with an ear-crushing explosion. B'Elanna reflexively dropped to the floor as crystalline shards crashed to the floor all around her. Screams of pain and shouts of surprise filled the air as humans and Chiar alike scattered. Plants were overturned and pots broke in the confusion. A pair of hard hands grabbed B'Elanna by the upper arms and hauled her partway to her feet. For a moment she thought it was Tom, then realized it was "her" thrall Chiar. Another thrall reached down and grabbed for her as well. They were surprisingly strong for their short stature.

"Thank you," she started to say, but then the air exploded from her lungs as one of the thralls punched her hard in the abdomen and the other clipped the side of her head. The moves caught B'Elanna completely off guard and stunned her with pain and surprise. One of the thralls flicked her combadge off her uniform, then the two of them began to haul her away, her feet dragging through the shards.

Kathryn Janeway slapped her combadge from her vantage point on the floor. Broken glass lay everywhere, and her ears rang with the aftermath of the shattering. She peered around a green-leafed plant. Several of the Chiar thralls had formed a group that was dragging something toward the perimeter of the ruined greenhouse. Most of the non-thrall Chiar had, like Janeway, ducked under bushes and plants. A few stood frozen by surprise.

Most of the *Voyager* delegates were out of sight—their combat training had doubtless driven them to take instant cover. A dozen or so Chiar that Janeway took to be security forces charged the retreating thralls. One of the thralls produced a short rod that before Janeway's eyes transformed itself into an energy pistol. The thrall fired, and one of the security Chiar went down. The security team produced their own weapons. All this Janeway took in and analyzed with a single glance. This was not her fight.

Janeway slapped her combadge. "Janeway to *Voyager*. Emergency beam-out for the entire delegation—now!"

The welcome blue shimmer fell over her. A moment later she was standing on a very crowded transporter pad. Officers in scuffed and dirty dress uniforms crouched, sat, or lay in the positions they had been occupying when the transporter grabbed them. They scrambled to their feet as Bethany Marija powered down the transporter from the control station.

"Head count," Janeway said. "Is anyone missing or injured?"

"B'Elanna!" Tom Paris looked around the transporter pad. "Where's B'Elanna?"

Bethany Marija tapped her boards. "I had a lock on her. She should—uh-oh."

"What is it?" Paris demanded, all but leaping off the pad and across the room. "Where is she?"

"We only got her combadge," Marija said.

"Here it is," Neelix said, holding it up.

Paris turned frantic eyes on Janeway. "Captain—"

"We'll find her, Mr. Paris," Janeway said with calm she didn't feel. "Mr. Chakotay, take an away team."

"Tuvok," Chakotay said, "Seven, Harry. Let's go."

The remaining officers quickly cleared the transporter pad. Tuvok, his face an impassive mask, opened the room's weapons locker and handed out phasers and phaser rifles. The three away team officers and Seven of Nine stood on the pad in a tight square facing outward, phasers at the ready.

"I want to go," Paris said.

Janeway put a hand on his arm. "You know the rules, Tom. You can't go on an away team to rescue a family member."

"Where should I set you down, sir?" Marija asked over Paris's protests.

"What are my choices?" Chakotay said.

"The feast hall has mountains on the north side and forest on the other three," Marija told him. "I can transport you to the mountainside, but it would be tricky."

"If someone kidnapped B'Elanna, it's doubtful they'd haul her up a mountain," Chakotay said. "Set us down on the south side of the feast hall."

Paris's face twisted into an expression of fear and worry as the transporter hummed to life and the rescue team faded away.

The forest faded into view around Chakotay and the others. His finger tensed on the firing button of his phaser, but there was nothing to shoot at, so he relaxed, though only a little bit. B'Elanna was out there somewhere, possibly injured, and it was his duty to find her. Not only was she his friend, but Tom would rip his lungs out if she disappeared.

Behind him lay the shattered remains of the greenhouse feast hall. Ahead lay a clump of buildings he assumed were more government property. Forest lay beyond the buildings and to his left and right. Sounds of frantic activity along with shouts and screams came from the greenhouse. Chakotay, Tuvok, and Kim scanned the area visually—he saw nothing—while Seven checked the tricorder.

"We've been gone for less than two minutes," Kim said. "Whoever took B'Elanna should still be in the area."

The tricorder beeped. "I have her," Seven said. "A Klingon-human lifesign approximately two hundred meters into the woods to the east. She is accompanied by six Chiar. I am also reading some kind of power source approximately fifty meters ahead of them."

"A vehicle?" Chakotay hazarded.

"Very likely," Tuvok said. "They would need some method of escape."

"Let's go, then." Kim started to charge forward, but Chakotay put a hand on his shoulder.

"Stand down, Mr. Kim," he said. "Seven, can you transmit B'Elanna's coordinates back to *Voyager?*"

"Certainly, but I doubt that will be enough to lock on to her and transport her to safety."

"It doesn't need to be," Chakotay said, and tapped his combadge.

B'Elanna's head was clearing despite the pain thudding through it. Options flashed through her mind, and she discarded them as quickly as they came. The Chiar had paused long enough to bind her wrists behind her, and there were six in the group, so fighting was not an option. She had tried to play possum to slow them down, but had stopped that once they reached the forest—the prospect of being literally dragged through the underbrush was unpleasant at best. She had finally settled on walking but stumbling as often as she could get away with to slow them down.

The Chiar spoke little, and without the translator in her combadge, she couldn't have understood them in any case. That they were kidnapping her was obvious, but who were they and why did they want her? Did they need her specifically or just someone from *Voyager?* Or was this a thrall escape that had grabbed her up on the spur of the moment as a handy hostage in case they got caught?

An irrational part of her mind flared with anger at Tom. Where the hell had he been when the Chiar attacked her? Didn't he see? Why hadn't he come after her?

Leaves and thin branches scraped past B'Elanna as the Chiar silently and efficiently hustled her forward. Her arms were starting to get cramped from the uncomfortable binding. She strained against it, but it didn't budge. And where was the captain? Why hadn't Janeway seen fit to come and get her? B'Elanna couldn't believe they didn't know she was missing. Why hadn't they—

Two dozen columns of blue light shimmered into existence around the party of Chiar. Before any of them could react, the startled group found themselves surrounded by over twenty Starfleet officers and crewmen, all armed with phaser rifles. B'Elanna instantly dropped to the ground.

"Freeze!" Chakotay snarled.

None of the Chiar moved. Then one of them gave a high-pitched wail that went straight through B'Elanna's aching skull. The other five joined in, their flat heads thrown back in apparent agony. Then they collapsed like broken dolls to the ground. After a moment's startled pause, Seven of Nine sheathed her phaser and took out her tricorder. B'Elanna suddenly realized her bonds had released themselves. She rolled over and sat up to massage her tender wrists as Seven examined the nearest Chiar.

"Dead," she proclaimed.

Kim knelt beside B'Elanna. "How do you feel?" he asked.

"I'm all right except for a headache," she said. "What happened to them?"

"Suicide?" Chakotay hazarded.

"I am reading no other Chiar lifesigns in the immediate area," Seven said. "We should be safe, but I believe it would be best to get Lieutenant Torres back to *Voyager* as soon as possible."

"Agreed." He raised his voice. "Good work, everyone. Prepare for beam-out. Seven, find out if the nanites on any of these Chiar are still active." He nudged one of the corpses with his foot. "If it's safe, I want to bring at least one back to *Voyager* for autopsy."

CHAPTER

5

SECRETARY NASHI KI made agitated chuffing noises from the viewscreen. *"Captain, I cannot find the words. Please accept our humblest and most horrified apologies at this incident. I hope most deeply that you will not judge all Chiar on the basis of what has happened. We took every precaution, but obviously it was not enough. Is Lieutenant Torres uninjured?"*

"She's fine, Secretary," Janeway said grimly. "A bit of a headache and a little shaken up, but not seriously hurt."

Nashi sighed. *"Praise to the moon for that."*

"And I am reserving judgment until we know more about what happened," Janeway finished. "Do you know who B'Elanna's kidnappers were?"

"We do not," Nashi replied in agitation. *"Though we have our suspicions. The feast hall windows were shattered by rogue nanites on a molecular level, I*

think to gain our attention. Afterward, they erased their own programming so we could not trace them."

"Captain," Tuvok said. "We are receiving a recorded transmission."

Janeway turned. "Source?"

"Unknown. Some sort of scrambler is interfering with my attempts to trace it."

Another Chiar stepped into view on the screen and muttered urgently in Nashi's ear. She looked at Janeway and said, *"Also we are receiving a recording."*

"On screen," Janeway said.

The screen blanked a moment, then showed another Chiar, this one with stripes that reminded Janeway of a zebra.

"I am Pek, leader of the Ushek-Sherekti Freedom Movement," said the Chiar. *"The disruption tonight of the feast was precipitated by our soldiers and was intended to gain the attention of the alien ship* Voyager. *We wish the people of* Voyager *to know that Nashi Ki and the Goracar Alliance do not speak for all of Chi, and any resources or information you share with them should also be shared with the Ushekti and Sherekti. We do not wish anyone to harm. We want fair treatment for the exploited and crushed people of Sherek and Ushek, and we plead with the aliens of* Voyager *to grant equal access to the wonders you bring the Chiar."*

The recording ended, and Nashi reappeared on the screen, her outer coating pale with anger.

"Terrorists," she spat.

Janeway thought a moment. It was impossible to know if this Pek was telling the truth or not. It did, however, make her position more complicated. She had no intention of interfering in Chi's internal politics, regardless of who might be in the right or in the wrong. The Prime Directive certainly forbade such interference, and Janeway wasn't inclined to disagree with it here.

That didn't, however, prevent her from trying to learn everything she could about the situation in order to protect herself and her people. But not necessarily from Secretary Nashi.

"We've met terrorists before, Secretary," Janeway said aloud. "Starfleet does not negotiate with them, and neither do we."

Nashi's coating darkened with relief. *"Thank you, Captain."*

"In the meantime, my engineering team would like to proceed with docking at your station so we can finish repairs before the next ion storm arrives."

"Of course. And the trade negotiations?"

"Should by all means continue," Janeway said. "I'll have Mr. Neelix contact you as soon as we have everything straightened up on this end."

They made their goodbyes, and Nashi vanished from the screen. Janeway headed for the turbolift. "You have the bridge, Mr. Chakotay," she said. "Though you might want to change out of your dress uniform first. I'll be in sickbay."

Down in sickbay, Janeway found Tom Paris hovering over B'Elanna, who was just getting up from a bio-bed. Her dress uniform was still dirty and strewn with a few twigs and leaves. The Doctor set down a hypospray.

"Our kidnap victim is perfectly healthy," he

replied to Janeway's inquisitive look. "No concussion and no injuries beyond some minor scrapes and bruises. A little analgesic to relieve the headache is all she needed."

"I'm glad to hear it, Doctor," Janeway said. "B'Elanna, were you able to learn why your captors came after you?"

The chief engineer shook her head. "They threw away my combadge, so I couldn't understand what they were saying. They were all dressed like slaves—thralls—but I don't know if they were in disguise or what." She outlined some of her suspicions about the kidnapping. "But I don't know anything concrete. Tom, don't do that. I can stand up on my own."

"Husband's prerogative," Paris said. "You'll have to live with it."

Janeway drummed her fingers on the bio-bed. "We received a recording," she said, and summarized it. "If this Freedom Movement was trying to get my attention, it certainly worked. But Starfleet doesn't negotiate with terrorists."

"Like the Maquis?" B'Elanna said, then added, "Sorry. It's been a difficult afternoon."

Janeway continued as if she hadn't heard the remark. "We still don't know if they wanted you specifically or if anyone from *Voyager* would have done."

"If they're looking for technology, it seems as if there'd be easier ways to go about it," B'Elanna said. "All six of them committed suicide rather than be captured, though I don't know how they did it."

"Speaking of which," Janeway said. "Doctor, what about the dead Chiar? Chakotay said there were no working nanites on it."

"I was just about to start the autopsy, Captain," he replied from a bio-bed across the room. A motionless Chiar lay curled up on it. Death made it look even smaller and not a little forlorn. The Doctor moved the sensor wand of his medical tricorder over the body, then dropped his hand. "Well. That was . . . simple."

Janeway moved over to him. "What do you mean?"

"If I tell you he—and it was a he—died of massive brain injuries, it would be like saying a warp core breach is rather dangerous." He checked the readout unit of his tricorder. "Preliminary scan seems to indicate that every cell in his brain was instantaneously severed from every other cell. Instant, painless death."

"Who needs cyanide capsules," Paris said dryly, "when you can commit suicide by nanite?"

The Doctor continued running the wand over the Chiar's body, his face wearing a look of concern.

"What is it, Doctor?" Janeway finally asked. "Not something that will endanger this crew, I hope?"

"No, nothing like that," said the Doctor distractedly. "But this poor creature was in terrible health before he died. Look at these readings. Borderline malnutrition, osteoarthritis, chronic subdermal lesions, and a tumor that would have metastasized and killed him within a few years."

"It doesn't look sick," B'Elanna observed. "Except that it's dead."

"Not on the surface," the Doctor agreed. "But many species can appear perfectly healthy until they surprise you by keeling over. Terran parrots, for one, actually are experts at hiding disease. I wonder if the others were in the same condition or if this one was unique."

"Study quickly, Doctor," Janeway told him. "We can't really hold on to the corpse for long."

"How are you going to explain our having a Chiar body on board, Captain?" Paris asked.

Janeway shrugged. "It must have gotten caught in the rescue beam-out, Mr. Paris. Once the *terrible* uproar over B'Elanna's injuries has died down, we'll 'remember' it's here."

"We could just keep it—him," B'Elanna said. "All the Chiar who know how many Chiar kidnapped me are dead."

"Even terrorists have families," Janeway pointed out. "I'm sure the Chiar have funerary customs, and they'll want to be notified."

"Well, I'm for engineering," B'Elanna said. "The ship isn't going to dock and repair itself."

"Are you sure you're up to it?" Paris asked.

"Tom," she warned, "the Doctor said I'm perfectly fine, and now I have all this nervous energy to burn off. I'm going to change clothes and get to work. I'll see you at supper."

"I don't consider leaves a good lunch," Paris complained. "I vote we eat early."

"Inertial clamps in place," Ensign Vorik reported. *"Voyager* is now stationary relative to the space station."

"Initiating umbilical dock." On the little engineering screen B'Elanna watched the collapsible tube extend itself toward the docking portal the Chiar had cleared of nanites. Everything was going smoothly but busily, which was fine with B'Elanna. As she had predicted, the work calmed her after the foiled kidnapping attempt. Just being in engineering helped. In engineering she was in charge.

"The docking area is still clear of nanites," Vorik said. "Seven of Nine's new scanning method appears to be effective."

"She told us it would be," B'Elanna admitted.

"Did you adopt the rest of her protocols?" Vorik asked.

"I've adopted some of them," B'Elanna said. "Especially the ones about nanites. She's the expert."

"Then why is she not here?" Vorik asked.

"Not her duty shift," B'Elanna said. "The protocols are in place, and I don't need her right now." *And it would negate the whole point of coming to engineering to relax.*

"Docking procedure complete," announced the computer.

"Well," B'Elanna said, dusting imaginary dirt from her hands, "let's alert the captain and go down to meet our new engineering friends."

She gathered up the twenty-odd on-duty engineers, including Vorik, and they trooped on down to the docking area. Captain Janeway was waiting for them on *Voyager*'s side of the docking tube.

"Just a reminder to all of you," she said. "We are not giving the Chiar any new technology. Do *not* under any circumstances work on a piece of equipment where the Chiar can see you. Bring it aboard *Voyager* for that. You may talk with the Chiar, of course—I encourage friendship and goodwill between us. But any information trading must come through me or Mr. Neelix."

The engineers nodded understanding. Janeway

turned to B'Elanna. "I look forward to reading your progress reports, Lieutenant." And with a nod to the team, she left. A certain amount of tension left with her. B'Elanna had for a moment thought the captain had intended to oversee the repairs herself, a move she was entitled to but one that would also indicate lack of confidence in her chief engineer. Exhaling silently, B'Elanna turned to her team.

"First priority is to get the warp engines repaired," she said. "Second is to scan the hull for potential weaknesses and breech zones. Get those fixed. The Chiar have plenty of waldoes, so we can take care of weaknesses on the outer hull without having to go outside. That's going to save us tons of time right there. Scan every single piece of Chiar equipment up-close and personal for nanites before you bring it aboard. Questions so far?"

There were none. B'Elanna handed out assignments, then turned to the docking tube portal and opened it.

The tube was a flexible biopolymer affair about three meters tall and reinforced with force fields interspersed with duranium ribbing. It made a ten-meter tunnel between *Voyager* and the Chiar station. At the far end lay the station entrance. B'Elanna headed for it, the engineering team behind them. It irised open as they approached, and the strong Chiar smell washed over them. B'Elanna gagged, realizing the Doctor's inoculation must have worn off and she had completely forgotten to renew it. It was like having perfume poured into her nose. The expressions on the team's faces told her they felt the same way, except for Vorik, who seemed unaffected.

"Nothing for it, troops," she said. "Maybe we'll get used to it after a few minutes. Meanwhile, try not to let it show."

The door opened on what looked like an empty cargo bay. No Chiar were in sight—they wouldn't give up their nanites even temporarily, and the agreement between the Chiar and *Voyager* was that no nanites would come close to the ship. Seven of Nine's detection and cleansing protocols ensured the integrity of the agreement. But the Chiar smell lingered.

"We could expose the bay to vacuum," coughed a crewman. "That would get rid of most of it."

"No," B'Elanna said. "We don't want to insult them. Just breathe normally, and after a while you won't even notice it. I hope."

The cargo bay door opened onto a long hallway with yet another iris door at the end. It opened when they reached it, revealing about ten Chiar. B'Elanna, who had indeed been getting slightly used to the smell, found her senses assaulted all over again. The smell was different, which meant her nose had to start over in learning to ignore it. She swallowed a cough and approached the lead Chiar.

"I'm Lieutenant B'Elanna Torres," she said. "Chief engineer on *Voyager.*"

The Chiar ducked. "Chief Engineer Vema of the Goracar Space Station. This is my husband and assistant primary, Pollu. It is an honor."

B'Elanna noticed the smell had changed slightly. It was sweeter, but still cloying. "Shall we begin, then, by going over what we need for the repairs?"

The work progressed smoothly. B'Elanna and Vema directed the handling of supplies while Pollu showed other members of the team how to operate Chiar waldoes. In less than an hour disembodied mechanical hands, some as large as a shuttle, reached across from the space station to *Voyager* bearing welding torches and other tools.

"It would go so much more quickly if you used nanites," Vema observed at one point.

"They're just not for us," B'Elanna said lightly. "But we do appreciate everything else you're doing."

"And we appreciate your bringing back Zedrel," Vema replied. "If he had not come back, I think the government might have dropped all warp drive research. Now we know it will work. Even if you cannot give us a working warp drive, you have brought priceless information. And we need it. We are crowded on our planet and need to expand into space."

They were standing in a double-wide corridor while a steady parade of Starfleet engineers with equipment-heavy gravity sleds trooped past. The corridor had started off pink but had lately faded into a garish blue-and-orange design of spots and speckles. Chiar decor seemed as variable—and in B'Elanna's opinion as tasteless—as their outer coatings.

They probably find our uniforms deadly dull, she thought. Another sled slid by, and B'Elanna checked a series of multiphase plasma regulators off the list on her padd. The Chiar's technology was proving pleasantly easy to adapt to *Voyager*'s needs.

"I've heard you're crowded," she said. "So you want to explore out there, huh?"

"I certainly want!" Vema said eagerly. "Being an engineer in space would be a challenge, and I wish to explore other places."

"But I do not," said her Pollu with just as much vigor.

Vema made a grin with her wide mouth and placed a hand on Pollu's flank, a gesture B'Elanna was starting to associate with Chiar affection. She also noticed Vema's smell had changed a little, taking on an overlay of . . . vanilla? Orchids? B'Elanna couldn't quite tell. It was still overwhelming and unpleasant. Next time she would definitely take a neural suppressor.

"It is a point of contention between us," Vema said. "I wish so much to explore space, but Pollu wishes to remain closer to home. Working on the space station seemed a compromise."

The scent in the corridor changed. B'Elanna turned and saw Zedrel approaching. The Chiar in the group exchanged greetings, and Zedrel turned to B'Elanna. His stare seemed penetrating, even wolfish. B'Elanna felt the hackles on her neck rise, but she couldn't say why.

"Lieutenant Torres," he said, "I have learned that your people usually eat at set times instead of grazing during the day. Have you eaten an evening meal?"

"No," she said cautiously. "In fact, I was just about to go off-duty to do just that."

"Then may I extend an invitation to you?" Zedrel said. "You had little chance to eat at the banquet, and I would greatly enjoy having a Starfleet engineer at my home. It takes approximately half an hour to reach the surface by shuttle, and another fifteen minutes of ground transport to reach my home, so it is not far."

A sharp, acidic smell punctured the air. B'Elanna glanced at Vema. B'Elanna was far from adept at reading Chiar expressions and body language, but the smell was something else. It said *anger* to B'Elanna, though she couldn't say exactly why. Was Vema mad at Zedrel for proffering the invitation? Did Vema simply dislike Zedrel, or had she intended to invite B'Elanna to dinner herself? It suddenly occurred to B'Elanna that none of the Chiar engineers had thralls with them, though several of them munched leaves they took from a sort of saddlebag thrown over their backs.

"Normally I would accept, Engineer Zedrel," B'Elanna said. "But I'm actually still a bit nervous after . . . what happened to me this afternoon. I need some time in my own space with my husband this evening."

"I understand completely," Zedrel replied, though he looked—and smelled—disappointed. "Another time, then."

"Another time," B'Elanna agreed.

"And you must also dine with us," Vema put in. "Our home is not as beautiful as Engineer Zedrel's estate, but it is comfortable. Your spouse is also invited."

"Thank you," B'Elanna said, feeling a little overwhelmed. "I'll ask him."

"Yuck!" said Tom.

"I feel the same way." B'Elanna sighed and slumped farther down into the couch cushions. The room was blessedly free of Chiar smells. When B'Elanna had gotten home, Tom had taken one whiff and ordered her into the shower before he would even kiss her hello, let alone sit at the dinner table with her. After a filling dinner of tender pot roast with mashed spicy *jeerina* root and a glass of wine, she was feeling human—and Klingon—again. Repairs would continue around the clock, but B'Elanna didn't need to be there for all of it. Not that she intended to stay away for long. She'd be up early in the morning, of course, and maybe she would just pop down for a quick look later this evening. The new injector coils would have to be realigned at every stage of installment, and—

"—refuse without appearing snobbish," Tom was saying. "What do you think?"

Caught out, B'Elanna backtracked furiously through the conversation to pick up the thread. "Right," she said. "No snobbishness."

Tom leveled her a hard look. "Your mind is on the repairs. I can tell."

"There's a lot to do," she protested.

"It can wait until morning," he said firmly. "Your team is well-trained. They know what they're doing." He slid closer to her on the couch. "Besides, I found a new cache of cartoons in the database, and you need to unwind."

He reached behind her to massage her shoulders. She rolled her head back, enjoying the work of his expert fingers. Maybe she should just relax after everything that had happened. The cartoons would help. Tom had introduced her to them, and at first she couldn't understand why he liked them so much. After constant exposure, however, she had to admit they were growing on her. Maybe all the violence was appealing to her Klingon side.

"And," Tom continued, still massaging, "we need to discuss Project Nine."

B'Elanna straightened. "Oh, no. Not tonight, Tom."

"You promised," he said. "And you always have some fake excuse for putting it off. 'I'm too tired' or 'The bolts around the warp core need tightening' or 'I was kidnapped by a bunch of aliens.'" He paused. "Okay, the last one was true. But the rest—"

She sighed. "All right. Project Nine. Let's get it over with."

Tom leaned forward. "I've already got someone lined up."

"Who?"

"Lieutenant Geraci. He'd be perfect."

"Geraci?" B'Elanna said in disbelief. "He's got nothing going for him. Unless you like the tall, broad-shouldered type," she said, reconsidering. "With deep, black pools for eyes. And a smoldering look . . ."

"You think he's cute?" Tom interrupted.

B'Elanna looked him up and down. "Maybe. Jealous?"

"Of Geraci? Get a reality link." He narrowed his eyes. "You're just trying to change the subject. Project Nine, remember?"

"Right." She sighed. "Project Nine. What do I need to do?"

"Not much, actually. I've already thought it all out. Here's the plan."

CHAPTER

6

"ENGINEER ZEDREL," SNAPPED SEVEN OF NINE. "You must leave this area at once. If you continue to follow me, you will be in violation of the Chiar-Federation Treaty."

Zedrel reared up slightly, then dropped back to the deck, bending his front legs in a combination of confusion and supplication that Seven had come to recognize over the last two days. She suppressed a sigh. They were standing in one of the corridors of the Chiar space station, one that led to the docking bay for *Voyager.* Seven was going off duty in a few minutes, and the holodeck—along with Commander Chakotay—was waiting. There was no time for foolish delays.

The Chiar space station was, like many other aspects of the Chiar culture, inefficient. Every square inch of wall, ceiling, and floor was covered with garish paintings and fractal mosaics that changed every few hours. The floor was sometimes inlaid tile, sometimes thick carpet, sometimes bare metal. Every time Seven looked at something she had seen before, it was different. This meant that Seven and the rest of the crew had to waste valuable time readjusting to their surroundings. The shifting colors, textures, and scenes also made it very easy to get lost on the station. Bethany Marija and the other transporter technicians had their hands full rescuing lost engineers and beaming them aboard *Voyager.*

The Chiar themselves didn't seem to mind the abrupt changes, nor did they have trouble adjusting. Seven suspected there was a pattern to it that she and the other crew hadn't perceived yet, or perhaps the Chiar's nanites guided them around the station. In any case, Seven found the entire place disconcerting. Although the idea of rejoining the Collective now made her shudder, at least every Borg vessel had been the same as every other of its class. She could have found her way around any of them even without the voices of the Collective to guide her. Likewise, the interior of *Voyager* changed only rarely. This made the Chiar alterations even more difficult to deal with.

And then there was the smell. Even Seven, who had thought she was above such petty problems, had been forced to take an olfactory inhibitor. The Doctor had examined the dead Chiar terrorist in great detail and had afterward informed the crew that the Chiar had, by human standards, an almost undeveloped sense of smell.

"The difference between them and you," he had said, "is the difference between a Terran dog and a human. The one I examined had enough scent glands to start a cologne factory, but in his eyes—or nose—the scent was barely strong enough to be noticeable."

As a result, the engineering crew began carrying hyposprays filled with olfactory inhibitors with them everywhere.

Finally there was Zedrel. He had taken to following the crew around like a half-grown puppy striving to fit in with adult dogs. He proffered dinner invitations, lunch invitations, recreational activities, and more. B'Elanna and Seven had so far managed to avoid them, but a few other members of the engineering team had been trapped into them. They said Zedrel always tried to grill them for information about the warp core, and it was a constant battle not to reveal anything. Also, Seven, Torres, and the others were constantly shooing him away from the restricted areas of the station. After some diplomatic persuasion from Janeway and Neelix, Secretary Nashi had reluctantly agreed that sharing Federation technology with the Chiar might upset the structure of their civilization and was therefore not a good idea. That didn't stop Zedrel, however, from trying to get a peek at everything he could. One wondered when he worked on his own warp drive. Seven usually felt a twinge of pity for him, but today had been a trial, and although Seven felt she had a nearly endless supply of tact for and patience with people, even she had her limits. Also, she was going off duty to meet Chakotay in the holodeck in a few minutes, and she didn't want to be late.

"You must leave, Engineer Zedrel," Seven said,

looking down at him. His head didn't quite reach chest height.

"I just . . . I just wanted to talk to Captain Janeway," Zedrel said. "It is important."

"Communication protocols are very clear in this matter," Seven replied. Around them, the corridor mosaics glittered and shifted, tugging at the corners of Seven's awareness. "All personal visits must be cleared with both Captain Janeway and Secretary Nashi. In my experience, they must also be pre-arranged at least four hours in advance. Personal communications, however, are handled by Commander Tuvok. Perhaps you should try your luck with him."

Zedrel ducked his head and slowly turned away, feet dragging. Seven sighed and relented.

"However," she added, "I might be able to give the captain a short message."

Zedrel perked up. "Gratitude! Please tell Captain Janeway that I have finished repairs on my warp drive. She promised to follow us in case something . . . fails to operate as planned."

"I will give her the message," Seven said solemnly.

Zedrel ducked his head again and trotted off, his nails clicking on the—for the moment—hard corridor floor. Seven was turning to head back for *Voyager*'s docking bay when the clicking sound ceased. Seven looked over her shoulder and saw Zedrel staring back at her. An odd look was back on his face, one she couldn't identify, though it reminded her of the look he had given her and Torres in the turbolift two days ago. A strange feeling rose in Seven's stomach. She tried to figure out what the sensation was, and couldn't. Stiffly she turned and marched through the docking bay.

Since the bay was devoid of nanites, it remained a safe, steady gray. Seven entered the umbilical passage to the ship. Two strips of light sectioned off a portion of the passage, and Seven halted in front of the first strip.

"Computer," she said, "deactivate force field alpha at umbilical passage. Authorization Seven of Nine omicron delta six."

The light winked out as the field deactivated. Seven crossed the barrier, and the force field immediately went up behind her. The field ahead of her remained active.

"Scanning for unauthorized nanites," the computer said. Pause. "Scan complete. Deactivating force field beta. You may proceed."

The second field came down, allowing Seven to cross into the docking bay. It went up again the moment she crossed the line. The airlock door slid open, and she entered Voyager's familiar corridors. Still the strange feeling remained.

Seven strode with quick, firm steps as she tried to analyze the sensation. It was an unpleasant one. She could still feel Zedrel's eyes on her, as if they were crawling over her skin. Also, the idea of fulfilling her recent promise to Zedrel felt repugnant. But why? The Chiar had done nothing wrong except stray too close to a prohibited area, and Seven had only promised to give Captain Janeway a simple message.

She was being ridiculous. As she headed for the holodeck, Seven of Nine firmly tapped her combadge to contact her captain and relayed Zedrel's message as dispassionately as she could.

"Thank you, Seven," Janeway said. *"I'll have to contact him. Janeway out."*

A few moments later Seven reached the holodeck and finally managed to push thoughts of Zedrel out of her head. Chakotay was nowhere to be seen.

"Computer," she said, "location of Commander Chakotay."

"Commander Chakotay is in holodeck one," the computer said.

Seven checked the panel outside the holodeck and found the playground program was already running. Chakotay must have already arrived and started without her. She tapped the panel, the holodeck doors whined open, and she entered. The moment Seven crossed the threshold, she changed. Her hair came down and formed itself into ponytails. Her jumpsuit shifted into sturdy denim play clothes. Her face became rounder, her body stockier. When it was done, the child Annika Hansen looked around the park.

The playground was the same as before, filled with shrieking children and lots of playground equipment. Seven—she still thought of herself by that name—looked around it uncertainly. The computer had reported that Chakotay was here, and the program was certainly running, but Seven saw no sign of—

Two hands landed on her shoulders. "Boo!"

Seven twisted like a cat and aimed a sweeping kick at the person behind her. Chakotay jumped straight upward just in time to avoid her foot.

"Hey, Seven," he said with a laugh. "Ease up. It's

kid time, remember? Little kids don't worry about security—that's an adult's job."

"You startled me," Seven said, pushing her blond ponytails behind her shoulders.

"That was the whole point," Chakotay grinned.

She looked at him. "Is this one of those actions human boys perform when they wish to show . . . affection for a human girl?"

"Uh, sometimes," Chakotay stammered. His face was flushed, and Seven realized that his boy self had no tattoos. "But not this time. I mean—"

Seven cut him off with a hand wave. "It is unimportant. What are we playing today?"

"Hide-and-seek. Come on—I've already got the others to set it up. Do you know the rules?"

"I have been researching childhood pastimes," Seven said. "I am familiar with this game. It strikes me as an excellent way to learn problem-solving skills."

"We're glad you approve," Chakotay replied gravely.

He led her over to a group of waiting children. Seven recognized them from the last time, including Tenna and Mel. Seven's stomach clenched when she saw the latter, and she had to remind herself that none of this, including Mel, was real.

"Who's It?" Tenna asked.

"Not It!" shouted Mel.

"Not It!" shouted Chakotay.

A chorus of "Not It!" quickly rose and just as quickly quieted. Seven blinked in consternation.

"Not It?" she hazarded.

"It's not a question, dummy," Mel said scornfully.

"You were the last one to say it," Tenna said.

"That means you're It! Home base is that tree. You have to count to a hundred by fives."

Seven obediently went over to the tree and hid her eyes against it, trying to find somewhere within her what Chakotay would call "the spirit of things." Chakotay seemed to be enjoying himself, even reveling in being a child again. Seven supposed she could understand why. Children had fewer responsibilities, were forgiven for transgressions that would land an adult in a great deal of trouble, and could play games while others were working. Seven, however, was having a hard time letting go. When her real self was the age she was currently pretending to be, Seven was cleaning trans-warp circuit tubes and upgrading shield rotation modules. There was always work to be done, and completing it efficiently in the manner prescribed by the Collective had filled her with pride, or as much of that emotion as anyone could feel among the Borg. Letting go of the need for efficiency and perfection was no easy task.

On the other hand, Seven loved a challenge.

"Five ... ten ... fifteen ... twenty ..." she chanted. Just because it felt like something Naomi Wildman might do, Seven allowed a certain amount of randomization in the amount of time between each number, adding a variation of up to half a second. Finally she reached a hundred and quickly spun around. None of the hiders were in evidence, though the several children who were uninvolved in the game continued playing among themselves.

Seven scanned the area visually. For an irrational moment she wished for a tricorder, then discarded the idea. Not only would it be cheating, it would remove all challenge—and therefore all fun—from the game.

And then a thought came to Seven. Perhaps the "fun" of being a child was not necessarily tied in with a lack of responsibility and the desire to play silly games. Perhaps it was that a child was in a position to meet challenges without having to worry about the consequences. If she lost the game, nothing would happen to her, and win or lose, she stood to gain a certain amount of personal growth. Perhaps that was what childhood fun was really about.

Seven decided to try it.

She edged away from home base, trying to look in all directions at once. This variant of the game allowed the hiders to make a break for home base before It found them, so she had to be careful. Where were they? Seven saw any number of hiding places—trees, boulders, small knots of other children, the overhead treehouses. Someone would certainly give themselves away if Seven waited long enough, but that sort of patience didn't strike Seven as childlike.

Then she caught a glimmer of movement from behind a waist-high rock about fifteen meters away. Seven wandered toward it in what she hoped was a casual saunter, surprised at how her heart was racing. The movement flickered again. Seven all but flew at the rock, leaped over it, and completely surprised Mel, who was hiding behind it. She tagged him on the shoulder.

"You're It!" she cried.

Mel got to his feet, eyes flashing. "You didn't see me. You cheated! You looked while you were counting."

Several other players rushed almost simultaneously from their hiding places and tagged the home tree. "Allee allee out are in free!" they chanted.

Seven found her temper rising at Mel's words. "I did not cheat," she said, putting her hands behind her back with forced calm. "You kept looking over the top of the rock and gave yourself away. It was a foolish strategy."

"You're a freak!" Mel shouted. "A weirdo freak who talks funny. You can't even talk right and you cheat."

Seven flushed. "I—"

"Freaky cheat! Freaky cheat!" Mel chanted. Then his fist hit her in the face. It hurt. Seven was so startled that she jumped backward and fell. She was only vaguely aware of the other kids running toward her and of Tenna shouting something at Mel. Anger and frustration tightened her chest. She had finally gotten into the game, had started to understand being a child and having childhood fun, and Mel had to ruin it. To Seven's horror she felt tears gathering in her eyes. She saw Chakotay running toward her as well. He couldn't see her like this. She couldn't let him.

"Computer," she choked, "end program."

The playground vanished. Chakotay, once again an adult, skidded to a halt in front of her. "Are you okay?"

Seven got to her feet. "I did not sustain serious injury," she said. Her voice remained rock-firm. "The safety interlocks would not allow it."

He still looked guilty. "Bullies are unfortunately a part of childhood," he said. "That's why the computer put one on the playground. But maybe we should delete him anyway."

"It would not matter," she said, heading for the door. "I do not intend to run this program again."

Janeway's combadge beeped. *"Engineer Zedrel is waiting to speak with you,"* came Tuvok's voice.

Kathryn Janeway set the data padd aside and tapped the tiny console of the communicator in her ready room. Zedrel's now-familiar features winked into view. He ducked his head in greeting. Janeway, who had the wrong sort of neck to duplicate the maneuver, nodded at him instead. The normally beautiful view outside her window was, at the moment, almost entirely blocked by the massive gray wall of the Chiar space station. Apparently the Chiar love of decoration only applied to interiors.

"Seven gave me your message, Engineer," Janeway said. "She said your warp drive is fully repaired?"

"It is, Captain," Zedrel said.

"Then congratulations."

"Gratitude," Zedrel replied. *"And how are the repairs to your own ship proceeding?"*

Janeway gestured at the data padd. "I was just reading the latest update. It seems we're pretty close to shipshape. We've already uploaded some of the programs we're trading, and I believe Mr. Neelix is overseeing receipt of the first dilithium shipment. Overall, things are going very well."

Zedrel shook his head from side to side, something Janeway recognized as minor amazement. *"Your people are extraordinarily efficient,"* he said.

Janeway couldn't help but grin. "Seven of Nine

sometimes begs to differ." She shifted to a more serious tone. "I assume you're calling because you want to test your ship and want us to follow you?"

"Yes, Captain. I am ready to run the test whenever you and your crew are available." He paused. *"I believe Secretary Nashi is rather hoping to view the test from your ship."*

"Is she? Well, I don't see why not. I'll have Commander Chakotay and Lieutenant Torres make the arrangements."

"You will follow me in your ship, then?"

Janeway shook her head. "That isn't really necessary. The *Delta Flyer* is better suited to the task. It's smaller and more maneuverable."

Zedrel gave her an odd look. *"But how will Secretary Nashi see the test?"*

"Our astrometrics lab will be able to keep on eye on them easily enough," Janeway said reassuringly.

"Astrometrics? What kind of—"

"Engineer, I don't want to seem rude," Janeway interrupted, "but if you wish to conduct your test and if the Secretary wishes to watch from our ship, there are matters I must attend to." *And answering your incessant questions comes low on my list.*

Zedrel ducked. *"Of course, Captain."*

The screen went blank. Janeway shook her head ruefully. Zedrel would probably keep her talking until the sun died if she let him. She called Chakotay into the ready room to start making arrangements.

Seven of Nine jabbed at the boards, and the astrometrics display drew back at a dizzying pace, as if a camera had fled backward through *Voyager*'s hull.

The Chiar star glowed yellow in the center of the screen, and a tiny replica of *Voyager* hovered nearby. It had moved several hundred kilometers away from the space station. The view swung to the right, revealing the sleek shape of the *Delta Flyer* next to Zedrel's needle-and-octagon ship. Both were moving steadily away from the planet under impulse power. Tom Paris and the Doctor, Seven knew, were aboard the *Flyer,* while Zedrel piloted his own ship solo. Seven was glad Zedrel was far away. She had the feeling if he were standing behind her, it would be exceedingly difficult for her to concentrate on the astrometrics display. It was hard enough keeping a stoic face after the incident in the holodeck.

The worst part about it was that she didn't know why it bothered her so much. A child which did not really exist had called her a name and had hit her once. The damage was so minor she had not even troubled the Doctor with it. But it did bother her. Every time she thought about it, it filled her with anger. She forced herself to push thoughts of the playground away and concentrate on her current assignment.

Behind Seven stood the Captain, Neelix, Secretary Nashi, and a small crowd of other Chiar, all safely ensconced in a protective force field manipulated by B'Elanna Torres. Several of them wore the matte outer coating that indicated enslaved service, and they passed steady streams of leaves and fruit to the higher-ranking Chiar. The Chiar, who were considerably shorter than the humans, stood on a platform so they could see better, and their outer coatings shimmered and shifted in clashing patterns.

Harry Kim waited nearby, tricorder in hand, to scan for stray nanites.

"I am ready to begin the test," came Zedrel's voice over the comm system.

"Our course is laid in to match," Paris reported from the *Flyer.*

"Bridge," Janeway said, "are you monitoring?"

"We are, Captain," Chakotay's voice came back. *"If there's any trouble the* Flyer *can't handle, we're ready to move in and assist."*

"And my medikit is primed and ready," said the Doctor cheerfully. *"With luck, I won't have to use it."*

The Chiar stirred within their force field. Captain Janeway stood motionless, hands behind her back. Seven wondered if she or one of the Chiar would give a speech and hoped they would not. Speeches were an unnecessary and inefficient use of time. It would take longer to give the speech than conduct the test.

But Janeway only said, "Whenever you're ready, Mr. Paris."

"On your own mark, Engineer Zedrel," said Secretary Nashi.

"Three . . ." Zedrel said. *"Two . . . one . . . engage."*

The Chi ship streaked away. An instant later the *Delta Flyer* shot forward and caught up. The display moved with them, keeping both ships in the center. Words and numbers ran in columns next to each vessel, indicating relative speeds, vectors, and warp factors.

"Both ships have achieved warp factor two," Seven reported.

"That means ten times the speed of light,"

Janeway translated for the Chiar. They made excited twittering sounds Seven had never heard before.

"I am increasing speed," Zedrel said.

"Everything looks steady from here, Captain," Paris put in. The ships moved faster.

"Warp factor two point three," Seven said. "Two point six. Two point nine. Warp three."

Secretary Nashi bobbed her head. "This is wonderful, Captain. It's working beautifully!"

"Congratulations," Neelix said. "You must be very proud of your engineer."

"Zedrel, your plasma conduits are overheating," Paris said. *"We'd better head back. Slow to warp two."*

"Agreed," Zedrel replied.

A hissing sound Seven took for disappointment issued from one of the Chiar. She turned in time to catch Janeway smiling at them.

"Well, I hope you have a celebration planned," the captain said. "It seems to have worked."

"But it did *not* work!" wailed Master Ree. His outer coating had paled with dismay. "The plasma whatever-they-are malfunctioned. How can we possibly celebrate when everything didn't go as planned? Zedrel will be so disappointed, and he will doubtless lose his government support, and he will not—"

"Master Ree," Nashi interrupted firmly, "Zedrel's ship has worked beautifully, and we will indeed hold a celebration. This is a monumental day for the Goracar Alliance. Captain Janeway, on behalf of the Chiar people, I extend gratitude to you and your crew for the assistance. You are all invited to our station for a celebratory event, one that will be uninterrupted, I promise."

"You are quite welcome," Janeway said. "And we would be delighted to attend."

On the astrometrics display, Zedrel's ship and the *Delta Flyer* moved steadily toward the station.

"We should return to the station, then, to make preparations," Master Ree said. "Can this be arranged, Captain?"

"Mr. Paris will be happy to bring you across in the *Flyer* once Engineer Zedrel has docked at your space station," Janeway told him.

"Captain, if I may," Neelix put in, his yellow eyes flickering toward Nashi, who pretended not to notice. He lowered his voice to a near whisper. "I, er, happen to know that Secretary Nashi was a tad disappointed that she wasn't able to experience the transporter."

Janeway looked at him expectantly. "Yes, Mr. Neelix?"

"If I recall correctly," he continued, "the problem is that the filters wouldn't, em, *process* the nanites so they could come aboard. But it shouldn't be a problem to transport them *off* the ship, am I correct?"

Janeway turned to Torres. "Lieutenant?"

"Doable," Torres said.

"Then would you like to try a transport, Secretary?" Janeway asked.

Nashi ducked. "I would indeed, Captain. Gratitude."

"Right this way, then. Seven, keep an eye on the ships and let me know if anything happens."

"Yes, Captain."

Staying within the confines of Torres's force field, the group of Chiar slowly made their way out of the astrometrics lab with Kim and his tricorder in tow. Seven watched them go, relieved without knowing why.

Janeway looked up at the transporter pad. B'Elanna Torres stood in the center, surrounded by a circle of Chiar. Janeway forced herself not to tap her foot with impatience. She wanted the Chiar off her ship, and in the worst possible way. She couldn't put her finger on exactly why or what was bothering her about them. It wasn't the smell—the force field kept that at bay. Perhaps it was just the idea that they were literally crawling with the same sort of technology that powered the Borg, or perhaps it was simply the strain of having to keep them shielded every second and moment they were on board. She didn't know how B'Elanna coped—the half-Klingon woman wasn't usually known for her patience.

The celebration was also unlikely to be rewarding. Everyone who attended would have to take the Doctor's olfactory inhibitor, making the food just as tasteless as it had been the first time around. And then there would be the careful scanning for unwanted nanites before the crew could return to *Voyager*, and no matter what Nashi said, there was the possibility of another terrorist attack, meaning Janeway and Tuvok would have to set up some kind of monitoring system and be ready to yank the attendees away on a second's notice.

The warp ship test bothered Janeway as well. The captain should have been able to share in the obvious joy the Chiar showed—or most of them showed. Instead, the entire affair made her edgy. Well, according to B'Elanna, all of *Voyager*'s repairs would be completed within twenty hours and they could be on their way before the next storm.

Secretary Nashi and her entourage shifted with impatience, excitement, or perhaps both. It had taken some doing to get the force field up the stairs, and then Bethany Marija had to follow Torres's curt instructions on slaving the shield to the transporter, but it was all done.

"You'll probably feel a slight tingling sensation," Janeway said. "Ready?"

"We are," Nashi said. Her outer coating glowed a happy pink.

Less than a day and we're out of here, Janeway told herself. *Almost done, girl. You're almost done.*

"Drop shield and energize," she said aloud.

A flash of light as the field came down. Instantly the group of Chiar were shrouded in a blue glow. Then they faded into nothingness, leaving Torres alone on the pad. A whiff of Chiar scent tanged the air, and Janeway, who hadn't taken an olfactory inhibitor that day, resisted the urge to fan the air with one hand.

"Transport complete, Captain," Marija reported.

"I'm not detecting any nanites left behind," Kim said beside her, tricorder open and flashing.

Janeway allowed herself a small slump in posture before tapping her combadge. "Janeway to bridge. Chakotay, set course for the Chiar station. I want these repairs completed by half-past hurry-up so we can get out of here."

"Acknowledged."

B'Elanna guided the shield generator's gravity sled off the transporter pad. "Half-past hurry-up?"

"Just something my grandfather used to say." Janeway smiled. "He was a . . . colorful man, by any standard."

"I don't know," Torres said doubtfully. "My own grandfather was—"

"Tuvok to Captain Janeway," Tuvok's voice interrupted. *"I am detecting an intruder in shuttlebay two. Security teams are underway."*

Janeway headed for the door, Torres right behind her. "Meet us down there, Mr. Tuvok."

As she and Torres hurried for the shuttlebay, Janeway's mind ran quickly over the possibilities. The obvious answer was that one of the Chiar had broken into the shuttlebay. But which Chiar? And what for? Had it broken in or somehow gotten lost? Janeway pursed her lips. She hated intruders on her ship. An intruder was a personal affront, a violation of her personal boundaries, and she was in no mood for treating them with kid gloves.

It took Janeway and Torres less than five minutes to reach shuttlebay two. When they arrived, the bay doors were open, and a pair of yellow-shirted security officers were standing watch, phasers at the ready. Janeway nodded to them as she jogged past, Torres on her heels. They found Tuvok, another pair of security officers, and an otherwise empty shuttlebay. Tuvok was staring at his tricorder. No sign of an intruder.

"Report, Mr. Tuvok," she said, reserving surprise and annoyance until she knew what was going on. Off to one side the *Delta Flyer* sat motionless near the outer doors. Beside it were two smaller, box-shaped Starfleet shuttles.

"There would appear to be no intruder in the shuttlebay," Tuvok replied calmly, "and Commander Chakotay reports the bridge has not detected any transporter traces. I have already ordered a sensor diagnostic."

"The Chiar?" Janeway said, her words echoing around the bay.

"Not likely," Torres put in. "They were with us the whole time, and they didn't leave the force field even once." She sniffed twice. "There's also the fact that there isn't any Chiar . . . scent in the air."

Janeway sniffed also, realizing B'Elanna was correct. She glared around the bay, trying unsuccessfully to mask her uneasiness. "I don't think it was a sensor malfunction," she said. "It doesn't feel right."

"Kim to Tuvok," came Harry's voice.

Tuvok tapped his combadge and acknowledged.

"Commander," Kim said, *"sensor logs indicate a transmission was made from the shuttlebay less than three seconds after the intruder was detected."*

"Source?" Tuvok asked.

"Unknown. It appeared to be some kind of data burst."

"It's got to be the Chiar," Torres muttered. "But how? They can't have gotten past our security when we were docked at the station. And even if they did, how did they hide for so long without being detected or leaving a scent? And where did they go?"

Exactly what Janeway had been thinking. "Excellent questions, Lieutenant. Think you and Seven can find the answers?"

"We'll get right on it," Torres said, already reaching for her own tricorder.

"One more thing." Janeway tapped her combadge.

"Janeway to transporter room two. Marija, can you confirm that all the Chiar arrived safely at their destination?"

Pause.

"The transporter log indicates all seven Chiar were beamed successfully to the station, Captain," Crewman Marija replied.

"So either it wasn't the Chiar," Janeway muttered, "or they've managed to fool our sensors. And our sense of smell." Her eyes darted about the bay. An unknown intruder on her ship. A level-two scan to start, maybe, see if there was any residual—

"We'll get it solved, Captain," Torres said in a firm voice.

Janeway looked at her blankly, then took the hint with a suppressed smile. "I have every confidence, Lieutenant. Carry on." And she made herself turn and leave the shuttlebay in the capable hands of B'Elanna Torres.

Whistling a cheery tune, Tom Paris opened the doors and strode nonchalantly into the shuttlebay. Inside, Seven of Nine was working a wall-mounted console with brisk, efficient movements. B'Elanna stood in the center of the bay, tricorder in one hand, padd in the other.

"How's it coming?" he asked brightly.

"It isn't," B'Elanna said, alternating glares between the padd and the tricorder. "If there was an intruder in here, he didn't leave anything behind that I can find. No DNA traces, no skin flakes, no hair follicles, no infrared signatures, no stray bacteria, nothing. If I didn't happen to know they were working perfectly, I'd say it must have been a problem with the sensors."

Seven continued working her console. Data flicked by faster than the human eye could read, but Tom doubted Seven was having any trouble keeping up. Although she had been removed from the Borg Collective years ago, she still retained many Borg characteristics, including the ability to scan data at startling speeds.

"You're not in uniform," B'Elanna continued, glancing up at him. "What's up?"

"My duty shift ended an hour ago," he said, moving behind her to massage her neck. Tom wore non-regulation blue trousers and a grass-green shirt, though his combadge was still fastened to his chest. B'Elanna's skin was warm under his hand. "Yours ended, too. I came down to see if you were going to eat. And we had *plans,* remember?"

B'Elanna shook her head and dodged away from him. "I'm not done yet."

Uh-oh, Tom thought with a chagrined glance at Seven. *She forgot. And after all that arranging.* "You need to take a break," he insisted. "Clear your mind so your subconscious can work at the problem. You don't want to become a workaholic, do you?"

"This from the man who once spent three full days of leave parked under the *Delta Flyer,*" B'Elanna snorted. Her tricorder continued to warble, and lights danced across it.

"That was recreation, not work," Tom protested. "And remember that we have . . . *things* to do?"

"Uh-huh. Well, this is recreation for me," B'Elanna said, not getting the hint. "A puzzle to solve."

She *had* forgotten, and he couldn't remind her directly. Not here.

"Now you sound like the captain," he said, and turned to Seven with sudden inspiration. "Help me out here. All I want is some time with my wife before she forgets what I look like."

Seven raised the blond eyebrow not obscured by a Borg implant. "You are asking me for advice on marital relations?"

"No," Tom said hastily. "We're talking about recreation. You've been working on that, haven't you?"

Seven gave a reluctant nod. "Commander Chakotay and the Doctor have persuaded me that the occasional hour or two on the holodeck can be . . . refreshing and educational. Which increases overall productivity," she added quickly.

"There you have it," Tom said. "What better excuse do you need, O my wife?"

"Dust," B'Elanna said.

Tom blinked. "What?"

"I'm getting more of that dust," B'Elanna clarified, eyes on her tricorder.

Seven walked over, footsteps loud on the hard deck plating. She peered over B'Elanna's shoulder. "Duranium, poly-steel, transparent aluminum, monostyrenoids, and particles of optic filament."

"Exactly the same stuff as before," B'Elanna muttered.

"What are you talking about?" Tom asked more insistently.

"We've been finding these patches of fine dust on the floor and walls," B'Elanna explained. "I can't account for them."

"How the heck do you get duranium dust?" Tom asked skeptically.

"All of these materials are found on board *Voyager,*" Seven told him. "More specifically, they are found in this cargo bay."

"But not as dust," B'Elanna finished.

"Sounds like you need to complain to the janitor." Tom grinned. "Look, are we on for dinner or not? And I have just the holodeck program for afterward. Won't take more than an hour, I promise. It's all *arranged.*" He stared hard at her. *Remember? Plan Nine?*

Something clicked in B'Elanna's brown eyes, and she closed her tricorder with a snap. Tom gave a relieved little sigh. He made a tiny gesture in Seven of Nine's direction. B'Elanna gave him an uncertain look. Tom gestured again.

"I'm—I'm not playing Captain Proton," B'Elanna said a little too loudly, "so don't even ask."

"Nope. I put together a historical montage of mid-twentieth-century newsreels for the movie theater program. We can see the twentieth century as the inhabitants saw it."

"In black and white with vocal narration?" Seven said dryly.

Tom shot her a smile. "Want to join us, Seven? You might like it. Dinner, too. Even you have to eat."

Seven had opened her mouth to reply when B'Elanna jumped in. "What a great idea! Dinner together and a movie. Just like in the twenties."

"Fifties," Tom corrected.

"Fifties," B'Elanna repeated. "Maybe we *should* take a break. How about it, Seven? Sounds like fun."

Seven looked from Tom to B'Elanna and back

again. Tom put his arm around his wife's shoulders and gave Seven yet another bright, guileless smile.

"It is unusual," Seven said slowly, "for a couple to invite another person to a recreational function. I believe the term for this is a 'third wheel.' Are you planning to invite—a fourth person?"

Paris's smile faltered a little under Seven's icy stare. "Well, I thought maybe Lieutenant Geraci might like to join us, too. He's a nice guy. Lots of fun."

Seven narrowed her eyes with cold calculation, and Tom resisted the urge to step back. "Is this meant to be a blind date?"

"It was all his idea," B'Elanna said, bailing out.

"Hey!" Tom protested. "You told me it would be a good—"

A high-pitched whine cut him off. Eight blue beams of light shimmered into existence around the cargo bay and resolved themselves into eight Chiar, their outer coating a solid gray. Each one carried a long baton. The Chiar smell smashed through the room. Tom stared, surprised into immobility, but B'Elanna was already moving. She dived for the floor and slapped her combadge.

"Security to—"

One of the Chiar flicked its baton in her direction. Instantly the device shifted from a simple baton into an alien weapon. Angry red energy flashed through the air and caught B'Elanna's shoulder before she could finish her sentence. She cried out and slumped on the floor. Four other Chiar closed in around Seven of Nine. She lashed out with a leg and connected with one Chiar's chest, but the kick bounced harmlessly off its hardened outer coating. Fear and

outrage shoved Tom into action. He shouted something incoherent and lunged for the Chiar who had
shot B'Elanna. It fired the pistol at him, and he
barely twisted out of the way in time. Scrambling for
balance, he reached for his combadge, but it was inexplicably gone. Seven's had vanished as well. Out
of the corner of his eye, he saw it gleaming on the
floor.

Two Chiar laid hold of Seven. She raised both
knees and aimed a double-footed kick that knocked
a third Chiar back a step. A fourth Chiar grabbed her
from behind. Seven struggled but couldn't shake
them off.

B'Elanna lay motionless on the deck. Tom turned
to attack the Chiar who had shot her, but it and the
other three were already galloping toward the group
that held Seven. One of them flicked its baton into a
boxy shape and spoke to it. Without the translator in
his combadge, Tom couldn't understand their language, but he did catch the Federation phrase *beam
away* among the alien words.

"No!" Without thinking, Tom vaulted into their
midst. The blue light shimmered, faded, and left
B'Elanna Torres alone in the shuttlebay.

"Track them!" Janeway bellowed at Harry Kim.
"Where the hell did they come from?"

"Scanning," Kim said. His hands worked frantically
for a moment, then he shook his head. "The background radiation from the ion storms and the Chiar
microwave emitters are scrambling the trail, Captain. I
can't tell where they've gone. I've lost them."

"Confirmed," Tuvok said.

"What happened, Commander?" Janeway said dangerously. "How did they get on my ship?"

"It would appear," Tuvok said with infuriating calm, "that eight Chiar beamed into shuttlebay two and beamed back out with Lieutenant Paris and Seven of Nine. I am also reading something similar to phaser fire in the bay."

"Doctor to bridge," came the Doctor's dry voice over the intercom. *"I am with Lieutenant Torres in shuttlebay two. She has been wounded by phaser fire and is unconscious, but I don't believe she is in any immediate danger. I am taking her to sickbay."*

"Hail the Chiar station," Janeway ordered. "I want to talk to Secretary Nashi and I mean yesterday."

"Hailing," Tuvok said.

"Mr. Kim," Chakotay snapped, "how did the Chiar get their hands on transporter technology?"

"I don't know, Commander," Kim said helplessly. "We were careful to make sure none of their nanites interacted with the ship's systems. We beamed the secretary and her people off the ship, but that wouldn't have given even Borg nanoprobes a chance to figure out how a transporter works."

"If the Chiar were able to smuggle any nanites aboard *Voyager*," Tuvok said, "it is quite conceivable they would be able to examine and create a schematic for a transporter. Their ability to use nanites for tool creation would accelerate the process, allowing them to build a working model fairly quickly."

"Except we never allowed their nanites to interact with the systems on board this ship," Janeway growled. "Mr. Kim, scan for nanites anyway."

125

"Already on it, Captain," Kim said. Pause. "Scan complete. No nanites on board."

Janeway thought a moment. "Mr. Kim, scan for nanites *outside* the ship."

"Captain?"

"Just do it, Mr. Kim!"

"Scanning." An alarm buzzed on Kim's console. "I'm detecting nanites, Captain. Several trillion on the hull and several trillion more floating nearby." His voice was incredulous.

"That's how," Janeway said, oddly satisfied even as her anger grew.

"A nanite cloud," Chakotay whistled from his chair. "They slipped into the shuttlebay when the *Delta Flyer* left to follow Zedrel's ship."

"And once inside the bay," Janeway concluded, "they explored *Voyager,* including the transporters. B'Elanna reported finding a very fine dust in the shuttlebay. I'll bet the nanites built a transmitter by lifting a monomolecular layer of various materials from inside the ship. They used it to send the data, disassembled the transmitter into its component molecules, and finished by disassembling each other to the molecule so there'd be no evidence."

"So the intruder Tuvok detected was the transmitter itself," Chakotay mused. "Seeming to come out of nothing and setting off the ship's alarms."

"Tuvok, get rid of them," Janeway ordered. "Now."

"I am working on it, Captain," Tuvok replied. "I believe I can borrow a page from the Chiar and route a microwave pulse through the deflector dish."

"Do it."

"And Secretary Nashi is hailing us," Tuvok concluded.

"On screen."

"Captain," Nashi said immediately from the viewer. *"Did something go wrong with your repairs? You have not docked with our station."*

"Eight Chiar just transported aboard my ship," Janeway snarled. "They shot one of my officers and kidnapped two of my crew. More terrorists, Secretary?"

Nashi's outer coating paled from red to white, and she backed up a step. Her wide eyes blinked rapidly over a mouth that worked soundlessly. *"Shot?"* she squeaked. *"Captain, is your crewman dead?"*

"Not yet," Janeway said, not backing down.

"Captain, please believe that I have no—" A pair of hands handed Nashi a thin sheet of plastic. She glanced down at it, reading rapidly, and her outer coating went dead black. *"Captain, I have just received news. Pek and his Ushekti terrorists claim credit for this as well. Their nanites invaded your ship during the test of the warp drive, and they copied your transporters. They have taken two of your crewmen as hostage. My people have already launched a full-scale search."* Nashi ducked her head twice and stared down at the floor. *"Please accept my deepest apologies, Captain Kathryn Janeway of the Federation Starship* Voyager. *I feel great shame for myself and my people. If I had any idea that this was going to happen, I would have immediately warned you and taken steps to help you secure your ship. It did not occur to me that Pek and his kind would be able to attack you directly. You may*

not believe this, but I assure you with all my being that it is so."

Janeway settled herself back and folded her arms, only slightly mollified. "How could the Ushekti attack my ship and my people when they are supposed to be imprisoned on their continent?"

"The imprisonment technology is imperfect," Nashi admitted. *"A few of them have now and then been able to escape. It is an entire continent, a difficult area to contain."*

"Why would they want Seven of Nine and Tom Paris?" Janeway asked. "Or were they going for Lieutenant Torres again and ended up with Tom and Seven?"

"Seven of Nine carries nanoprobes in her systems," Tuvok said. "She is a logical target. Perhaps the Ushekti wanted both her nanoprobes and Lieutenant Torres, but Lieutenant Paris got in the way, or was taken by accident."

Janeway sent him a curt nod. "Secretary, I am bringing my ship in orbit around your planet. We have powerful sensors that will aid in the search, and I will also be assigning people of my own to work with yours." Her tone made it clear that this was not a request.

Nashi ducked her head again. *"Of course, Captain. We are happy to have your assistance."*

"Mr. Tuvok, assemble search parties," Janeway concluded. "You're going to be very busy for a while."

CHAPTER
7

LIEUTENANT TOM PARIS tried to rattle the barred window set low into the cell door. It didn't budge, but at least it was something to do. He put his forehead against the metal shafts and tried to peer into the stone-walled hallway without success.

"Hey!" he yelled. "Hey! Who the hell do you think you are, huh? Hey!"

"There is no point in shouting, Lieutenant," said Seven of Nine. "It only wastes energy."

Tom looked over his shoulder at her. She was standing in the exact center of the cell, hands clasped behind her back, hair unruffled, gray eyes calm. Only her missing combadge showed that anything was out of place. Tom figured the Chiar nanites must have somehow made both hers and his drop off in the shuttlebay.

"It's my energy to waste," he said. He didn't mention that it kept his mind off B'Elanna.

The cell itself was low-ceilinged, barely tall enough for a human to stand upright, though it was plenty high for a Chiar. The walls were of worked stone and mortared solid. The floor was some species of concrete, perfectly flat and smooth. The only window was the heavily barred one set into the door. A low stone wall partially hid a strange-looking toilet Tom hoped he wouldn't have to use. The cell contained not a single chair or bed, and it smelled strongly—very strongly—of Chiar. Tom sighed and drummed his palms on the cold, heavy bars. He had seen more than his share of jail cells over the years and even had the dubious distinction of serving time with Harry Kim in one of the worst prisons this side of the Cardassian empire. No matter where they were, though, all jails seemed to have one common trait—they were near impossible to escape from.

Near-impossible.

"Since you are no longer shouting," Seven said, "I assume you are attempting to formulate a plan for escape."

"Thinking about it," Tom said.

"Then it may interest you to know that I have already examined our . . . quarters in minute detail."

Tom remembered that Seven's Borg implants gave her a visual acuity denied to most humans. "Yeah? Find any weak spots?"

Seven paused. "No."

"Right." He bent to examine the door more closely. No hinges or knob on this side, though there was an imposing-looking lock. Tom grunted in frustration. The last thing he remembered from *Voyager* was leaping at the Chiar attacking Seven and the familiar tingle of a transporter.

. . . a burst of red energy, B'Elanna going down with a cry . . .

He and Seven had materialized here with no sign of the Chiar, meaning he hadn't had a chance to see the operation of the cell door.

"Do you think the lock would respond to your nanoprobes?" he asked.

"No. It contains no technology my probes could assimilate or control. It appears to be a primitive deadbolt."

"Primitive enough to keep us locked in," Tom said. "I'll bet B'Elanna's chewing the walls by now, assuming she isn't . . . assuming she's all right." He paused and wet his lips. "Do you think she's all right?"

Seven nodded. "I am certain she is. I am also certain it will go badly for the Chiar who laid hands on her husband once she catches them." She didn't add, *if B'Elanna wasn't killed when the Chiar attacked.* That and her oddly phrased assurance actually made Tom feel better. A little.

. . . B'Elanna going down with a cry, the sound of her body hitting the metal deckplates . . .

Although he heard no sound, the sudden increased smell gave Tom warning. He glanced at Seven, who nodded. They had already gone into battle crouches when the lock clunked and the door slid open with surprising speed. Three Chiar entered the cell and fired pistols before either human could react. Energy slashed the air. Seven and Tom both collapsed to the floor as B'Elanna had done, though Tom remained conscious. He couldn't tell about Seven. His brain had seized up, and he was unable to think or move. He realized he was twitching, but he felt no pain.

One Chiar kept its pistol trained on Seven's motionless form. The other two took Tom by his upper arms and dragged him from the cell. The world wavered, spinning in and out of focus. Tom was vaguely aware of his legs and stomach sliding along the cold floor and of Chiar voices echoing around him. He couldn't understand what they were saying, and a small part of him realized it was because his universal translator was contained in his missing combadge.

And then he was being hauled onto a low table. Restraints were clamped around wrists and ankles. The twitching eased, and his mind began to clear. The Chiar smell was strong, overpowering. Tom twisted his head around, trying to keep the panic from rising in his chest. The table was in what appeared to be a kind of medical lab, with white walls and floors and with equipment scattered across gleaming metal tables. A pair of Chiar stood to one side, watching him, while the two who had brought him into the lab exited through a solid-looking door. The remaining Chiar conversed among themselves for a moment, then approached the table.

The first Chiar's outer coating shimmered and danced in pastel colors, while the second swirled various shades of blue. The pastel Chiar leaned over Tom. The smell grew stronger and Tom's eyes teared up. He opened his mouth to breathe.

"And now comes the probing, right?" Tom said, still fighting panic. "Are you sure my insurance covers it?"

The pastel Chiar said something. Its voice reminded Tom of a cat hacking up a hairball.

"Really? I like the chocolate ones myself," he said.

Pastel Chiar reached for Tom's neck. He tried to twist away but couldn't move far. The Chiar attached something to Tom's collar without actually touching his skin.

"That's better," Pastel said. "Now it can understand us and we, it."

" 'It'?" Tom echoed.

Pastel brushed a hand over its outer coating and came up with a simple black disk. It affixed the disk to Tom's forehead, where it made a cool, slightly sticky patch. Then it dipped a hand into what seemed to be a pocket in its outer coating and retrieved a black sphere set with lights and readouts. It ran the sphere over Tom's body, and the object warbled much like the medical tricorders the Doctor used in sickbay.

"A fine specimen," Pastel commented. "In fine health. Fit for work, certainly."

A pang hit Tom's stomach. "Work? What the hell are you doing to me? Why did you grab us? How did you get a transporter? What—"

Blue tapped a button, and a scream tore itself from Tom's throat before he could stop it. He kept screaming until Blue released the button.

"B'Elanna," he croaked when it was over. The smell didn't seem as important now. His throat was raw and aching.

"Proceed with mnemonic disruption," Blue ordered. Pastel nodded and turned to one of the tables. The Chiar selected what looked like a pistol capped by a clear glass dome filled with a fluorescent orange liquid. Pastel put the barrel on Tom's neck. It was cold, and he cringed away from it. There was a hiss, and the orange liquid slowly drained away. Tom stared up at the Chiar for a moment, his stomach clenched so hard it hurt.

"Tell me what you're doing," he gasped.

"It won't take long," Pastel said. "The nanites are efficient."

And Tom's eyes went blank. Memories flickered through his mind like the movies at the holographic Bijou: tottering after a gray kitten across green grass . . . swooping higher and higher on a playground swing . . . whooping with exhilaration on a joyride in his father's shuttle . . . holding back tears at the funeral of three friends from the Academy . . . smells of stale synthehol and poorly cooked food at the bar where he first met a Maquis operative . . . being thrown to the deck as the Caretaker snatched *Voyager* into the Delta Quadrant . . . meeting B'Elanna for the first time and wondering how anyone could stand to work with her . . .

"B'Elanna," he whispered again. His eyes slid shut.

"Where's Tom?"

A tight smile appeared on the Doctor's face. B'Elanna, who had seen the expression many times before, took it to mean he wasn't going to answer right away. Fear clutched at her chest.

"You've been hit with a neurophasic disruptor," the Doctor said calmly. "You aren't in any condition to—"

B'Elanna struggled to a sitting position on the narrow bio-bed so she could look around. The other beds were empty—no Tom, no Seven of Nine. The place was well-lit and immaculately clean. Through a glass wall she could see the Doctor's private office. Worry gnawed at B'Elanna's stomach. If Tom wasn't in sickbay and the Doctor wasn't saying where he was, it could only mean something was badly wrong.

"Lieutenant," the Doctor said, "I must insist—"

"You always insist, Doctor," B'Elanna said. "If you won't tell me what happened to Tom, then I'll have to find out myself." She pushed herself off the bed and groaned as the floor rocked dizzyingly beneath her. Her limbs quivered. A strong arm guided her gently and firmly back to the bed.

"You aren't going anywhere," the Doctor said, taking up a hypospray and racking an ampule into the handle. "But not to worry—another injection and you'll be . . . well, if not in top shape, at least functional. I don't suppose I could persuade you to take a nice long nap to complete your recovery." He pressed the hypospray to B'Elanna's neck and the medication hissed into her bloodstream. B'Elanna sighed and the room steadied.

"Tell me what happened to Tom," she said in a deadly tone, "or I'm going to visit your databanks with a *bat'leth*."

The Doctor sighed. "He and Seven were kidnapped by the Chiar."

"*What?*" She sat up again. The Doctor made no attempt to hold her down. "How? And how long was I out?"

"You were unconscious for about half an hour," the Doctor said. "As for the other question, I have no idea. The captain has already mounted search parties."

B'Elanna jumped off the bed. The room swayed slightly, but she ignored it. "I have to go. Thanks for—"

The main doors swished open, and Captain Janeway entered the bay. "How's the patient, Doctor? If she's awake, I'm sure she'll want to know—" Janeway caught sight of B'Elanna's face, pale and sweating. "Ah. I see she is and she does."

"Captain—what happened?" B'Elanna asked, startled at how desperate she sounded.

Janeway quickly explained. "We're scanning Chi for human lifesigns," she concluded, "but it's slow-going. The microwaves and background ionic radiation keep interfering with the sensors." Janeway's low voice became quiet and soothing, which only made the knot in B'Elanna's stomach bigger. "We'll find him, B'Elanna, and Seven, too. Don't worry."

"Right," B'Elanna said. "Tell a *targ* not to bite the hand that feeds it. Which team am I being assigned to?"

"None," Janeway said firmly. "You know the protocols—you're too emotionally involved. Besides, I need you back overseeing the final repairs. Thankfully we already received one shipment of dilithium from the Chiar. We can easily make do with what we have so far."

"Captain, I can't—"

"You have your orders, Lieutenant," Janeway interrupted, steel in her voice.

"Captain," the Doctor interjected, "I feel it would

be better if the Lieutenant remained in sickbay for another hour to rest."

Janeway looked B'Elanna up and down. B'Elanna tried not to fume, but didn't entirely succeed. "If you think you can keep her here," Janeway said, "you have my blessing."

She turned and left. B'Elanna glared daggers at the doors. Tom, her husband, was down on the planet somewhere, and the Chiar were doing who-knew-what to him. And to Seven. Hot anger flashed in her blood. Her jaw clenched, B'Elanna strode for the door, ignoring the protests of the Doctor behind her.

A few moments later she entered engineering. Fewer than a dozen crewmen were at work, not nearly as many as should have been. B'Elanna surmised that the missing people were currently involved in the search for Seven and Tom. Icheb stood near the two-story blue pillar that made up the warp core. He caught sight of her as she strode toward him. The nausea and wooziness had mostly abated by now, and she wasn't going to let either feeling slow her down.

"Lieutenant," Icheb said. "You have recovered." He was young, still in his late teens by human standards, but frighteningly intelligent and already useful to have around engineering when they were short handed. Like Seven of Nine, Icheb was a former Borg drone the *Voyager* crew had severed from the Collective, and like Seven, he had retained some of his Borg implants. In his case, a thin band of silver ran past his left eye and down the outer side of his nose.

"Yeah, I'm shipshape," she said. "Why aren't you

on one of the search teams looking for Tom and Seven?"

A hint of a grimace crossed Icheb's solemn face. "The captain informed me that I was too emotionally involved to take part in the search, and she ordered me to assist with the final repairs."

"There's a lot of that going around." B'Elanna put her hands on the board next to his. Her touch automatically logged her into the computer and engineering systems. "What's the status of the repairs?"

He looked at her in puzzlement.

"What?" she demanded.

"It seems unlikely," Icheb replied in his low voice, "that you are so eager to work on repairs when your husband is in the hands of Chiar terrorists."

B'Elanna tapped at the board without really looking at it. "What's the *status*, Icheb?"

"All systems are on line and functional," Icheb said promptly. "Nine systems still require minor repairs that will take us twelve to fifteen hours to complete under current conditions. We could complete these repairs in less than two hours if we were docked at the Chiar station, but Captain Janeway refuses to allow it."

"Good for her," B'Elanna muttered.

"However, the ship," Icheb finished, "is fully functional."

B'Elanna crossed the circular room to one of the panels lining the walls. "What about long- and short-range sensors?"

"The ion radiation is still interfering with them," Icheb said. "But they have been fully repaired. If it weren't for the radiation, they would be functioning normally."

B'Elanna checked the readouts on the sensor systems. The data was interspersed with chunks of static, and the images were spotty. She ground her teeth. There had to be a better way to look for Tom. She couldn't stand by and wait, no matter what the captain said.

"Lieutenant," Icheb said, "correct me if I am in error, but if the sensors are fully functional, they do not require our attention."

B'Elanna's fingers continued to move over the boards and her eyes never left the displays. "They require *my* attention, Icheb." She paused a moment, lost in thought. "If the sensors can't scan for human lifesigns," she mused aloud, "I wonder if there would be some way to locate Tom and Seven visually."

"Lieutenant?"

More brisk tapping of sensors and an image of Chi winked onto a screen. In orbit were a single moon, one space station, and an entire series of satellites of varying shapes and sizes, each one emitting signals that, as a side effect, helped the sensors locate them.

"Look at this." She gestured at the screen. "They have hundreds of pieces of junk in orbit, and most of them are equipped with cameras, both infrared and normal spectrum."

"Lieutenant, the captain said—"

"All we should have to do," B'Elanna continued, ignoring him, "is link the satellites together and upload images of Tom—and Seven—to the link. If a satellite camera sees one of them, we'll know exactly where they are."

The satellites continued spinning around the planet, their orbits marked in rings and ellipses of differing colors. A spark ignited behind Icheb's dark eyes. Seven was a sort of surrogate mother to him, which explained the "emotional involvement" Janeway wanted to avoid in the search.

"We will have to contact the Chiar," he said. "We will need their security protocols and specifications for each of the different satellites."

Kathryn Janeway entered engineering, expecting to see Torres flat on her back under an instrument panel or up to her elbows in bioneural gel-packs. The activity would keep the lieutenant's mind off her husband. Instead, Janeway found her chief engineer talking intently to a sensor display with Icheb standing beside her. Icheb caught sight of Janeway and coughed once. Janeway narrowed her eyes and made for the pair. Torres straightened, and Janeway caught sight of a Chiar on the display screen.

"Captain," Icheb said.

The words *What the hell is going on here?* were on the tip of Janeway's tongue, but she bit them back. It wouldn't do to show friction in front of what might be an enemy, despite the fact that Torres was clearly *not* working on the final repairs to the ship and instead seemed to be working with the Chiar. Janeway had the distinct feeling she knew exactly what B'Elanna had been working on.

Janeway felt her temper fray. The constant diplomatic dance with the Chiar had been a daily strain. The mysterious kidnapping of Paris and Seven added another stressor to the mix, and Janeway was still trying to figure out if Secretary Nashi was trustworthy. The ship was still slightly damaged, another ion storm would arrive in a few more days, and now she had an officer who was flagrantly disobeying orders. The delicate relations with the Chiar and the sympathy she felt for Torres's position were the only things that kept her from snarling.

"What's this?" Janeway asked, trying for a neutral voice. She got a near growl instead.

"Captain, this is Engineer Pollu," B'Elanna explained. "We met during the repairs at the station. He's an expert on the Chiar satellite system."

"I see." The tone was a little more dangerous now. Torres seemed to notice and she shifted uneasily. Icheb had already edged away.

"An honor to meet you, Captain," Pollu chuffed. His outer coating cascaded through a rainbow of dizzying colors on the little screen.

"The honor is mine," Janeway replied automatically.

"I think I've found a way to track down Tom and Seven using the Chiar satellite system," Torres said, and went on to explain. "Engineer Pollu thinks it'll work."

"Most definitely it would," Pollu agreed. *"Give me a few hours to assemble the necessary protocols and it will be done."*

"If you gave me access to the satellite grid," B'Elanna said to him, "I could help. Get everything together faster."

Pollu ducked his head nervously. *"I am unsure that would be . . . em, appropriate, Lieutenant Torres. Our technology is governed by a complex series of laws, and I am not sure granting to you access would be . . . em, allowed, especially under the treaty*

Secretary Nashi negotiated. I wish not to offend," he added hastily. *"But I have no authority to—"*

"Of course," Janeway said, and put a tight hand on Torres's shoulder. "My chief engineer is just a little too eager sometimes. She didn't meant to put you in a difficult position, Engineer. Accept my apologies."

"No, no, no," Pollu said. *"Do not . . . em, that is, it is necessary not . . . the honor of working with your culture is . . ."*

"Well, I think you have a fine idea here," Janeway said brightly. "Engineer Pollu, we appreciate your help more than you can know. Please contact me personally when you have the protocols set up, and we'll go from there."

"Of course, Captain." The image winked out.

"What the hell did you think you were doing?" Janeway snapped at Torres the instant Pollu's image had vanished. "I gave you a specific order, Lieutenant, and you deliberately disobeyed it. Not only that, you entered into unauthorized diplomatic negotiations with a species that may or may not be friendly to us and almost put him into a bind to boot."

"Captain," Icheb put in, "I was as much at fault as Lieu—"

"Stay out of this, Icheb. I'm willing to assume that Lieutenant Torres used her authority as chief engineer to persuade you to disobey my orders when you wouldn't otherwise have done so. I wouldn't push it further."

Icheb shut up.

"That's my husband down there, Captain," Torres shot back. "If disobeying orders gets him back here in one piece, then put me on your list of troublemakers."

"Oh, you're already there, Lieutenant," Janeway replied evenly. "You're already there. The only reason I haven't put you on report is that I'm worried about Tom and Seven, too, and I think that your idea just might work. But in the meantime"—she raised her voice—"computer, restrict Lieutenant B'Elanna Torres from all extravehicular communication and remote sensor access until further notice. Authorization Janeway rho six omega."

"Captain!" Torres protested. "You can't just—"

"Don't tell me what I can and can't do on my ship, Lieutenant. You have your orders. I expect you to carry them out." Janeway stared hard at Torres.

Torres's jaw clenched. "Yes, Captain," she said smartly. "Whatever you say, Captain. I'll get right on it, Captain."

Janeway continued to stare at Torres until the other woman turned away. Without another word, Janeway left engineering and decided to take the long way back to the bridge turbolift. It took two corridors of walking for her to cool off.

"And now the star specimen," said the auctioneer. She was tall for a Chiar, almost a full head taller than the rest, and she stood with her assistant on a dais which was surrounded by more Chiar. The thrall blinked up at her from the bottom of the short flight of stairs that led up to the platform. He was breathing through his mouth to keep the smell of over a dozen Chiar at a bearable level. His wrists were bound in front of him, and his mind was maddeningly empty. No matter how hard he tried, he couldn't remember his name or where he lived or anything about his past. He couldn't even remember what species he was, though it was obvious he was not Chiar. His heart beat faster. Why couldn't he remember? He should know this sort of thing about himself. Shouldn't he?

The auctioneer's assistant tugged on a chain attached to the thrall's shackles, and he stumbled up the stairs to the dais. He was wearing an outer coating like the auctioneer and her assistant, though his was dull black instead of a rainbow riot. The coating slid and moved around his body like a living thing. It was an unnerving sensation. Shouldn't he be used to it? He didn't remember owning any other clothes, so this should feel natural.

The dozen or so Chiar in front of the dais shook their heads and chuffed with interest, their outer coatings shimmering and shifting with excitement. Their smell intensified somewhat and changed as a result. The group stood in a domed hall, well-lit by a crystalline skylight. A table in the back groaned under the weight of several potted plants, "rare and delicious as befit a gathering of the hidden elite," as the auctioneer had said.

"And now our final item. This is an actual specimen of the species known as *humans*." The auctioneer spoke the alien word with a strange accent. "It, and others like it, arrived in our system on the vessel known as the Federation Starship *Voyager*."

So he was a human, whatever that was. The thrall shook his head. He remembered nothing about a starship, nothing about arriving. His earliest memory was of waiting at the bottom of the stairs to the dais.

His heart started to beat faster. Why couldn't he remember?

"We have acquired this particular *human* through our own secret channels," the auctioneer went on, "and we offer it up for sale in this special venue for our most discriminating customers. For your safety—and our security—its memory has been disrupted, so it remembers nothing of its previous life. We have included a translation program free of charge."

Over a dozen pairs of Chiar eyes stared at him, muttering among themselves and munching leaves. His face grew hot with embarrassment and anger. He held his wrists defiantly before himself and stared right back at them.

"Naturally complete discretion is required, and we cannot acknowledge any involvement should anyone ask awkward questions after the sale. Now, shall we begin the bidding at twenty decaquads?"

"Twenty decaquads!"

"Twenty-one!"

"Twenty-four!"

The bidding continued to escalate and none of the Chiar stayed out of it. They gesticulated wildly, shaking their heads and chuffing their excitement. The musty smell intensified as the bidding escalated, but eventually the number of bidders slowed.

"Two hundred decaquads!"

"Two hundred ten!"

Long pause. "I have a bid of two hundred ten, my friends," said the auctioneer. Her voice was high and flutelike. "Is there another bid? Two hundred fifteen? There is no other thrall like it on the planet, and there never will be again. Do I have two hundred fifteen?" the auctioneer said.

The auctioneer had said he was a human. Did that mean anything? Was it a clue?

"Three hundred!"

Silence. The thick, musty smell hovered in the air like an invisible fog.

"Three hundred decaquads," the auctioneer repeated. "Is there another bid?"

No answer.

"Very well. If there are no other bids . . ." The auctioneer paused meaningfully, but no one said anything. "Sold, then, for three hundred decaquads."

All the Chiar but one shook their heads and chuffed. The thrall looked at the one who didn't move. This was his new owner, then. The idea made his stomach turn. The audience parted to let the winner approach the dais steps.

The chuffing and whispering continued as the thrall found his legs moving of their own accord, forced into motion by his own outer coating. The assistant led him down the steps and handed the leash to the winner with a duck of her head. A computer voice said, "Monetary transfer complete. Three hundred decaquads in exchange for one thrall and one puppet program set to expire in seventeen days. Do you wish to extend the time limit of the program?"

"No." The winner's outer coating swirled scarlet.

"Gratitude for your purchase," the assistant said.

Auction over, the other Chiar had broken into small chattering groups. A few wandered back to pluck leaves from the plants at the back of the room. The winner looked up at the thrall.

"You may refer to me as Master Zedrel," he said. "Your name"—he paused, and his smell shifted, became lighter—"is Tom Vu. Do you understand?"

When Tom didn't answer, Master Zedrel gave him a sharp jab in the shoulder, and a light jolt shot through Tom's neck and arm.

"Yes, Master Zedrel," Tom said.

"Then I will take you home."

Zedrel led Tom up a hallway toward a door, collecting congratulations and envious stares from other Chiar along the way. Tom towered a full head over all of them, and he felt conspicuous.

Zedrel pressed a hand to the door, and it irised open. Outside, an awning hid the sky. Zedrel hustled Tom into a long and low vehicle with six wheels. Another Chiar, also clad in solid black, sat at the controls. Tom tried to get a look at his surroundings, but Zedrel got into the vehicle, forcing Tom to follow before he could do more than turn his head. Getting in was awkward with bound hands.

The interior of the vehicle was blue, plush, and reeked of Chiar. It was large enough to qualify as a small room. Several plump cushions occupied the floor. Tom noticed that he was getting used to the Chiar smell enough to breathe through his nose a little. For this he was grateful—his tongue had dried out from all the mouth breathing, and he felt thirsty.

Zedrel lowered himself to one of the plush cushions. A harness grew out of it and held Zedrel in place. The side windows were tinted, and the windshield wasn't visible from the floor, so Tom couldn't see out.

"There are a few things you learn must, Tom,"

Zedrel said, "since you have no proper memory. First, under the type of contract I bought you under—"

An illegal one? Tom wanted to say, remembering the auctioneer's words about discretion. But he held his tongue, remembering the jolt he had already received.

"—I own you completely. I need not pay you or even feed you if I wish. I can punish you in any way I like. However, you are valuable, and I care not to punish even my most worthless thralls unless they disobey." Zedrel raised his voice. "True, Nylo?"

"Yes, Master Zedrel," said the driver. "Gratitude."

Tom said nothing.

"Second," Zedrel went on, "you should know that the nanites in your coating are slaved to mine. When we arrive at my estate, you will not go out of doors, nor speak to anyone but me and the other thralls. You will wait on me as my new personal attendant."

The vehicle made a sudden correction that threw Tom slightly off balance. The scent in the car also changed, becoming sour, almost astringent. Tom's nostrils widened. The new scent was coming from Nylo.

"I will download appropriate programming into your coating. Do you understand?"

Tom didn't like the sound of that. He wanted to yank open the door and jump out of the vehicle. But he said, "Yes, Master Zedrel."

The journey didn't last long, though without a timepiece Tom couldn't tell for sure. Zedrel spent the time alternating between humming to himself and reading from the thin sheets of plastic the Chiar used to hold and transmit data. Tom sat and bore it, not knowing what else to do.

The vehicle stopped and the door opened. Zedrel led Tom out of the car. Overhead, the sky was a glorious blue. Ahead of him lay a low, sprawling building on a lush lawn of some kind of dark green, springy plant. There were no other houses in sight, but a high stone wall stretched away in the distance. The air smelled heavily of Chiar musk, and from over the wall Tom could hear crowd and vehicle noises as from a crowded city.

"My estate," Zedrel said. "Go inside."

Tom stared up at the sky. Somewhere up there was supposed to be a starship, a *Federation* starship. The auctioneer had said it was his home. But he couldn't remember anything about it.

"Tom!" Zedrel snapped. "Move!"

A jolt of pain, and Tom's legs moved him into the open door mere centimeters in front of him. Then he was in a low-ceilinged room of rough-hewn wood. A fireplace took up one wall. Cushions and low tables peppered the floor. Several black-coated Chiar came forward, their smell again overpowering. Zedrel came inside, and Nylo shut the door behind him.

"You may not outside go, Tom," Zedrel instructed. "I do not wish . . . certain people accidentally sight of you to catch. Do you understand?"

The scent in the room shifted. Tom realized the source was Nylo. It dawned on Tom that whenever the Chiar underwent an emotional shift, their scent changed as well. More important, they seemed unaware of it—they couldn't smell themselves. Nylo had felt something at Zedrel's orders to Tom. He had also felt something when Zedrel had announced that Tom was going to be Zedrel's attendant. Was it anger? Jealousy? Relief? Tom didn't know. But ability to smell his captors' emotions had to be an advantage.

Now he just had to figure out how to use it.

Seven of Nine stood stiffly in her cell as the Chiar she had privately designated as "A" stared at her through the bars on the door. According to her internal chronometer, the Chiar had taken Paris away nine hours and thirteen minutes ago. The need to regenerate was beginning to grow within her, and Seven was at a loss for what to do about it. Most humans would have just stretched out on the chill concrete floor and gone to sleep, but Seven couldn't do that. The only way she could "sleep" was in her regeneration unit back on *Voyager*. Here, the fatigue could only grow.

"Give up," Chiar A said.

Seven didn't answer. She could understand him because the Chiar had fastened a translator onto her jumpsuit while she had lain stunned in the cell. Seven had considered tearing the device off and destroying it as an act of defiance, then had decided it would probably be best if she were able to understand what her captors were saying.

"You will be in pain," A said. He was one of the Chiar who had taken Tom Paris away. "It is fun to watch, but it wastes time. We will begin again soon, and you cannot stop us."

His tone reminded Seven of Mel from the holodeck playground. Seven noted an impulse to rush across the cell and reach through the bars to punch his face. But she didn't dare. A held a weapon and he was outside the cell. Punching him would accomplish nothing.

Though it might make you feel better, whispered an inner voice that sounded strangely like B'Elanna Torres.

Then Seven realized she didn't want to hit A as much as she wanted out of the cell. She wanted to be free of the helpless feeling. On the holodeck she could end the program whenever she wished and make the bully go away, but here she could not.

"This will be fun to watch," A said then with a wide Chiar grin. "Are you ready, little human? Here they come."

And another wave of nanites rushed over Seven's body. Seven knew she couldn't truly feel them crawling over her, but it seemed as if she could. Her skin itched with their tiny claws and shivered from millions of microscopic touches. Seven's nanoprobes let her know exactly where each invading nanite was and what it was doing. They skittered over her skin, slipped into her pores, invaded her bloodstream, marched over her cybernetic implants, looking, feeling, tasting every bit and piece of her. They were trying to copy her Borg nanoprobes both in structure and programming.

A cold drop of sweat slid around Seven's ear. She couldn't let the Chiar get their hands on Borg nanotechnology. The potential consequences were frightening. Seven had no idea what might happen if Borg programs got into whatever nanite-drive network the Chiar used, but she doubted it would benefit *Voyager*—or the Chiar.

The Chiar nanites had taken several angles on the attack. Some of them had tried to hack into her internal network. Another set had tried to capture and dissect Seven's nanoprobes on the spot. This group attacked her probes and tried to carry them off.

Fortunately, Seven retained control over her nanoprobes just as the Chiar kept control of their nanites, and she was able to stay one step ahead of the invaders. She retuned her security protocols at random and changed the micro-frequencies that her nanoprobes used to communicate with each other. She sent regiments of probes to rescue their fellows when they were captured or in danger, and the few who were actually removed from her body she ruthlessly shut down and erased.

Unfortunately, all this took a great deal of energy and concentration. Seven had received no nutritional supplements since her arrival in the cell. Her blood sugar was running low, and her electrolyte balance was tilting. Although her augmented mind was far stronger than any normal human's, eventually even her stamina and concentration would dissolve, leaving her nanoprobes open to the Chiar.

Seven's nanoprobes literally crushed fifteen thousand Chiar nanites and ejected twenty thousand more. Her probes scavenged parts from the vanquished nanites to build new nanoprobes and replace those she had lost. She shifted communication frequencies again and set up a new security grid.

"Give up, little human," A called. "Come. You must. You have no power here."

One part of Seven considered letting the Chiar have their way. It would be poetic justice if the programming and designs her kidnappers were attempting to steal ended up turning on the Chiar.

No, she told herself. *That would not be right.* But still the idea—and the temptation—persisted, no matter how she tried to ignore it.

Seven's stomach rumbled, a phenomenon she disliked. Pain thumped at the back of her head, and she recognized it as a hunger headache. Seven ignored these sensations and kept her attention on the next wave of nanites even as her anger grew.

CHAPTER

8

"THE REPAIRS ARE FINISHED, Captain," Torres said. *"Voyager* is in peak shape. At your order, we have taken on no more supplies of dilithium, but between the stores that survived the ion storm and what we already received from the Chiar, we should be fine."

Captain Janeway nodded from her chair and set the data padd on her desk. Her ready room windows showed their normal starscape since her side of the ship faced away from the planet Chi.

"Fine work, Lieutenant," she said. "And how are *you* doing?"

"As well as can be expected, Captain," Torres replied in a flat, neutral voice.

Janeway looked at her. Black circles hovered under Torres's eyes, and her hair hung in listless strings. Her black-and-yellow uniform was rumpled, and although that could have come from long hours spent on the final repairs, Janeway had her doubts.

"There's still no sign of Tom or Seven," Janeway told her. "We're still looking."

"I know."

Janeway leaned forward. "B'Elanna, I didn't put you on search detail because Starfleet regulations are very clear. People rarely make good decisions when the safety of a loved one is involved. You know that, don't you?"

"Yes, Captain."

Why was she justifying this? Torres knew the regulations and the reasons as well as Janeway did. Yet, Janeway felt an uncharacteristic need to explain. She knew the desperate worry behind the other woman's brown eyes. It hurt to see B'Elanna in pain.

Well, living with that sort of thing was part of being a captain, wasn't it? There was no need to blather on about why she was enforcing the rules. Still . . .

"I know you want to help find Tom," she found herself saying, "but I can't put you on any of the teams. I'm sorry."

"Yes, Captain." Torres remained standing in front of Janeway's desk, as if sensing the captain's ambivalence. Janeway's jaw worked back and forth.

"Of course," she continued, "it's a shame that the chief engineer is completely excluded. Although it's an . . . appropriate step, it could be to *Voyager*'s detriment."

"Yes, Captain."

Janeway sighed and gave up. "If you were to . . . talk to some of the search people and give suggestions—no orders, just suggestions—and on your own time, of course—I suppose that wouldn't be breaking any regulations now, would it?"

Torres's expression did not so much as twitch. "Of course not, Captain. I have a lot of . . . suggestions. And I'm off duty now."

"Well then, Lieutenant," Janeway waved a hand. "Why are you wasting your downtime in the captain's ready room?"

Torres vanished out the door. Janeway took a sip of Neelix's bitter coffee and stared out the window.

"My name is Boleer and you will do as I say."

Tom nodded, wondering if he was breaking any rules by staring. Boleer, whose outer coating was matte black, was missing an eye and her head was flatter than usual. An accident? Punishment? Or had she been born that way? She deviated from the norm and was probably considered rather ugly by Chiar standards, though to Tom she was rather interesting. With a start, he realized he was thinking of Boleer as "she," though the Chiar sexes had no outward differentiation. It was her smell, he decided. There was something about her scent that the auctioneer and her assistant had shared and Zedrel and Nylo had not.

"It is my duty to show you your duties," Boleer continued. "If you do not do as I say, you will be punished."

"What do I call you?" Tom asked.

"Boleer will do," she said. "I will teach everything you need to know, or at least, that which your outer coating is not programmed to make you do. Come with me now and I will show you the house."

Zedrel's home was spacious and, from Boleer's

tone of voice, clearly luxurious. Tom had no frame of reference. Were human homes typically this large or not? He didn't know. The ceilings and rough-hewn beams were uncomfortably low, and he had to duck in order to go through the doorways. The floors changed from soft carpeting to bare wood to smooth stone even as Tom walked across them. Colors danced and flickered on sections of wall and ceiling, and Tom supposed they were meant to be art, though he understood none of it. Boleer showed Tom a music room and a game room—he didn't recognize any of the objects in either place as games or musical instruments—storage cellars, guest rooms, and a library. The entire house reeked of Chiar, though Tom was at last getting somewhat used to it. It still stank, but at least his eyes had stopped watering.

They ended the tour in Zedrel's personal suite. Zedrel himself was nowhere to be seen.

"The master is in his study," Boleer said in answer to Tom's question. She gestured at a closed door. "Do not disturb him there unless he asks. Otherwise he becomes angry. What is it?"

Tom blinked, realizing he had been staring again. "I'm sorry."

"You find my looks odd?" she said. There was a definite challenge in her voice and a glint in her single eye. Tom smelled the sharp, stringent scent he had gotten from Nylo earlier. Did that smell indicate anger?

"I think they're interesting," Tom said. "I mean, many Chiar look similar to me, but you're . . . unique. It's kind of . . . I don't know . . . *comforting* because I know who you are. I like it."

"You *like* the way I look?"

"I—yes. I suppose so."

The anger smell faded, replaced by a gingery sort of scent. "I see." She paused. "You have seen the entire house. Now I will show you your duties. Come."

"Is there a bathing room?" Tom asked as she headed for the door. "I didn't see one."

Boleer turned and peered at him. "Bathing? You mean for cleansing the skin?" At Tom's nod she said, "Your nanites will cleanse your skin, and your outer coating will not accept dirt in any case. Now come."

They went down a set of narrow stairs and through another room to a door. It irised open before they reached it, and Tom smelled Nylo. A moment later the Chiar stepped through the doorway. A bit of yellow leaf clung to his lower lip. He stopped when he saw Tom and Boleer.

"Excuse us," Boleer said. "I need to show this new thrall the kitchen garden."

Nylo didn't move. Instead he looked hard up at Tom. The air filled with the pungent smell of anger. Tom retreated a step.

"So you think you will wait on Master Zedrel," Nylo said.

Tom shrugged, then realized Nylo would probably not understand the gesture. "That's what he says."

"You will not last." The yellow leaf moved as Nylo spoke. "I will see to that."

"Look," Tom said, "I didn't ask for the job. If it were up to me, I'd be out of here so fast I wouldn't even leave a warp trail. You want to wait on Zedrel—"

A jolt of pain flashed through him. Tom yelped in hurt, surprised.

"He is *Master Zedrel* or *the Master*," Boleer put in. "You must call him that even in his absence or your nanites will react."

"He is too stupid to learn," Nylo spat.

"You've got something hanging," Tom said, and dabbed at his own face. Nylo slapped his chin and whipped the leaf away. "I guess you Chiar have never heard of napkins, huh?"

Abruptly Tom found himself slammed and held against the wall. Nylo's anger smell was overpowering, enough to make Tom gag. The Chiar were clearly strong for their size. Nylo's grip was hard as duranium. His eyes, glaring up into Tom's, were equally hard.

"You make a fool out of me?" he hissed.

"You do a pretty good job on your own," Tom choked out over the smell.

"Leave him, Nylo," Boleer ordered.

"Shut up, One-eye."

"If you damage him, the Master will be angry," Boleer replied icily, "and I will ensure he finds out."

Nylo glared pure hatred at Tom for a long moment. Then he gave Tom one more shove against the wall before letting him go and stalking away with all the dignity he could muster.

"What's his problem?" Tom said.

"He has been the Master's personal attendant for twelve years," she said simply.

Tom rubbed his shoulders where Nylo had gripped him hard enough to bruise. "I told him I don't want the job."

"And he is not angry at you," Boleer told him.

"Oh, yeah? Then why slam me against the wall?"

Boleer ducked her head. "The Master is immune to his anger. You are not. Now come. I will introduce Muaar."

The room beyond turned out to be what Boleer said was the kitchen, though it looked to Tom more like a big greenhouse. The floor in the room remained unchanging white and black tile, and the walls were made of glass panes. Pots and flats containing a rainbow riot of plants and shrubs stood in orderly rows. Some of the windows were so transparent as to be invisible, and they let the sunlight pour over certain plants while translucent windows provided more indirect lighting for others. The place was crowded with yet more overwhelming smells, and Tom wondered if he'd ever be able to take a scent-free breath again.

A female Chiar—Tom could smell her gender—was plucking leaves from a green plant and dropping them into a bowl. Boleer ducked her head to her and introduced Tom.

"This is Muaar," she finished. Tom wasn't sure what to do, so he nodded.

"You're the alien, then?" Muaar said. "The Master's new attendant?"

"I suppose."

Muaar looked him up and down, and Tom became acutely aware that his black outer coating was not normal clothing for him.

But what is *normal clothing for me?* he thought. A moment of despair dropped over him. He didn't know who he was or where he was supposed to be. His proper place couldn't be here, in this houseful of strange creatures who expected him to do strange things. He *had* to have a past—if he could just remember it. Did he have a family? A job on board the starship? He had no way of knowing.

"You are strange," Muaar pronounced. "But it is not my place to question the Master. Here." She thrust the bowl into his hands. "Take it to him."

In the presence of food Tom suddenly realized how hungry he was. And how tired. When had he last eaten and slept? He couldn't remember.

"Where do I sleep?" Tom asked. "I'm about ready to drop. And I haven't eaten in a while."

Muaar looked surprised. "You sleep in front of the Master's door, of course."

"Of course," Tom echoed faintly. "And food? Do we peons get to eat?"

In answer Muaar stripped a large handful of leaves from a random bush and handed them to Tom. "The thralls of Zedrel are fortunate," she said. "Any time you are hungry, come and get something to eat. The Master has ordered it so. In many other household, thralls only eat at prescribed times. But eat first—it is unseemly for a thrall to eat in the presence of the Master."

Tom accepted the leaves with his free hand. He crammed a few into his mouth. They were juicy and oddly sweet. Boleer led him out of the kitchen and up the stairs to Zedrel's suite. They reached Zedrel's bedroom door just as Tom finished his leaves. Boleer was reaching out to open the door when it irised open with a *snap* and Nylo marched stiffly out. Every muscle was rigid, and the anger smell was so thick Tom could almost touch it. Nylo paused when he saw Tom and Boleer. Then he shot Tom a look of pure poison before stalking away.

"What was that about?" Tom whispered.

Boleer ducked her head in a Chiar shrug. "Just feed the Master his leaves as he asks for them. I will see you in the morning."

She herded Tom through the door and closed it behind him. Tom looked around the room. At the moment the low-ceilinged room was decorated entirely in shades of green. A subtle ivy pattern twisted through the walls. In the center of the room was a giant round cushion. Zedrel reclined in the middle of it with all four legs folded beneath him. He was looking at one of the plastic sheets the Chiar used for paper and tapping it with a stylus.

"Matrix increase by eight-point-two-six always leads to cascade failure, but if I adjust the magnetic field and graviton quotient to compensate . . ." He scribbled with the stylus, and figures moved on the paper. "Of course, that means I will have to increase the plasma flow by—what? At least four percent, which will put a strain on the induction coils for a few seconds. Can I strengthen them without harming the ratio of—hello, Tom. Well, do not just stand in the doorway like a rock. I am hungry."

"Yes, Zed—Master Zedrel," Tom said.

He sat down by the edge of the cushion and handed Zedrel a few leaves from the bowl. Zedrel turned his main attention back to the plastic sheet. Every so often he held out his hand, and Tom placed more leaves in it. From his current vantage point Tom could see the plastic sheet was covered with numbers, calculations, and diagrams. Even though he couldn't read the numbers, he recognized the diagrams as the configuration of a basic warp system—

And how did I know?

—and he could see where Zedrel's mistake lay, exactly why the matrix refused to remain stable above warp two. He thought about pointing it out to Zedrel, then clamped his lips shut. Not only was he not sure it would be acceptable for a thrall to offer advice, Tom didn't want to help Zedrel any more than he had to. Being in this place felt wrong, and he didn't want to give away anything that might help him escape. Exactly how holding secret knowledge of a warp system could help him get away, he didn't know, but he had no idea what might come in handy and what might not. Best to keep his mouth shut.

As if reading Tom's mind, Zedrel turned to Tom at that moment. "Tom, do you know anything about warp drives?"

The lie popped out before Tom could think. "No, Master Zedrel."

"I suppose not. But it was worth a question. More leaf."

Tom handed the last ones over, and Zedrel munched them down. Then he sighed, pushed aside the diagram, and settled down on the pillow. Without any command from Zedrel that Tom could see, the room went dark. Tom heard Zedrel shift around a bit, and a few moments later his breathing deepened into sleep. Tom didn't know what else to do but feel his way to the door, curl up on the floor, and do the same.

Chakotay watched the children laugh and scream their way through one of their endless games of tag.

He recognized Tenna and Mel and most of the others, though they looked much smaller now that he was an adult. The idea of joining the children in the game didn't hold much appeal, either. Not without Seven here. Strange how when Seven was here, the game was interesting and fun. Now it seemed like a waste of time for an adult.

What did the Chiar terrorists want with Seven—and Paris? Were they interrogating her? What about her regeneration alcove? How would she rest without it? What would happen to her if she went too long? The worry nattered at him, and he suddenly wished he had never offered to help Seven with her playground program. Then he might not be in this mess. She was a crewman and a friend. That was all she should be to him.

Except, as his father would say, there was *should be* and there was *is,* and we fight for the one while we deal with the other.

Chakotay sighed. "Computer, end program."

The shrieking children vanished, and Chakotay stared at the blank hologrid for a long time after they disappeared.

"You clumsy idiot!"

Tom looked at Muaar, then down at the mess of red pottery shards and black dirt at his sandaled feet. A small bush lay in the mess, its yellow leaves already wilting, and a sharp scent from Muaar's body scored the already reeking air. The anger smell.

"Have you no idea how difficult it is to grow this species?" demanded Muaar. "Do you?"

"I'm getting an idea," Tom answered.

Muaar made a disgusted sound and bent her two front legs to kneel and rescue the little bush. Her normal, nonangry scent was still clearly different from the male thralls, and Tom had added that bit of information to his growing mix. So far, he had learned to distinguish gender, pain, hunger, boredom, and anger. It was strange how the Chiar seemed completely unaware that their scent broadcast bits of information, and Tom had so far seen no reason to enlighten them.

Muaar straightened, cradling the wilting bush. She was short, even for a Chiar, and her bulbous eyes always looked to Tom as if they were about to leap out of her head. Her outer coating was a soft gray instead of black, and Tom had learned it meant she was in charge of all Zedrel's thralls, including Tom.

"Clean up the big pieces," she said. "I'll see if I can save this before it dies. It's one of the master's favorite snacks." And then, before Tom could react, her hand lashed up and slapped him across the face. The unexpected blow actually drove him to his knees and made the room rock back and forth. Muaar swiped at Tom's forehead. Something cool and wet stuck there, and when Tom put a bewildered finger up to check, he found dirt.

"Don't touch that!" Muaar snapped. "You will keep that mark until tomorrow morning, and then perhaps you will learn to be less clumsy." She turned and marched away with the little bush.

Tom stared muzzily after her until the room stopped moving. A rage boiled within him and he wanted to lunge for the stupid Chiar. She had *slapped* him? Who did she think she was? He tensed to spring to his feet. Then he remembered how the

Chiar had taken over his body movements. Anger warred with practicality, and the latter eventually won out. Tom silently began gathering up shattered pottery shards, but his hands were shaking.

Around him the garden room was light and airy in the morning sunlight. The glass ceiling was twice as high as any in the rest of Zedrel's house, and Tom usually liked that—he didn't feel as if he was going to crack his head on a low beam. The garden room provided most of the household food, and three Chiar thralls did nothing but tend the plants. The one Tom had dropped was originally going to be part of Zedrel's next meal.

The familiar scent struck him before he heard the voice. "Do you require assistance?"

Tom didn't look up. "Sure. Gratitude, Boleer."

"Were you aware it was me before I spoke?" Boleer asked as she knelt next to him.

"I could smell you," he said before remembering that he had intended to keep his olfactory prowess to himself. The words had just popped out. Fact was, Tom knew, he was lonely and wanted at least one person to talk to. Muaar thought he was clumsy, Nylo hated him, and Zedrel treated him like a pet. The rest of the household staff avoided him as much as possible. Only Boleer had been friendly.

"You could smell me?" Boleer repeated. She gathered up a small pile of pot shards. "How do you mean?"

"Each of you has a different scent," Tom explained. "I can tell you're there long before you say anything. I could probably track you outside."

Boleer cocked her head. "How do I smell?"

Tom thought a moment. "You smell like . . . Boleer. I can't describe it better. You have a smell, Muaar has a smell, Ze—Master Zedrel has a smell."

"Is it unpleasant to you?"

Very, Tom almost replied. "It's . . . strong," he said instead. "I sometimes wonder why you can't smell it."

"It is because you are an alien," Boleer said sagely.

They worked in silence for a moment, and the pile of shards grew. Dirt gritted beneath Tom's fingernails. Tom stole several glances at Boleer's oddly shaped head and missing eye.

"How did you . . ." he began, then tried again. "Who was it that . . . what did—?"

"You mean my eye and head," Boleer said.

Tom nodded, slightly embarrassed. "If it's painful to talk about, then—"

"It is no more painful than anything else about being a thrall," Boleer said. "My previous owner had a temper, and I was stubborn. I tried to escape one day but was caught before I even left the city. He was displeased and he did this to me. Later he decided that he no longer wished to keep such a deformed servant in his household, so he sold me. My price was very low because I am now so very ugly."

The last statement was made matter-of-factly, as if she were discussing Zedrel's favorite food, and Tom's heart turned inside his chest.

"Were you born a thrall?" he asked.

"Now you try to flatter me, Tom Vu," Boleer said. "I am not so young as to be born after the war. My father was Goracar but my mother was Ushekti. My father and my sister—half sister—thought I was an embarrassment and had little contact with me, though Father sometimes sent money to my mother. And then he died, and then the Ushekti were conquered by the Goracar Alliance. Many of us were made thralls. Those who were not were either killed or denuded of their nanites, which to a Chiar is much the same thing."

"What happened to your sister?" Tom asked. "Couldn't she help you?"

Boleer ducked. "I have no contact with her. Now that I am a slave, I am twice the embarrassment, especially now that she has attained a certain level of power in the Goracar government. Sometimes I think Master Zedrel bought me because I am a novelty like you. You are a member of an alien race, and I am the disfigured half sister of a powerful politician."

"Have you ever thought about trying to escape again and go home?"

Boleer's head reared back. "No, Tom Vu. Such a thing is impossible. I would like to see my people again, but that will never happen, and it is unwise to speak of such things unless you wish to be made as ugly as I am."

"I don't think you're ugly," Tom said. "I think you're unique."

"More flattery. And you have said that before." She dropped the last bit of broken pot into Tom's pile with a gritty *clink* and stood up. "I find you are not very ugly, either."

Tom blinked. "Do many people think I'm ugly?"

"Of course," Boleer said lightly. "You have only two legs, your neck is deformed and short, and your eyes are so small. But I find it interesting to watch you walk."

"You do?"

Boleer ducked her head. "It fascinates me that you do not tip over."

Tom had to laugh. At that moment a chime sounded.

"Tom," came Zedrel's voice, transmitted by his outer coating, *"bring me some* hrugar *tea and a plate of* afgar *leaves. Make sure they're ripe."*

"Yes, Master Zedrel," Tom said. He hated calling Zedrel *master,* so he opted for *Master Zedrel,* which felt marginally less repulsive. Sometimes he could convince himself he was an adult servant addressing a child, although he didn't know where that reference came from.

"You must complete your task," Boleer said. "We will talk later."

She left, and Tom straightened with a gritty double-handful of broken shards. After a moment the pile of muddy earth left at his feet seemed to dissolve, melt away, and vanish entirely. The house nanites at work. Pot shards were too big for them to handle efficiently, but garden dirt was no problem, easily moved to the surrounding garden pots. Tom dropped the pottery into a waste receptacle and went to the end of the garden room that attached to the house.

At the house end of the garden room lay a kitchen, including a stove, refrigerator, heater box, and counters. Clay pots and metal utensils hung from hooks or stayed in closed drawers. Muaar was at one of the counters, easing the bush Tom had damaged into another pot. The yellow leaves had wilted further, and she was chuffing to herself in annoyance. Tom headed for the stove. Like all the counters and tables in the house, it was too low for him, and as he leaned forward he felt a small backache creeping in from all the bending he'd been doing lately. A pile of blue-green moss sat next to the stove, on which a large pot of water maintained a rolling boil. Tom dropped a square of the moss into a carafe and followed it with boiling water. *Hrugar* tea, Zedrel's usual drink. While it was steeping, Tom caught up a plate and went back to the garden area, where he gathered several handfuls of reddish *afgar* leaves, being careful to select the darkest ones he could find. Armed with carafe and plate, he left the garden room to head for the stairs and Zedrel's chambers. By now he could find it with his eyes shut.

It had been almost two days since his arrival. In those two days Tom had taken the chance to explore Zedrel's house from top to bottom without Boleer as a tour guide. For all its rustic appearance, the place was quite luxurious. The continually changing decor still twisted his brain, but he was getting used to it. Artwork appeared and disappeared from the walls in mere hours. Floor coverings ranged from thick carpets to woven straw to scrubbed wood. The floor pillows, which seemed to be the only form of furniture, changed color and texture from one moment to the next. The nanites and thralls handled most of the changes, and if there was a pattern. Tom couldn't see it.

The dozen or so thralls in the house handled many duties, though the only ones Tom recognized were cooking and gardening. No one seemed to clean anything, and Tom assumed the nanites handled most of that. Like most of the thralls Tom's duties were actually fairly light. Since the Chiar didn't eat formal meals so much as nibble constantly, bringing Zedrel his food was an almost constant task, but not a difficult one.

On the stairs Tom encountered another thrall, one whose name he didn't know, though he did recognize its—his—smell. Tom had privately christened him "Two-Day Sushi" after his scent. Sushi, noticing that Tom was laden with plate and carafe, started to make way, then stared at Tom's forehead. Sushi's scent changed, becoming a bit harsher, and he made a single barking sound Tom knew was a form of laughter. This laughter, however, contained a sharper edge. Sushi continued down the staircase, still barking.

What the hell was that all about? Tom wondered, then remembered the mark Muaar had put on his head. It must have something to do with that, but what? He started to put a hand to his forehead, then his arm stopped of its own accord—his outer coating had hardened to stop him from wiping the mark away. After a moment it released him, and he dropped his hand. Grimacing and feeling a bit confused, Tom continued up to Zedrel's chambers. Zedrel, his outer coating flickering red and yellow, sat on a high velveteen cushion facing a wall outfitted with a communication system. He was bent over a sheet of the plastic Chiar paper but looked up when Tom entered.

"Tom, I want you to—" Zedrel caught sight of the mark on Tom's forehead. He shook his head once and chuffed hard. His outer coating pinked with mirth. "So Muaar has selected you for humiliation, has she? What irony! I do not know if such a thing means anything to an alien."

Humiliation. So that was why Two-Day Sushi had laughed at Tom. Zedrel was right—it meant nothing to Tom. He hadn't even been entirely sure that Sushi had been laughing.

"Sit," Zedrel ordered.

Silently Tom settled himself. He didn't want to remain silent. A big part of him wanted to tell Zedrel exactly what he thought of him and his reeking house. Barring that, he wanted to crack jokes and make smart remarks. The Chiar smell made them a natural target. Instead, something kept Tom quiet. It wasn't nanites but rather an internal instinct. Or was it some kind of training? He didn't know, and this fact was both maddening and frightening.

Zedrel reached down with one hand, and Tom put a leaf in it. The Chiar munched the leaf and continued to peruse the plastic sheet of paper, his outer coating a contented green. Colors, pictures, and letters swirled as nanites marched information across the paper. Tom wondered if it was more warp calculations, but he couldn't tell—from his current perspective everything on the paper was upside-down and backward. Every so often Zedrel tapped the sheet or made marks on it with a stylus. Tom provided a steady stream of leaves and handed him the tea carafe at intervals.

A chime issued from the communication system, and words scrolled across the screen. Zedrel chuffed once, swiped a hand across his plastic sheet to clear it, and looked up. Just as had happened with the lights on his first night, the communication screen responded with no order that Tom could see, though by now he knew it reacted to Zedrel's nanites. Another Chiar appeared. Tom, sitting below screen level, thought that he probably wasn't visible to the caller.

"Undersecretary Ree." Zedrel ducked his head in greeting. "What is the honor?"

"Engineer Zedrel," Ree said. *"I hope you are well."*

"I am."

They exchanged further words of politeness, then Ree said, *"Why have you withdrawn, Engineer Zedrel? Your warp drive is a success, and I would think—"*

"I am continuing my work, Master Ree." Zedrel brandished the sheet. "There are data to interpret, modifications that must be made."

"Alone?" Ree sounded puzzled. *"What about your team?"*

"There are some things which I must do in solitude, Secretary." Zedrel's hand dropped below screen level and brushed over Tom's hair. The touch made Tom's skin crawl. What if he jumped up, popped into Undersecretary Ree's view? It was obvious that Zedrel didn't want anyone to know he had Tom. Maybe he should find out exactly why. Tom tensed to leap to his feet—

—and froze. His outer coating had hardened into an immobile shell. Tom's muscles strained against it, but it was as if he were wearing a frozen suit of armor.

"I am now working on something very delicate, Undersecretary," Zedrel continued, "and I do not wish for disturbances. That is why I have cloistered myself. I have not the time for appearances in public or visitors in private. I hope you understand."

"Engineer Zedrel," Ree said, *"your project is truly of the highest of importance. We need you at your—"*

"Do you speak for Secretary Nashi?" Zedrel interrupted mildly. "You know I answer directly to her and her only."

Ree ducked his head. *"I . . . do not speak for her in this matter."*

"I see." Zedrel paused, and Tom added a new smell to his growing catalog—smugness. "Has the search for the missing . . . person shown any success?"

"It has not," Ree said with another head-duck. *"The Inspection Bureau is extremely upset. They are searching everywhere and getting nowhere. My nephew is an investigator, you understand, and he told me last night that—"*

"Yes, well it is a great pity. I really should not keep you, Undersecretary. Greetings to Secretary Nashi."

The screen blanked. Zedrel sipped *hrugar* tea while Tom sat at Zedrel's feet and forced himself to think about what he had just learned. Zedrel was an important person, an inventor who had just made some kind of breakthrough—a warp engine?—but he was hiding from the public. It didn't take a genius to see that the reason Zedrel had withdrawn was because of Tom. It also seemed obvious that Tom was the "missing person" Zedrel spoke of, and that Tom wasn't supposed to be here.

The old feeling of outrage returned. Tom wanted—needed—to run, get out of this reeking house. Last night, in fact, he had already tried it after the household had fallen asleep. But he found that whenever he tried to open a door or window, his outer coating would freeze him in place. He couldn't lay so much as a finger on a windowpane. His nanites had been programmed to keep him from making a run for it.

Zedrel had said earlier that Tom wasn't to go outside. That and the way his outer coating acted told Tom that getting outside for a while would somehow help him escape. The only trouble was, he was physically unable to do so.

As if reading Tom's thoughts, Zedrel said, "Tom, it would be folly for you to attempt to reveal yourself to anyone outside of this estate. Your nanites are programmed to prevent it. If you make continued attempts, you will experience pain and accomplish nothing."

Zedrel held out his hand for another leaf. Tom gave one to him, wishing he could give the job back to Nylo. Nylo deserved it.

And then, like a glass of water thrown into his face, the idea hit him. He stared at the shimmering walls as his mind worked furiously, examining the possibility from all angles. It looked sound.

Zedrel drank some tea and reached idly for his plastic sheet again. Tom wanted to rush out of the room to set his idea into motion, but of course he couldn't. At long last the last leaf disappeared into Zedrel's wide mouth. Tom got to his feet without a word, took up the dirty dishes, and headed for the door. Zedrel didn't stop him or even seem to notice. The bare floor turned into a thick carpet beneath Tom's sandals.

Downstairs, Tom dumped the dishes in the kitchen and went looking for Boleer. He eventually found her kneeling by herself in one of the workrooms. She held a strange object between her forelegs. It looked something like a book, but with a lot of odd protuberances. A bit of cloth hung from one end, and Tom realized she was weaving on a small loom.

"The Master allows hobbies," she explained as he squatted next to her. "I weave this cloth with very little nanite help. It takes long, but I find it satisfying. Do you have a hobby, Tom?"

Tom thought. "I don't know," he said at last.

"We will find one for you," Boleer said. "It is good for the mind to relax." She paused. "You still have Muaar's humiliation mark on your forehead. One moment, and I will laugh at you." Her head reared up and she made a mechanical barking noise toward the ceiling. "There. I have fulfilled my duty to Muaar. I hope you were not too overwhelmed with humiliation."

Tom smiled. He liked Boleer's dry humor, but he hadn't come to see her just to talk. "Listen, Boleer—I need your help."

"With what?" Another centimeter of cloth edged out of the loom.

Tom lowered his voice. "I want to get out of here. I want to go home."

"Do you?" Boleer said with none of the surprise or shock Tom had expected. Even her scent remained unchanged.

"I don't belong here" was all Tom could say.

Boleer stopped weaving. "And where would you go? Even if you could escape from this house, you could not blend with other Chiar or hide among them. The Master would find you, and quickly."

"My people could find me," Tom said, "but I think

I need to be outside. Master Zedrel doesn't want me to set foot outdoors, and I think it's because my people would immediately know where I am if I did. But my nanites won't even let me knock on a window."

"Tom," Boleer said gently, "I finally learned to adjust to thralldom. You will do the same."

"I don't *want* to adjust," Tom said, barely keeping his voice level. "Boleer, it's as if even my blood knows being here is wrong. I don't know what my home—my ship—is like, but I know I have to go there. Will you help me? Please?"

She looked at him with her single eye for a long moment. Then she said, "I have already lost much. What would a bit more be?" She added wryly, "Especially for someone who does not think I am ugly."

"If we do it right," Tom said with relief, "there will be no risk to you at all."

"I find that difficult to believe."

Tom took one of her hands in his. It was soft, like fine leather. "Boleer, when I get out of here, I promise I will find a way to free you, too."

"Now you are telling stories," Boleer replied shortly, and took back her hand. "I said I would help you. You need not say empty things in order to persuade me."

Tom started to protest, then snapped his mouth shut. She had agreed, and that was the important thing. "All right, then. First I need you to go talk to Nylo."

"You! Human!"

Tom's stomach tightened with tension. So it

began. He turned, though he knew from the smell who it was. "Hey, Nylo old buddy."

They were in the greenhouse. Tom, armed with a pair of pruning sheers, was snipping yet another meal for Zedrel. Unlike rooms in the rest of the house, the floors and walls of this room remained the same—tile floor, wood walls, lots of big windows. The windows were why Tom was spending as much time as possible there. He needed them if he wanted his plan to work.

"I have heard certain things about you," Nylo snarled.

"Oh?" Tom said. "Like what?"

"I know now why I was removed as the Master's attendant," Nylo said. His anger smell made the air thick and heavy. "You told the Master that I was incompetent. You told him that I disliked my job."

Not the brightest star in the cluster, are you, Nylo? Tom thought. *Since I didn't even know you were Zedrel's attendant until he announced I had the job.*

"On my planet we have a saying, Nylo," Tom said aloud. " 'If the shoe fits, wear it.' I mean, you must have been pretty awful to have your position handed over to an ugly alien like me. I guess I should thank you. If you weren't so bad at the job, I wouldn't have it right now. Gratitude."

Nylo fixed Tom with a hard stare, though some of the effect was lost because the Chiar had to stare upward to do it. The anger smell increased, and Tom knew he was on the right track. He wondered if this was how it felt to be an empath.

"I don't know a whole lot about Chiar customs and all that," Tom continued, "but I figure being the

Master's personal attendant must be a pretty high-ranking position. I show up and you get demoted. That must be pretty humiliating. I've heard some people talking, that's for sure."

"Talking?"

"Yeah. You know how it goes. 'Nylo couldn't hack it as the Master's personal attendant, so the Master had to buy a new one.' 'Nylo must have been doing a pretty rotten job for the Master to replace him with some weird creature.' 'We knew Nylo was going to lose it, and it was only a matter of time.' That sort of thing. Everyone's talking about it."

"I see." Nylo's anger scent strengthened until Tom was almost gagging. Tom settled himself back until he was almost leaning against one of the large greenhouse windows. His outer coating tingled a warning.

"I figure they must be right," Tom went on. "Zedrel keeps going on about how good a job I'm doing. Muaar doesn't like me, but so what? Zedrel says I'm the best personal attendant he's ever had. Lots better than you, anyway. He says you messed up a lot. He's even thinking of giving you one of these." He pointed to the earthen mark on his forehead. "Except he wants to make it permanent. You know—a tattoo? Anyway, I just wanted to thank you for—"

Nylo leaped. He slammed into Tom's chest, shoving him violently backward. They both crashed through the greenhouse window. Tom's outer coating instantly hardened into immobility. Pain exploded as Nylo's fist smashed Tom's face. The anger smell blew into a full rage stench that turned Tom's stomach. He lay flat on his back, unable to defend

179

himself or even move. Nylo crouched on Tom's chest and punched him again. Tom's head snapped sideways and he saw stars. Overhead, the sky was a perfect blue.

Another punch, and another. Voices swirled around him. His body tingled, and he thought he caught an odd shimmer of blue light. The world went gray. Blood from the broken glass trickled down his neck. Another voice, firm and self-assured.

And then the pain ended. Tom had time to sigh once with relief before letting the gray fade to black.

"Attention, Lieutenant B'Elanna Torres," the computer said. "Lieutenant Tom Paris is now aboard *Voyager.*"

B'Elanna's heart jumped and she stood up so fast, her chair fell over. The other people in the mess hall turned to stare. "Computer, location of Lieutenant Paris?"

"Lieutenant Paris is in sickbay."

For a tiny instant B'Elanna considered calling for a site-to-site transport to get her to sickbay in an eyeblink. She almost as quickly discarded the idea. Site-to-site was reserved for emergencies, and she was in enough trouble as it was. B'Elanna bolted from the mess hall and rushed toward sickbay. Several members of the crew flattened themselves against the wall in her wake. B'Elanna didn't even notice. Tom was alive and back on *Voyager.* Relief so intense it made her limbs weak warred with new worries. Why had he been taken to sickbay? A routine checkup? Or had something gone wrong?

The Doctor looked up at her as she entered. "He's

right here, Lieutenant Torres," he said before she could speak. Tom lay on a bio-bed, though B'Elanna couldn't see him very well around the Doctor.

"Let me see," she said, trying to push past him. The Doctor intercepted her with a strong arm.

"Lieutenant," he said, "I want you to be careful. He's been through a lot, and a Klingon welcome-home hug would only exacerbate his injuries."

B'Elanna peered over the Doctor's shoulder. Tom was lying pale and motionless on the bio-bed. He was naked except for a blue sheet the Doctor had thrown over his lower body. For a horrible moment B'Elanna thought he was dead. Then she saw his chest rise and fall with his breathing and knew he was only unconscious or asleep. There was blood on his face, and his nose looked strange.

"What's wrong with him?" she demanded. "No runaround, Doctor, I'm warning you."

The Doctor turned back to his patient, and B'Elanna followed him. "He has been severely beaten. His nose is broken, two teeth have been knocked out, and he has numerous bruises and contusions on his face and chest. He has been unconscious since he arrived, and I intend to keep him that way until I have finished treatment. It will be less painful."

"Who did this?" she snapped.

"One of the Chiar, I assume." The Doctor placed a gentle hand on Tom's nose to realign the broken bone, then plucked an instrument from a tray and shone a red light on the injury. When the Doctor removed his hand, the swelling was reduced. "If you want to help, you can get something to wash the blood off his face."

B'Elanna hurried to the sink and wet a sterile cloth. "Is he going to be all right?"

"I think so. His injuries are superficial, and experience has taught me that Mr. Paris has a very hard head."

B'Elanna let this go. Gently she wiped blood off Tom's face as the Doctor continued his work. Bruises and abrasions vanished beneath the blue light of the Doctor's dermal regenerator. When he was finished, he reached for Tom's mouth and carefully pried it open. B'Elanna saw the gaping holes left by the missing teeth, and her temper boiled.

"It'll take a day or two to grow replacements from his stem cells," the Doctor said, shining the regenerator over Tom's bloody gums. "I can make sure the stumps don't hurt in the meantime so he can eat solid food. And kiss his wife, while he's at it."

The main doors hissed open. Janeway and Chakotay entered, closely followed by Harry Kim.

"How is he, Doctor?" Janeway asked without preamble.

The Doctor repeated what he had told B'Elanna. B'Elanna, meanwhile, twitched the sheet up to Tom's shoulders.

"How did you find him, Captain?" she asked. "I programmed the computer to watch the transporter log and alert me when he came aboard, but I don't have any details."

"It was your idea that did the trick," Janeway told her. "A Chiar satellite caught a glimpse of him lying on his back on someone's front lawn. His image matched the pictures the Chiar programmed into the satellite network, which alerted us to his location. After we knew where he was, the rest was easy."

"Seven of Nine wasn't with him?" B'Elanna said.

Chakotay shook his head. "No sign of her. The system is still keeping an eye out."

"Why was he lying on someone's front lawn?" B'Elanna asked. Anger tinged her voice. "Who was beating him like this? And what happened to his clothes?"

"We aren't completely sure what was going on," Harry Kim said. "The captain is making inquiries. We do know that the transporter detected a solid coating of Chiar nanites. It filtered them out during transport."

"I'm going to wake him now," the Doctor put in. "He might know where Seven is being held."

"That's why I'm here, Doctor," Janeway said. "I'm glad to see him safe. Waken away."

The Doctor pressed a hypospray to Tom's neck. Medication hissed into his bloodstream, and a few seconds later Tom's eyelids fluttered open. B'Elanna grabbed his hand. She had never been so glad to see the color blue. He groaned and tried to sit up. The Doctor pressed him back and raised the bed to a sitting position instead.

"Relax," said the Doctor. "You're safe in sickbay."

"How do you feel?" B'Elanna asked.

"Fine. A little dizzy, I guess."

"That's to be expected," the Doctor said. "You took several blows to the head, though none of the damage was permanent."

"Okay," Tom said. "Good. That's . . . good."

"Are you in any pain, Tom?" B'Elanna asked.

Tom looked at her. "Who are you?"

B'Elanna blinked. "What?"

"I asked who you are."

"I'm . . . B'Elanna. Your wife."

He laughed, then looked uncertain.

B'Elanna Torres stared at her husband in shock as the Doctor quickly ran the scanning unit of his medical tricorder over Tom's head.

"He has amnesia," the Doctor reported.

"No kidding," B'Elanna said.

"I knew that," Tom put in at the same time.

Janeway stepped forward, a concerned look on her face. Behind her, Chakotay and Kim looked equally worried. "Can you be more specific, Doctor?" she said.

"Certainly. If I'm not interrupted, that is."

B'Elanna fixed the Doctor with a hard stare. It was easier to focus on being annoyed with the Doctor than on the fact that Tom didn't seem to have the faintest idea who she—or anyone else—was.

"Certain functions in his cerebral cortex are being disrupted," the Doctor explained, eyes on his tricorder. "Something is keeping the neurotransmitters that transfer memory from the cortex to other parts of the brain from activating. His memory has gone dormant, in other words."

"Hel*lo!*" Tom waved a hand in front of the Doctor's face. "Patient sitting right in front of you!"

"Sorry." The Doctor closed his tricorder. "Tell us exactly what you *do* remember, Mr. Paris."

"Tell me who you are first," Tom countered.

To her horror, B'Elanna found herself blinking back tears. Her throat thickened. She slid back a step and turned away as Janeway approached the bed. This was stupid. The last time she'd cried was when Chakotay had told her that their friends in the Maquis had all been killed or arrested, and even then she hadn't cried in public. She wasn't going to do it here, either.

"I'm Captain Kathryn Janeway," the captain was saying. "This is Commander Chakotay and Ensign Harry Kim. He's your best friend, Tom." Kim nodded uncertainly.

"Okay," Tom said. "I'm with you so far."

"You're a member of the crew on the Federation Starship *Voyager*," Chakotay said. "You and Seven of Nine were kidnapped by the Chiar."

"Seven of Nine? Is that a name or a serial number?"

B'Elanna swallowed tears and composed herself. Amnesia or not, he was still the Tom she knew, a man who covered fear and nervousness with jokes and insults. The realization that he was scared helped a little.

"We were the ones who rescued you," Kim said, and explained about the satellite system.

"So that's why he didn't want me to go outside," Tom said, half to himself.

"Now it's your turn, Tom," Janeway said. "What do you remember? Start at the earliest memory you have."

He did so, beginning at the auction. B'Elanna listened to his story with growing fury. He had been put up for *sale?*

"Why were you so sure that going outside would help you escape?" Janeway asked at one point. "Besides the obvious, I mean."

Tom shook his head. "A lot of little things. The person who bought me seemed afraid that if I even poked my nose out a doorway, the wrong people would somehow see me. I figured that anything he didn't want me to do should go right to the top of my list."

"It's good to see you haven't changed," Kim observed, and B'Elanna silently concurred.

"Anyway," Tom said, shooting an annoyed glance at Kim, "I managed to pick a fight with Nylo, and he shoved me out a window. I was just hoping to get outside for a while. I didn't think he'd pound me like a sledgehammer. I was paralyzed by my outer coating and couldn't fight back. Next thing I knew, I was waking up here."

"And you still don't know who we are," Janeway said. "This place doesn't look familiar?"

"Not in the slightest." He looked down. The sheet had slipped to his waist. "Shouldn't I be wearing something?"

The Doctor nodded at B'Elanna, who headed for a wardrobe. As she reached for a blue sickbay jumpsuit, she noticed her hands were shaking. Tom didn't recognize her, didn't seem even the slightest bit interested in her. After everything they'd been through, she was going to lose him like this? Her throat closed again as she rifled through the soft cloth, looking for a suit that might fit.

"Where did you find me?" Tom was asking back at the bed.

"As I said, you were on an estate on the Sherek continent," Janeway explained. "It's a postwar protectorate of the Goracar Alliance."

"Okay." Tom's tone made it clear this meant nothing to him.

"Who bought you?" Chakotay asked. "We haven't been able to learn that yet. All we know are the coordinates of the spot we beamed you from."

Tom said, "His name was Zedrel."

B'Elanna spun. The jumpsuit she was holding tore with a loud ripping sound. *"Zedrel* bought you? Engineer Zedrel? That slimy son of a—"

Janeway held up a hand, but her face looked serious. "We don't know that, B'Elanna. There may be more than one Zed—"

"Another Chiar called him Engineer Zedrel," Tom said. "And he just made some kind of breakthrough with a warp drive."

"He's *dead,*" B'Elanna howled. "All that time he spent staring at me like I was some fascinating animal. I thought he was trying to weasel technological data out of me, but he wanted a *slave?* I'm going to *kill* him, Captain. I swear I—"

"B'Elanna." Janeway put a calming hand on her shoulder. Tom looked on with interest. "We'll handle Zedrel. A bigger priority now is finding Seven."

B'Elanna opened her mouth to contradict, then clamped her teeth shut. The captain was right. They had to find Seven. Was she suffering from amnesia, too?

"Tom," Chakotay said, "were there any other humans on Zedrel's estate?"

"Not that I saw."

"I really need to give my patient a more thorough examination," the Doctor said pointedly. "In private, if you don't mind?"

"And I need to have a talk with Secretary Nashi,"

Janeway said, heading for the door. Chakotay and Kim reluctantly followed. "Doctor, keep us posted."

"That I will," the Doctor muttered. He was already running the small scanner over Tom's head again.

"This isn't private if you're here," Tom said. "Banana, right?"

B'Elanna's face hardened. A hint of annoyance was starting to wear through the worry. Here they were trying to help him, and all he could do was make smart remarks. She knew why he was doing it, but now it was starting to annoy her. B'Elanna folded her arms without budging.

"Right," Tom said. "How about those clothes, then?"

"You want them?" B'Elanna said. "Get up and get them. Here, I'll help." She reached for the sheet as if to yank it away. Tom snatched it around himself.

"Knock it off," he sputtered. "Get your thrills somewhere else."

"Don't move, please," the Doctor murmured.

"Yeah, your head might fall off," B'Elanna added.

"That happen to you?" Tom shot back. "Are those dents in your forehead from when it hit the floor?"

"Listen, you ungrateful—"

"Ah, love." The Doctor looked down at his tricorder with a small smile. "It shows itself in mysterious ways. Or so I'm told."

B'Elanna shut up. She glared at Tom. Tom glared back. The Doctor sighed and reset his tricorder.

"Already we have arrested Engineer Zedrel, Captain," Nashi said from the viewscreen. Her outer

coating was red with agitation. *"He will be punished under harshest law, I give you my promise."*

"Forgive me if I sound skeptical, Secretary," Janeway replied tightly. "But Engineer Zedrel is a hero to your people. He designed your warp drive. It's hard to believe he'll receive—"

"Nevertheless, Captain," Nashi said. *"It will be done."*

Janeway folded her arms. She was standing in the exact center of her bridge instead of sitting in her ready room because the bridge was an imposing place of power, a place that controlled weapons and in which people worked and scurried about under Janeway's command. The entire scene was designed to make it clear that Janeway was in control. Was Nashi aware of this or not? Hard to tell.

Nashi stood in her office, which currently had bare green walls. None of the usual functionaries shared the screen with her. A gesture of submission? Again, hard to tell.

"Secretary," Janeway said, "there is still the matter of my other missing crewman. Does Zedrel know anything about her?"

"Ask him yourself, Captain." Nashi barked a command, and Zedrel marched with stiff steps into range of the screen. His outer coating was a solid thrall gray, and he was careful to keep his head lower than Nashi's. *"Zedrel has confessed to his crimes. I will send you a copy of his words immediately, but you may interrogate him here and now."*

Janeway shot Tuvok a glance. He quirked an eyebrow.

"Captain, I will be frank, and please give me your

189

belief," Nashi said. *"This is a disaster beyond night-mare for all of Chi. An alien civilization appears in our system, a peaceful civilization which goes out of its way to help us—twice. Then a minority group twice perpetrates acts of violence on you, our benev-olent visitors. It must make all of Chi look barbaric and warlike to you. The Chiar are not such as that, Captain, and we are all hoping that the actions of a violent few will not destroy relations between our people."* Nashi paused, then ducked her head. *"Cap-tain, if you wish it, I . . . I will turn Zedrel over to you for whatever punishment you deem necessary."*

Janeway's expression didn't change. She was get-ting better at reading the Chiar, and Nashi sounded sincere, but Janeway couldn't tell for sure. She wanted to trust Nashi, believe her words, but a spark of suspicion remained. Suddenly Janeway was tired of being suspicious, tired of wondering who was lying to her and who was not. If Seven of Nine hadn't been missing, she would have sent *Voyager* back on course for the Federation at warp nine with-out a backward glance.

"Thank you for your offer, Secretary," Janeway said. "But that won't be necessary. My main priority is to find Seven of Nine."

"And ours as well," Nashi agreed. Zedrel kept his head low.

"I would, however, like to ask Zedrel a few ques-tions."

"And he is eager to answer." Nashi stared down at Zedrel with fiery eyes. *"Very eager."*

"Engineer Zedrel," Janeway began.

"He has been stripped of his title and family

name, Captain," Nashi interrupted. *"Zedrel is now his only name."*

"I see. Zedrel, then. What role did you play in the kidnapping of my two crewmen?"

Zedrel lifted his head. Nashi made a sharp movement, and Zedrel's gaze instantly dropped to the floor. His segmented neck stiffened, moving his head down. More nanite tricks?

Zedrel muttered something Janeway couldn't hear.

"Speak!" Nashi barked. *"Answer her questions and perhaps you will be allowed to atone for your crime!"*

Janeway shifted a bit uncomfortably. No doubt Zedrel deserved what was happening to him, but Janeway had never been a fan of public humiliation as a method of punishment. She also wasn't sure if Nashi meant what she said or if she was grandstanding for Janeway's benefit.

"I had no role," Zedrel replied to the floor.

"Then how did you learn Lieutenant Paris was up for sale?"

"I have many contacts who know my tastes," Zedrel said. *"Though the one that informed me of Lieutenant Paris's sale is an anonymous one. When I heard one of your . . . people would be available on the black market, I knew I must attend the bidding."*

"Why?"

Zedrel moved his eyes, sneaked a look at Janeway. *"I have been fascinated with your kind from the first time I saw you. Your people are beautiful and unique, and I had to have one of you. Many people think I created the Zed—the warp drive in order to explore space, yet I was truly seeking alien life-forms. I found them, and my dream was within my grasp. But I kidnapped no one, Captain. All I did was advantage take of what came my way."*

Janeway's stomach turned. Maybe Nashi's attitude toward Zedrel was right after all. "Did you see Seven of Nine at the auction?"

"No."

"Was there any indication that she would be up for sale at a later time or that she'd already been sold?"

"No."

"He is telling the truth, Captain," Nashi said. *"My nanites watch his physiological responses and would inform me of any falsehood."*

"Secretary, you said Tom and Seven were kidnapped by Ushekti terrorists. If I remember correctly, you said the Ushekti and the people from the continent of Sherek banded together to attack your people—the Goracar Alliance."

"True. It was the southern continents against the northern ones. Fortunately the Alliance won. The Ushekti refused to surrender, so we imprisoned them with the microwave generators. The Sherekti did surrender, and they are now our protectorate. I suspect the terrorists put Tom Paris up for sale to make money for their cause."

"Why did your people go to war, Secretary?"

"Trade. Economics. Many reasons, all intertwined. It is all very complicated, as any such conflict must be, but in simplification, the Sherekti attacked first, we retaliated, and we won."

The turbolift doors opened, and the Doctor strode onto the bridge. The mobile holographic emitter that allowed him to leave sickbay made a small black triangle on his upper arm. He approached the captain while Nashi spoke.

"We have a problem," he murmured.

"Can't it wait, Doctor?" Janeway murmered back. "I'm rather busy."

"I know. The comm system wouldn't patch me through to you. But I also need to ask our . . . hosts a few questions about Lieutenant Paris."

Janeway raised her voice. "Secretary Nashi, this is our chief medical officer. He has been examining Tom Paris, and he would like to ask you a few questions."

Nashi ducked her head affirmatively.

"Secretary," the Doctor said, "I'm having difficulty tracing the exact source of Mr. Paris's amnesia. Can you give me more information or put me in contact with someone who can?"

"I will you tell what I can," Nashi said. *"I imagine it has something to do with the nanites in his system."*

The Doctor raised his eyebrows. "I detected no nanites."

"You must look more closely, Doctor . . . Doctor . . ." Nashi ducked her head again. *"Apologies, but I have forgotten your name."*

"Just 'Doctor' will do."

"Very well. When Tom Paris was . . . taken, he was no doubt injected with a series of starter nanites."

"Starter nanites?" Janeway said.

"Nanites are self-replicating," Nashi said. *"They build copies of themselves as needed out of whatever materials are available. In a Chiar—or human—system, they would build copies of themselves from materials in the hosts's body."* She held out an arm. *"Many, though not all, of our body nanites are or-*

ganic in nature. They use DNA and RNA for memory storage, and they often mimic different types of cells."

"A form of retrovirus," the Doctor said. "One that the transporter biofilter wouldn't necessarily detect, since the nanites would blend into his body cells."

Chakotay spoke up from his chair for the first time. "Then why did the biofilters detect Chiar nanites when we tried to beam them aboard?"

As I said, not all our nanites are organic," Nashi explained. *"Your biofilters probably detected our nonorganics. Internal nanites, such as might interfere with memory, are usually organic. Whoever installed them would not have had much time to familiarize himself with your physiology, and using nanites created from your crewman's own organic material would automatically easier be to introduce."*

"So I've been looking for the wrong thing," the Doctor mused aloud.

"A possible truth."

"What do the nanites do in a thrall's body, Secretary?" Janeway asked.

Nashi ducked her head in surprise. *"They ensure loyalty, Captain. They can deliver pain or even take over a thrall's muscles to force obedience. They can also alter a thrall's brain chemistry, though this is time-consuming and very complicated. I doubt it was done to Tom Paris."*

"But what about the amnesia?" the Doctor asked.

Nashi chuffed once. *"Of that specifically I know nothing, Doctor. I am quite sure it is connected to the nanites. You should also beware of simply remov-*

ing them, however. Removing internal nanites is potentially devastating. I shall ask in the medical community to see if anyone knows of a precedent and inform you when I hear of something useful."

"Thank you, Secretary," the Doctor said. "I should return to my patient." And he left the bridge.

"Again, Captain, I must offer you our humblest apologies. Zedrel"—she gestured at him—*"will be punished."*

"Your apologies are acknowledged," Janeway said. "Contact us again if you come across any information for us."

Nashi ducked her head. The screen went blank. The instant the frequency was closed, Janeway turned to Harry Kim at ops.

"Mr. Kim, can you break into the Chiar computer network?"

"Captain?" Kim asked in surprise.

"I want you and Mr. Tuvok to scour the Chiar networks," Janeway said. "See if you can track down any information about Tom and Seven being put up for auction, now that we know it happened. The news of their sale must be recorded *somewhere,* black market or not."

"The Chiar encryption methods are formidable, but not impossible to breach," Tuvok said.

Janeway leaned against a railing. "You sound like you've already explored a few areas, Mr. Tuvok."

"A simple precaution," Tuvok replied. "I assure you I was not detected. As Seven of Nine might say, I thought it might be more . . . efficient to conduct a preliminary survey."

"I see," Janeway said archly.

Harry's console beeped and he raised a sheepish hand. "While we're confessing . . ."

"Yes, Mr. Kim?" Janeway brought her head around. "Do continue."

"I initiated a search when Nashi mentioned black market sales. Tuvok was right—their encryption methods aren't impossible to break. Tom was held in an enclosure in the Sherekti desert not far from the ocean coastline. I just now got the coordinates, but the place is protected by force fields so we can't beam in. I also can't find any reference to Seven, but—"

"But it's a good place to start. Mr. Chakotay, assemble a team and check it out."

Chakotay rose, gestured for Tuvok and Kim to join him at the turbolift. Janeway watched them go, then wet her lips and sat in her chair to do that one thing Starfleet captains everywhere hated doing:

Wait.

CHAPTER

9

THE TRANSPORTER BEAM FADED. It was followed by a flash of blue light from the fist-sized sphere on Chakotay's belt. Chakotay's phaser rifle was set against his shoulder and he found it was aimed at a house-sized boulder. Beside him, Harry Kim had already flipped his own weapon over his shoulder by the strap and was consulting a tricorder. Tuvok kept a watchful eye out, as did Crewman Bethany Marija and Ensign Paul Christopher.

They were standing at the bottom of a cliff. A dry canyon over two hundred meters wide spread out before them, littered with rocks and boulders. A hot, dry wind rushed over them. Sand stung the inside of Chakotay's nose, making him want to sneeze. Blue lights on the sphere at his belt winked quietly to themselves, indicating operation within normal parameters.

"No lifesigns in the immediate vicinity!" Kim

shouted over the wind. It whistled between the rocks and boulders. "But there's a force field in the cliff behind us. Sensors can't penetrate it."

As one, the group turned to face the cliff wall. Paul Christopher, a stocky security officer with dark hair and hazel eyes, raised his own tricorder. "The outer coating of rock is a hologram!" he yelled. "The force field is beneath it. I'm reading a fluctuation in the energy patterns about ten meters to the left. It looks like one of the field generators has a small malfunction, and it's made a weak point in the generators' overlap."

"Security sensors?" Chakotay bellowed.

"Plenty," Christopher replied. "But they're reading us as sand devils thanks to the sensor disruption unit."

Chakotay automatically touched the sphere on his belt. "It won't fool them for long. We need to get inside. Now!"

Heads bent against the wind, the quintet moved toward the place Christopher had indicated. The cliff face looked perfectly normal—chunky, red-brown rock rising almost straight up to a clean sky.

"Here!" Christopher pointed. The others huddled around him. Sand scoured Chakotay's face and hands, sifted grit down inside his uniform. Marija grimaced, looking as uncomfortable as Chakotay felt.

Harry Kim checked his own tricorder. "The only way in is to disrupt the field and make a run for it."

"They will know we are here!" Tuvok shouted.

"No choice!" Chakotay boomed. "If Seven's in there, we have to get her out."

"If we concentrate phaser fire right there"—Christopher pointed—"we should disrupt the force field enough to let us through."

As if on cue, all five readied their rifles.

"One . . . two . . ." Chakotay shouted, "three!"

Five red beams flashed through wind and blowing sand. A portion of the rock rippled, distorted, and melted away, revealing a field of pulsing gray energy. Chakotay held down his trigger. He smelled ozone and singed silicon. Beside him, Marija, Kim, and the others held their own beams steady on the disruption. The force field shimmered under the onslaught. Chakotay wondered how many alarms they had set off, how many Chiar were mustering themselves to meet the invaders.

A hole opened in the field, one just large enough for two humans to pass through side by side.

"Go!" Chakotay barked.

Tuvok and Christopher leaped through the opening, followed by Christopher and Marija. The hole started to close. Chakotay dived through and felt the tingling shock along his sides as the field brushed his body. He landed hard, jolting the air from his lungs. Tuvok hauled him gasping to his feet in one smooth motion— Vulcans, Chakotay remembered, were stronger than they looked—and they all hurriedly looked around.

They were in an indentation of the cliff, wide but shallow. Less than three meters in front of them, the rocky wall—the real wall—had been carved into a two-story fortress. It reminded Chakotay of cliff-dweller homes he had seen back on Earth as a boy, except the doorways possessed metal doors and the windows were covered with glass or plastic. The second floor jutted out over the first, though, giving the group some cover from above as they grouped near the closest door.

Hold on, Seven, he thought. *We're coming for you.*

Kim and Christopher were already working on the lock, tricorders in hand. Chakotay, Tuvok, and Marija readied their phaser rifles and formed a protective half-circle around them. The area was perfectly quiet, and Chakotay heard his own heart pounding in his chest. It was a relief to be out of the wind, but how long before the Chiar came for them? The quiet was eerie, deafening.

"Is Seven in there?" he asked Marija. She shifted her rifle into a one-handed grip and flipped open her tricorder with the other.

"I'm reading a human lifesign," she said. "If it isn't her, someone from the crew is taking a very unauthorized shore leave down here."

"You have coordinates?"

"Yep."

The force field had already resealed itself, and the hologram had been reestablished, leaving the indentation only dimly lit. A quartet of generators set into the edge of the indentation held the force field in place. Lights winked over three of them in a steady pattern, but the lights on the fourth were different. Chakotay assumed it was due to the malfunction Christopher had mentioned.

"Got it!" Kim announced, and the door irised open. Instantly phaser fire ripped through the air. All five humans dived for the sandy floor. Half a dozen Chiar stood several paces up the corridor, firing energy weapons. Chakotay took hurried aim and fired back. He hit one of the Chiar dead on. Its outer coating flared orange for a moment, and it took a single step backward. Surprised, Chakotay rolled aside as a red beam plowed the ground next to him. Marija shot at another Chiar, who also took nothing more than a backward step before returning fire. She yelped and ducked away from the doorway. Kim, Tuvok, and Christopher had already plastered themselves against the cliff wall beside the opening.

"Their outer coating is absorbing our phaser energy!" Kim said. "They're probably using it to power their own phasers."

Backs still against the wall, Tuvok and Christopher wordlessly tapped the controls that upped their phaser power. In perfect tandem, they whipped into the opening and fired a volley.

"One's down!" Christopher shouted, then grunted as a return blast caught him in the shoulder. His rifle dropped to the ground. Christopher barely flung himself back around the corner and out of range. He clutched his shoulder, panting. Tuvok dodged away as well. More phaser beams shot through the doorway and fizzled harmlessly against the force field wall.

"Now what, Commander?" Marija asked.

"We can't get through this," Chakotay growled. "I was hoping to be deeper inside before we caught resistance."

"So what do we do?"

"Cheat." Chakotay raised his rifle and fired it across the little cavern. The beam struck the malfunctioning generator, which promptly exploded in a shower of green sparks. With a hissing crack, it shut down. The force field stuttered and shimmered. Chakotay aimed again, this time at the second generator.

"Kim and Marija, get the other two!" he shouted. "Tuvok, lay down suppressive fire. Keep 'em busy!"

Marija and Kim took aim. Tuvok dodged into the doorway long enough to fire at random and nip back out again before the Chiar could draw a bead on him. Three phaser beams flashed into life, focusing on the three generators. In moments all three were hissing piles of metal and polymer. The field fell apart like disintegrating chain mail. Chakotay slapped his combadge as the hot wind rushed through the recessed area, dragging sand with it.

"Chakotay to *Voyager*," he snapped. "Can you get a lock and beam us out of here now that the force field is down?"

"Yes, Commander."

Another volley of phaser fire lashed out of the doorway. Chakotay felt the heat on his face. He gritted his teeth.

"Marija, send them Seven's coordinates," he ordered. "See if they can beam her out, too."

"Done, sir."

"I can't get a lock, Commander," the transporter technician reported. *"She's too far underground."*

Chakotay swore. They had to get Seven out *now*. If they retreated, the Chiar holding Seven captive would only move her. He thought furiously. They could beam down multiple strike teams, attack the fortress in force. Or would the Chiar see that as an act of war? They were already on shaky ground as it was, violating who-knew-what Chiar codes and laws by now. A handful of people might get away with it, but a small army was something else entirely. Dammit, they were *this* close to Seven.

Close to Seven . . .

Chakotay tapped his combadge again. *"Voyager,* can you beam us inside the fortress? Get us closer to Seven?"

"One moment, Commander." Pause. More phaser fire, this time from above. Another group of Chiar had apparently gone up to the second-floor windows to rain energy down from that vantage point. The smell of scorched sand filled the air. Chakotay flattened himself against the wall and thanked his ancestors that the second-story overhang prevented the Chiar from firing at any of them directly. Unfortunately, it meant the five of them were completely hemmed in. Christopher struggled to his feet, still nursing his wounded shoulder, and snaked a hand toward his phaser rifle, which was lying in the doorway. A burst of beams from the corridor forced him to snatch his hand back, empty.

"I think we can do it, Commander," the technician said. *"One level above her there's a corridor that we can penetrate."*

"Energize, then. And beam Ensign Christopher directly to sickbay."

The familiar blue light folded itself around Chakotay. The fortress wall faded and was replaced by a stone corridor. Chakotay, who had still been backed up against the fortress wall, lost his balance for a moment now that the wall was no longer there. Beside him, Tuvok and Marija held their rifles ready while Kim checked his tricorder. Lights were flashing in the empty corridor, and alarms blared about intruders.

"This way," Kim said, striding ahead. "There's a stairwell. Seven's down there."

They were halfway down the stairs when the other group of Chiar opened fire.

Seven of Nine sat on the cold stone floor of her cell. She did not normally sit, did not feel comfortable doing so. But her leg muscles were fatigued after standing for so long without regeneration. It had been almost two days now. Her captors had brought her water and some rudimentary nutritional supplements, but not enough to meet her needs. Thirst dried her tongue and hunger chewed her stomach. Tendrils of her hair straggled around her face and neck. None of these things were what truly bothered her now, though.

She was alone.

This was not a new sensation. When Captain Janeway had severed Seven from the Borg Collective and cut her off from the comforting minds of billions of drones, Seven had felt alone, crushingly, terribly alone. Eventually she had come to learn that cooperating with others for either functional or recreational tasks was a way of coping with loneliness, even alleviating it. But now her friends were gone. She hadn't even seen any of her captors long enough to interact with them. The empty cell yawned around her, echoing and silent. Seven had never been this alone for so long before. Even when she had been forced to put the crew into stasis so she could fly *Voyager* though a dangerous nebula, she had had the Doctor for company and plenty to do to keep her occupied. Here in the cell, she had nothing to do, no purpose, no company. It frightened her.

Why hadn't anyone from *Voyager* come to her aid? They had to know she and Lieutenant Paris were missing. And what had happened to Paris? She had heard his screams while she lay stunned on the floor, and they hadn't brought him back to the cell. Was he dead? She had no way of knowing, and the worry gnawed at her along with the loneliness and boredom.

Another problem was nanite attacks. So far six waves of them had washed over her. Seven had fought off all six and spent considerable time reworking codes and systems in readiness for the next wave. This did give her something to do, but she didn't know how much longer she would be able to hold out. Her mind was already fogging from hunger and fatigue, and it was only a matter of time before she made a mistake and the Chiar gained access to her nanoprobes.

A sound from the hallway brought her head up. Phaser fire, but faint. Seven scrambled to her feet and tried to look out the tiny, barred window on the cell door, but she couldn't see anything. She held her breath, straining to listen. There it was again. Phaser fire, this time interspersed with the gallop and clatter of Chiar claws on stone. No human voices that she could hear. Were the weapons Federation or Chiar? Seven couldn't tell.

"I am here!" she yelled out the window. "I am here! I require assistance!"

A slight rumbling noise got her attention. Seven turned around in time to see part of the cell wall change color. A human-height circle of stone lightened from gray to white. As Seven stared, the white part of the wall crumbled and puffed into fine white dust. Seven coughed as it caught in her throat and threatened to clog her lungs. After a moment the dust cloud cleared, revealing a single Chiar standing in a round tunnel. The Chiar smell assaulted Seven's olfactory senses. Seven found herself thinking of the Chiar as female.

"This way," the Chiar said. "Quickly!"

Seven backed up a step. "Who are you?"

"Your rescuers. A rival faction is attacking this installation. Once they find you, they will kill you. Hurry!"

More phaser fire, louder this time. Seven turned her head and shouted out the window again.

"Are you a fool?" the Chiar said, hurrying forward and clutching her arm. The smell made Seven's tear ducts spring to life. "You'll lead them right to you."

Seven listened. No one responded to her shout, though the phaser sounds continued.

"My name is Maski," the Chiar said. "I am here to rescue you before the others kill you. Will you come or not? I cannot risk my life here much longer."

Seven hesitated, caught between choices. If Maski was lying and her friends from *Voyager* were out there, then she needed to remain where she was. On the other hand, if Maski wasn't lying, Seven would be dead. And if she went with Maski, she would be out of this cell. Once she was away from here, she would attempt to contact *Voyager* herself.

"Very well," Seven said. "Rescue me."

Maski lead Seven into the round tunnel. Seven had to duck to avoid cracking her head on the roof. The phaser fire grew distinctly louder. After Maski and Seven had gone a few meters, Maski drew a universal tool from her outer coating. It flicked and shifted shape into an energy weapon. She fired at the roof of the tunnel. It rumbled and collapsed in a cloud of white dust that left Seven coughing. Some kind of breathing filter, Seven noticed as she gasped for air, had already covered Maski's face. The advantage of nanite-driven clothing. Another flick, and the energy weapon changed into a flashlight.

"This way," Maski said, though there was only one direction to go. She drew Seven along, and they both vanished down the tunnel.

A red spark appeared at the cell door's upper left corner. It moved, describing an oval that followed the door's outline. Sparks showered down and vanished against the stone floor. Eventually, the spark touched the spot where it had started, and the door fell inward with a loud *thud* that raised a cloud of white dust. A human head appeared above a phaser around the jamb, followed moments later by a second head. Chakotay, face streaked with sweat, swept the room with the barrel of his rifle. Bethany Marija did the same. Both of them took in the sight of the rubble pile opposite the door. The heavy scent of Chiar hung with the dust on the air.

Marija looked at Chakotay and said, "She's gone."

Seven of Nine forced herself not to wolf the food she was given, nor did she allow herself to gulp the water. The boat leaped and rocked beneath her, but she barely noticed. This was the best food she had ever eaten, whatever it was. Some kind of fruit, a series of dense, chewy leaves that reminded Seven of bread, water dipped up from the river. All of it, delicious. Seven was amazed at how hunger could enhance the routine experience of physical sustenance.

The boat leaped forward, almost flying up the river. It was a small craft, only a little larger than a shuttle, with a deck that was partly hidden by a canopy. The motor was nearly silent, meaning the only sound was the rushing hiss of the hull slashing silvery water. Maski and another Chiar—male—were the only two people aboard besides Seven. Neither spoke much. Maski piloted the boat, holding herself in place by gripping with her front paws a set of handles bolted to the deck. The other Chiar sat doglike behind her, clutching a similar set of handles. Seven had been forced to sit as well, bracing herself against the hull to keep from sliding all over the deck. The Chiar seemed to have no concept of chairs or seat belts. Seven bit off another mouthful of fruit. She had heard of motion sickness and had wondered if she would suffer from it. Apparently not. Not a hint of nausea touched her stomach and her appetite remained strong. And the helpful wind kept the strong Chiar smell from becoming overpowering.

Overhead, the canyon walls rose to meet a ribbon of perfect blue sky. Peering around the canopy, Seven could see each sedimentary age in the stone. Every level was a different color, like a rainbow caught in rock. The river at the bottom of the canyon was studded with rocks and boulders, which Maski avoided with graceful ease. Air rushed past Seven's face, and a fine spray misted over her. The canyon walls blurred past. Seven found the feeling oddly exhilarating. She had spent the vast majority of her life on one spaceship or another, where a strong breeze meant the presence of a deadly hull breach. Here, on this fast boat, the wind was to be expected, even enjoyed. Tom Paris had a minor obsession with speed, and Seven had always scoffed at it. Why would someone who piloted a starship be fascinated with vehicles that reached a velocity of less than two hundred kilometers per hour? Now she had an idea. On a starship, speed was an abstract, a number to be recorded. Out here, it was *real*, something that pushed her against the hull and stole the breath from her lungs. After days of confinement it was glorious.

Seven swallowed the last of the food and took a long drink from the canteen.

"It was good?" the other Chiar asked.

"Yes," Seven said. "What is your name?"

The Chiar tightened his grip on the floor holds. "I am Pek."

"The leader of the Ushek-Sherekti Freedom Movement."

"You have heard of me—of us." Pek made it a statement.

"I viewed the recording you made after your failed attempt to kidnap B'Elanna Torres," Seven said. A moment of bewilderment came over her. "I had assumed that the Freedom Movement was the one who kidnapped me. Now it would appear I was in error. Were you also not responsible for the attempt on B'Elanna Torres?"

"We were and we were not," Pek said. "There are many factions within the Movement, and one of them did attempt to kidnap your B'Elanna Torres. They did not have my support, however. I was not even aware the attempt was being made until the faction was already carrying it out."

"You made the recording," Seven pointed out. "That would indicate your support."

"This is true," Pek admitted. "I did record the message, but only in order to make it appear that the Movement acts under a united front. If the Goracar Alliance knew the Movement was in any way divided, they would exploit that weakness. Myself, I believed—I still do believe—that the best way would be to persuade you to come to us of your own free will."

"Then who *did* kidnap me?" Seven demanded.

"I do not know," Pek said.

"They used our name," Maski said, speaking for the first time since Seven had boarded the boat. "After you were captured, Seven of Nine, the kidnappers sent a letter to the Alliance government stating that we had taken you and your friend Tom Paris. But that is untrue."

"I see," Seven said. "But you have captured me now."

Pek ducked his head. "This is hardly a capture, Seven of Nine. You came of your own free will, as I hoped you would."

"My choices were limited," Seven pointed out. "What is our destination?"

"It will be easier to show you than tell you," Pek replied easily. He had a smooth, low voice that reminded Seven oddly of Chakotay. "You are one of the *humans* from the starship, so you know little of our people."

It was a statement, not a question, so Seven didn't answer.

"How much have you been told of the war between the Goracar Alliance and the Ushek-Sherekti?" Pek asked.

"I know a little."

"Please. Tell me what you know."

The boat slowed somewhat, then put on a sudden burst of speed. Maski's attention remained on the river.

"The Ushekti and Sherekti attacked the Goracar Alliance," Seven said. "The Alliance fought back and won. It took Sherek as a protectorate, but Ushek refused to surrender, so the Alliance imprisoned the Sherekti on their own continent with a microwave pulse."

"That was . . . succinct," Pek said in a quiet voice. "Three years of war and deprivation and death compressed into three sentences."

"I do assume it was more complicated," Seven told him. "But I have not yet had the opportunity to study your history."

"Your succinct summary is actually somewhat incorrect," Pek said. "It was the Goracar Alliance who attacked first. To be specific, the Alliance attacked the Ushekti space station."

Seven blinked. "The space station was built by the Ushekti?"

"Indeed. The Alliance constructed a series of shuttlecraft made for war and attacked by surprise. We Ushekti were caught unprepared and lost the station within an hour. It also destroyed any hope we had of perfecting warp technology."

A flock of birdlike animals with four legs exploded into the sky as the speedboat approached. Their outraged cries and screeches echoed against the canyon walls as they swirled upward.

"Then Engineer Zedrel did not develop warp drive?" Seven said.

Pek ducked his head, chuffed once. "He did and did not. He is—was—wealthy and powerful, and he was able to . . . persuade the Alliance government to give him the specifications the Sherekti had already developed. He promised that he would finish it, and I suppose this he did, but the work was stolen." Pek chuffed again. "This is not to mean Zedrel is not a brilliant design engineer. He is. But Zedrel is also used to purchasing what he wants. He wanted to purchase a guarantee of heroism and a place in history."

"It would appear he has succeeded," Seven said. "Why did you say he *was* wealthy?"

Pek ducked. "It was he who purchased your colleague Tom Paris. He has since been arrested, and Paris was returned to your ship. Zedrel can no longer be counted among the wealthy or the powerful. Perhaps it was a group of criminals who kidnapped you in the first place, with the simple intent of selling you to the highest bidder."

Relief washed over Seven. So Lieutenant Paris wasn't dead. But she didn't let her attention wander from the conversation. "You sound pleased at Zedrel's disgrace."

"Perhaps I am. Among my people, he is a thief and a monster."

"You are Ushekti," Seven observed.

"Yes."

Seven digested this. "I am . . . uncertain how to react."

"You need not react at all."

"I disagree. There are multiple factions on your planet, and yours seems to be determined to bring me into some kind of struggle for power. I can see no other reason why you would kidnap—or rescue—me."

Pek shifted, clutched the handhold more tightly. His outer coating shifted into green swirls. "Correct."

"I cannot interfere. I also have no way of knowing who is telling me the truth and who is lying, or who is distorting the truth due to faulty perception."

"That is why I will show the truth you rather than tell you." He turned to Maski. "Is there any sign of pursuit?"

"No," Maski said, eyes on the river. "The invasion of the base was a sufficient distraction, and our motor is not creating enough of a trail for anyone to follow."

"How did you tunnel into my cell?" Seven asked Maski.

"Nanites. It took most of a day. The people holding you captive failed to put any antinanite controls in your cell, or it would have been impossible."

Seven braced herself again as the boat swerved. "They continually exposed me to nanites of their own. I suspect antinanite controls would have been counterproductive to their goals."

"It is your nanoprobes that make you so valuable to the Chiar of whatever alliance." Pek paused. "The more I think of it, the more likely it seems that you were kidnapped by criminals who used our name to throw investigators off their trail. They were probably hoping to sell your nanoprobes."

"How did you know of my nanoprobes?" Seven demanded.

Pek's outer coating darkened. "Like many of the Goracar, Secretary Nashi does not hold her tongue when her thralls are present. I think she forgets that many of her household are Ushekti. Her nanites prevent them from acting against her personal safety but they do not prevent enslaved Ushekti and Sherekti from talking. Word of you and your capture filtered back to us very quickly, and we set out to rescue you. We ensured that the people on your ship would find the black market computer trace that would lead them to the fortress. When they attacked and provided a distraction, Maski was able to tunnel in and bring you out."

Seven considered this. "You tricked *Voyager* into attacking the fortress and tricked me into escaping my own rescue. And you expect this to make me sympathetic to your aims."

Pek made a low, husky sound and dropped his head so it was lower than Seven's. "I did. It was the only way I could conceive. Please understand, the Ushekti are desperate. I mean no harm to you or your people. We need your help and saw no other way to get your attention."

Seven decided to reserve judgment for a later time. "What help do you need?"

"Again, I will show you when we arrive at Ushek. It is easier to see than to describe."

"What if I do not wish to go?"

Pek and Maski whipped their heads around to look at her in alarm. Both chuffed hard.

"We are approaching a large rock," Seven said, pointing.

Maski made a choking, guttural noise and turned her attention back to the river. The boat swerved and a boulder rushed past. The breeze had become cooler. Pek continued to look at Seven.

"Seven of Nine of the Federation Starship *Voyager*,"

he said. "You are not our captive. There is a communicator on this craft. With enough time you can no doubt find a way to use it to contact your people, and they will take you home using this wonderful transporter I have heard about. You may begin to do so at this very moment, and we will not stop you. But I am hoping that, since you have heard the Goracar side of the story, you will also wish to hear of events from the Ushekti. How fair is it to see only one point of view?"

Seven said nothing.

"After the Goracar Alliance stole our space station, Zedrel"—Pek made the same choking noise Maski had a moment ago—"created a nanovirus that rendered most of our nanites inoperative. It affected approximately four-fifths of the Sherekti and Ushekti populations. My people and the Sherekti were left defenseless against the forces of the Goracar. The Sherekti surrendered, but we did not. After devastating our homeland, the Goracar imprisoned us and made Sherek their 'protectorate.' The Alliance has been bleeding resources away from Sherek for a decade now, enslaving the people and taking their lands, their food, their water. Meanwhile, we Ushekti were left to starve in our prison. Once Sherek is bled dry, I am sure the Goracar will come to Ushek to take what little *we* have."

"Why was this done?" Seven said. "What began this war?"

"Lack of resources," Pek replied simply. "Our planet is overpopulated. People go hungry everywhere. The Goracar decided the only way for them to survive was to conquer their neighbors to the south. And now Zedrel"—another choking noise that Seven began to take for profanity—"has perfected a stolen warp drive. This will make possible the colonization of other worlds. Lack of resources will no longer be a problem. But do you think the Goracar will share this discovery with the Ushekti and Sherekti? Even though without us the warp drive would not exist?"

Seven sensed the question was rhetorical and therefore didn't respond. Instead she said, "You still have not stated our destination."

"We are currently on the Sherekti continent, and soon we will be at the Center Sea. Ushek is on the other side of it."

As if on cue, the canyon suddenly widened, then ended altogether. The little boat shot out into a wide, blue ocean. The canopy flapped a bit in the new wind, and Seven smelled the salt.

"How far is Sherek from here?" Seven asked.

"Nine hundred twenty-seven kilometers," Maski reported.

Seven blinked. "At our present rate of velocity it will take us several days to travel that far."

Pek and Maski both chuffed and barked in amusement. "Seven of Nine," Pek said, "we are better-equipped than that."

Maski's outer coating turned a vibrant blue, and the boat changed. The hull flattened and the prow spread until the craft was a blunt square. The canopy spread, became transparent, then tinted itself, forming a bubble over the deck. Seven felt vibrations and rumblings underneath herself and realized the engines were reforming as well. The boat left the surface of the water and shot forward like an arrow. Maski continued to pilot, though the blue coloring left her outer coating.

Seven assumed she and her nanites were responsible for the transformation. Now that the deck had become a sealed cabin, the Chiar smell returned in full force, but Seven was able to ignore it as unimportant. Instead she turned her gaze to Pek.

"Why did you not use this form of the craft before?" she asked.

"A hover engine is too easy to track from orbit," Pek replied, "and we required stealth. As it is, we'll be spotted, but by then we'll have reached our destination and we can abandon this craft."

"Is that not expensive?"

Pek shook his head and lowered it. "We acquired it through . . . a nonmaterial method of exchange."

"You stole it."

"If you wish," Pek said. "We had no choice."

Pek, Seven noted privately, seemed to say that a great deal.

"We will reach the beachhead in eighty-four minutes," Maski said.

"You may wish to sleep," Pek said.

"I cannot," Seven said. "I can only regenerate in a special cubicle aboard *Voyager.* I am unique in this regard."

Pek stared. "You haven't slept since you've been captured? Aren't you tired? Are you in medical danger?"

"Your nutritional supplements have largely alleviated the physical fatigue," Seven told him. "As for the mental fatigue, I can go four or five days without regenerating before I begin to feel any ill effects."

"With luck"—Pek sighed—"that will be time enough."

CHAPTER

10

TOM PARIS SAT PERFECTLY STILL on the bio-bed as the Doctor ran yet another instrument over his head. The little flashing lights were giving him a headache.

He was also scared.

His name was Tom Paris. He was a Starfleet lieutenant aboard a ship named *Voyager*. He was newly married to a half-Klingon woman named B'Elanna Torres. His best friend was Ensign Harry Kim, a science officer who had a penchant for falling in love with unattainable women. He had the best doctor in Starfleet. All these things he knew because the Doctor had told him so.

Tom remembered none of it. It all sounded like someone else's life. No matter how hard he tried, his earliest memory was still the slave auction. And when he remembered that particular event, his face burned with alternating doses of anger and humiliation. The whole thing frightened him. He had a whole life out there. Granted, it was an impossibly weird life, but it was *his,* and it had been stolen from him. He hadn't had much time to think about it in Zedrel's home—he'd been too focused on escape. Now, however, there was nothing to focus on but B'Elanna and the Doctor and their discussion of his memory loss.

"Now that I know what I'm looking for," the Doctor was saying, "I am detecting a whole series of nanites. They're made out of materials from your own body, Mr. Paris, which is why my earlier scans didn't detect them."

"What are they doing, Doctor?" B'Elanna asked. She was still there; in fact, she had refused to leave. Tom wished she would. The way she kept staring at him, like she was simultaneously upset for him and angry at him, made him uncomfortable. The fact that the Doctor had found a whole bunch of nanites in his brain didn't help.

"They are suppressing his memory. I noted before that something was keeping the memory centers in his cerebral cortex from interacting with the rest of his brain. Now I know what's doing it. I just don't know how to stop it. Yet."

"Can't you just remove the nanites?" B'Elanna asked.

"Secretary Nashi advised extreme caution about that," the Doctor said. "I can see why. The nanites are created from your own neural tissue, Mr. Paris. Many of them are performing brain cell functions. If I simply removed them at this point, it would be like giving you a lobotomy. I don't think it advisable at this stage."

Tom's stomach clenched. "Is it permanent?"

"Too early to tell." The Doctor set the scanner down. "There are many avenues to explore, and I still have to talk with a Chiar doctor. Meanwhile, I want you to do something. You can help, Lieutenant Torres."

Tom cast B'Elanna an uneasy glance. "What?"

The Doctor pressed a black disk to the skin under Tom's left ear. It stuck there when he drew his hand away. "This is a cortical recording device," he said. "It measures and records mnemonic activity. I want a long-term scan of your brain activity, and this will give it to me."

"What do you want me to do?" B'Elanna asked.

"Most people with full amnesia lose personal memories but retain their skills and knowledge," the Doctor explained. "Take your husband down to the holodeck and run these simulations with him." He handed her a padd. "See exactly how much he re-members. Then take him on a tour of *Voyager*. Perhaps it will jar his memory."

"Sounds like fun," Tom said. "Do I get to put on any clothes or should I just do a Julius Caesar imitation with this sheet?"

"A good sign," the Doctor observed, tapping another padd in approval. "He remembers something of history and literature. I'll monitor him from here. Off you go."

Tom wrapped the sheet firmly around himself and ducked behind a privacy screen so he could don the clothes B'Elanna had handed him. Blue shirt, black trousers, socks, and bootlike shoes, the soft feel of fabric on skin. The past stretched behind him like a dark hallway, but if he concentrated on the small things, he wouldn't have time to be scared about it.

When he came out from the screen, B'Elanna handed him a vaguely triangular bit of metal. "You'll need this, too," she said.

Tom fastened the combadge to his shirt without thinking. The Doctor made another note on his padd. Suddenly Tom wanted out of sickbay, where his every move was noted and recorded. He headed for the door without a backward glance, and B'Elanna, caught off-guard, had to trot to catch up.

"That was rude," she said out in the corridor.

"What was?"

"Just leaving without thanking the Doctor or saying goodbye."

Tom shrugged, strode quickly. "I couldn't stand it in there anymore."

A man and a woman Tom didn't recognize stopped as they were about to pass him. "Good to see you back, Tom," one said. Tom nodded and they continued on their way. Who the hell were they? Good friends? Simple acquaintances? Relatives? He didn't know.

"Look, we're only trying to help you," B'Elanna was saying next to him.

"Yeah, well I wish people could help me without staring at me all the time and talking about me as if I'm not there." He strode faster. "I'm starting to feel like a laboratory specimen."

B'Elanna stopped. "Tom, can I ask you something?"

"What?" he said without pausing or looking back at her.

"Where are you going?"

Tom halted, blinked in consternation. "The captain," he said. "I need to see the captain."

"What for?"

"I made a promise," Tom said. "And I need to keep it. Will you take me to see her? I . . . I don't remember how to find her."

B'Elanna gave him a long look. "All right. Computer, locate Captain Janeway."

"Captain Janeway is on the bridge," replied the computer.

"Let's go, then," she said, and led him toward a turbolift. Once inside, she ordered it to take them to the bridge. As the lift rose silently, B'Elanna turned to Tom. "Banana?"

"What?"

"You called me *Banana* back in sickbay. And you laughed when you found out that we're married."

Tom flushed. "Yeah, well—sorry. It just seems weird that I'd even go out with a Klingon, let alone marry one."

"But you know I'm a Klingon," B'Elanna pointed out. "Or half of one. And you know what a Klingon *is*. That's a start."

"Maybe," Tom replied doubtfully. "How long have we been married?"

She told him. "So we're not even newlyweds anymore."

"Wow," he said. "So we . . . you know . . . sleep in the same bed?"

"That's what married couples do."

Tom wasn't sure what to say in response, so he didn't say anything at all. An uncomfortable silence fell over the two of them. Tom sneaked a look at

B'Elanna, who kept her eyes on the deck indicator above the door. She was definitely pretty, he had to admit, even if she was a little bossy. He searched his memory, looking for something, anything, familiar about her. Nothing turned up.

The turbolift doors snapped open on what Tom assumed was the ship's bridge. People hurried about their tasks under the watchful eye of a dark-haired man with odd markings tattooed on his face. He nodded at Tom, who nodded back without recognition. Janeway was bent over a station and talking to a dark-skinned man with pointed ears.

"Secretary Nashi has insisted that her people conduct the investigation of the installation where Seven was held," the man said. "She said she wishes to set the situation right for us without our help—a matter of Chiar pride, I believe—and that her investigators' findings will be immediately forwarded to us. The data brought back by Mr. Kim would seem to indicate the place is used to research nanotechnology, though in what little time he was allotted, he found nothing to indicate who was performing the research."

"Did the Goracar authorities arrest any Chiar?" Janeway asked.

"They did not. The Chiar who were captured all committed suicide in the manner of the earlier attackers."

Janeway grimaced. "Well, I suppose we'll just have to wait to hear more from the Goracar investigators, then. Try to learn everything else you can, though."

The man nodded and turned back to his station.

"Captain," B'Elanna said, and Janeway turned. "Could we have a word in private?"

"Of course," she said. "In my ready room?"

A moment later Tom found himself beside B'Elanna facing Janeway across her ready-room desk.

"What can I do for you both?" she asked. "Any progress?"

"Not yet," B'Elanna said. "Tom says he has a favor to ask."

To his embarrassment, Tom realized that thoughts of B'Elanna had momentarily distracted him from the reason he had asked to see the captain. He floundered for a moment, then blurted, "Boleer."

Janeway raised an eyebrow. "Is that a name?"

"It's a person," Tom explained. "A Chiar thrall who helped me escape Zedrel. She started the rumors about Nylo being incompetent. That got him even madder at me, and I was able to goad him into throwing me out a window so you could find me. I promised that once I got away, I would help her escape, too. She likes to weave," he finished lamely.

Janeway waited a moment, but Tom didn't continue. "Tom, I'm not sure what you're asking me to do," she said finally. "I loathe the idea of slavery as much as you must, but we're pushing the Chiar on a lot of fronts right now."

"Captain," B'Elanna put in, "Zedrel has been arrested, hasn't he? What happens to the thralls when their owner is in legal trouble?"

"What are you getting at, B'Elanna?" Janeway asked.

"If Zedrel is under arrest, maybe his thralls will

be put up for sale," B'Elanna said. "We could buy Boleer outright."

Janeway looked shocked. "I can't truck with—"

"We'd set her free, of course," B'Elanna interrupted.

Janeway drummed her fingers on her desk as Tom shot B'Elanna a grateful look. He couldn't remember anything about Starfleet regulations, and it was hard to think of ways around them as a result.

"I agree with your point of view," Janeway said, "but the Prime Directive—not to mention a few dozen other Starfleet regulations—does not allow for the purchase of slaves by Starfleet officers, whatever their intentions."

"What about Neelix?" B'Elanna said. "He's not in Starfleet. He's not even a Federation citizen."

"Captain, Boleer helped me escape," Tom said. "I'd still be down there snipping leaves and smelling Chiar if it weren't for her. I—we—owe her."

A long moment passed. Tom held his breath. Finally Janeway puffed out her cheeks and reached for the comm unit on her desk. "Let me contact Nashi's office and see what they have to say."

A few moments later a Chiar named Madam Ree came on the little screen. Janeway seemed to recognize her. Ree explained that Nashi herself was busy, but she, Madam Ree, would be honored to act in her stead. Tom suppressed a small shudder. Looking at a Chiar, even one that wasn't Zedrel, made him remember the feeling of outraged helplessness he had been living with for the two days since the auction.

"I understand the secretary must be a very busy person," Janeway acknowledged. "And I merely have a legal question. What will happen to Zedrel's thralls now that he's confessed to buying illegally acquired aliens?"

"That will be decided as part of his sentence," Ree stated. Her voice was quick and clipped. *"Since he has been stripped of his family name, his family lands will be forfeit as well. Almost certainly his thralls will be sold off."*

"You know, I think that's the first time I've actually heard her speak," B'Elanna said in a voice that carried no further than Tom's ear.

"Undersecretary Ree," Janeway said, "I would consider it a great . . . favor if Ambassador Neelix were allowed to acquire one of the thralls from Zedrel's household. A thrall named Boleer."

Madam Ree ducked her head. *"Captain, the Chiar are happy to do* Voyager *a favor, and this would be simple to arrange. It is hardly worth mentioning as a favor."*

"Gratitude, Undersecretary," Janeway said, and Tom let out a small relieved sigh. "I will have Ambassador Neelix contact you immediately to arrange the details, including the"—Tom saw Janeway's jaw clench—"selling price."

"I am sure it will be reasonable," Ree said.

"I literally bought her for a song," Neelix explained. He, Tom, and B'Elanna were walking quickly toward transporter room two. "A Talaxian lullaby my grandmother used to sing. The Chiar find alien music fascinating, you know, and even a single song is valuable to them."

"Thanks for agreeing to this, Neelix," Tom said, trying not to stare at the Talaxian. Tom didn't remember him, but that was becoming par for the course now. In any case, Neelix seemed a nice enough guy, if weird-looking and a little chatty.

"Happy to help," Neelix said. "I was just talking to Seven about slavery before you two were . . . er, removed from the ship, and I thought to myself that it would be nice to help a few of the downtrodden on Chiar. Seven's views on slavery are a little strange, I have to say."

"You did tell Boleer that if she wants to come on board *Voyager,* she can't have any nanites with her, right?" B'Elanna said.

"Oh, yes," Neelix said as the trio turned a corner. "But she said one more disfigurement couldn't hurt, whatever that meant."

"One of her previous owners disfigured her as a punishment," Tom said. "Zedrel never fixed it, either."

"The guy just sounds nicer and nicer every time I hear about him," B'Elanna said.

The transporter room doors hissed open. Bethany Marija was on duty at the console, and her fingers were already moving over the controls. The Doctor waited beside her.

"The Chiar have sent me your friend's coordinates," Marija reported. "I have a lock on her, so we can bring her up whenever you want."

"What are you doing up here?" Tom asked the Doctor.

The Doctor brandished a hypospray. "The Chiar smell being what it is, I thought it prudent to come up with something to suppress it. Studying the dead Chiar agent gave me enough information to come up with an agent that should suppress our visitor's more active scent glands without harming her. She won't even notice a difference."

"Then energize," Tom said.

Blue light cascaded over the transporter pad. When it cleared, Boleer was blinking down at them. The heavy smell of Chiar filled the room. For a moment Tom was back at Zedrel's feet, his head growing numb from the way Zedrel constantly stroked his hair, and a wave of nausea washed over him. Before anyone else could react, the Doctor stepped up and pressed the hypospray to the base of Boleer's neck. The smell almost immediately lessened, though it was still noticeable.

"Welcome to *Voyager*," Neelix said. "Never mind the Doctor—he just needed to inject you with a little something to make sure you don't catch anything from us. Better safe than sorry, you know."

Looking a bit dazed, Boleer carefully descended from the platform. Her claws clicked on the stairs. With a start, Tom noticed a light coat of ash-blond fur covered her body. He hadn't seen it before. Her head was still slightly squashed, and a dark socket indicated where her missing eye should have been.

"I feel naked," she said in a hushed voice. She looked down at her body. "I *am* naked."

"We can replicate something to cover you if you like," B'Elanna said. "Though you look fine to us."

Boleer ducked her head. "No, thank you, Master. I need to get used to a lack of nanites, and it would be best if I did it all at once."

"Don't call me *Master*," B'Elanna said almost sharply. "We don't keep slaves here."

Neelix cleared his throat. "If I may, Lieutenant?"

His voice took on a deeper, solemn note. "Boleer, by the power vested in me, I hereby release you from bondage. You are no longer a thrall."

Silence hung in the transporter room. After a moment Boleer ducked her head. "I feel no different."

Neelix chuckled. "Perhaps it'll take a while to sink in."

"It's good to see you, Boleer," Tom said. "I told you I'd help you escape."

"You did," Boleer replied. "Though I did not believe you. I thought you were lying—or insane. Gratitude."

"I like her," B'Elanna observed. "She speaks her mind."

"Gratitude," Boleer said to her. "Who are you?"

"This is my . . . spouse," Tom said. "B'Elanna Torres."

Boleer's single eye sparkled. "Ah! Then you have your memory again!"

"No." Tom shook his head. "I'm just taking everyone's word for it." He made the other introductions.

"What happens next?" Boleer asked.

"Uh, well," Tom said with an uneasy glance at B'Elanna. "I'm not entirely sure."

"If you ask the captain for asylum aboard *Voyager*," B'Elanna said, "she'll probably grant it and you can stay here."

"Or you can return to Chi," the Doctor said. "I can probably give you a holonovel or an opera recording that you can sell so you'll have something to start a new life with. It's completely up to you."

Boleer hesitated. "I would like to stay here for a time while I decide, if I may. Is there any work I can learn to do to earn my place?"

"You can certainly stay," Neelix said, "but as our guest. There's no need for you to work. Please. Come this way and I'll show you to some quarters you can use until you make up your mind."

The group went toward the door, leaving Marija at her station. It opened as they approached, and Boleer halted in confusion.

"How did you do that?" she asked. "You have no nanites to tell the door to open."

"The doors have sensors that notice our approach," Neelix explained.

"And what if you are not authorized to enter a particular place?" Boleer said.

"The sensors know that, too, and the door won't open."

Boleer walked uncertainly through the opening. Tom and the others went with her. Tom found himself feeling oddly bashful. He had promised to help Boleer escape. That he had done. Now, though, he wasn't sure what to do, and he gratefully let Neelix take the lead.

"Perhaps you'd like to see the ship?" Neelix was saying. "We could take you on the same tour Secretary Nashi had, if you like."

Boleer's skin twitched like a horse's. "That would be fascinating, Mas—Neelix."

"And I'd like to examine you in sickbay," the Doctor put in. "That missing eye . . ." He clucked his holographic tongue. "We can replace it."

Boleer halted and rotated her head to face him. "You can give me my eye back?"

"It would be my pleasure to regrow it for you," the Doctor said.

"Regrow? Not replace it with an artificial implant?"

"All it takes are a few stem cells," the Doctor replied cheerfully.

Boleer's neck folded down rather like an accordion, and she looked overwhelmed. "Could you take me to the quarters you mentioned? I feel a bit . . . strange."

"Of course," Neelix said quickly. "What was I thinking? This must be a lot to handle all at once. You'll probably want something to eat as well."

Trailing a continual stream of light chatter, Neelix led Boleer away. Tom watched them go with B'Elanna and the Doctor beside him. He realized he was getting hungry.

"Now what?" he said.

"Well," the Doctor said, pointing to the cortical recording device still stuck to Tom's neck, "you were supposed to be on the holodeck trying to reconstruct your memory two hours ago."

"Shucks," Tom said automatically. "Missed it."

B'Elanna tapped a wall display and called up a schedule. "It looks like holodeck two will be free at eighteen hundred. We could eat supper and go right down there."

"An excellent idea," the Doctor said. "Keep me posted on your progress, Mr. Paris. I'll continue with my end in sickbay."

After the Doctor left, B'Elanna turned to Tom with an uneasy look on her face. "So. What do you want for supper?"

"Anything but leaves," he said as she led him away.

When they reached what B'Elanna said were "their" quarters, Tom halted just before the door slid open. He tried to see if anything about the door looked familiar. It didn't. It was just one of several dozen anonymous-looking doors that lined the corridors of the ship. B'Elanna noticed he wasn't directly behind her as the door slid open.

"What are you waiting for?" she demanded in the entrance.

"I'm trying to soak up the ambience, okay?" he snapped.

B'Elanna looked ready to retort, then clamped her lips shut and stalked into the room beyond the doorway. Tom entered more slowly.

So this is where I live, he thought.

The quarters didn't look in the least familiar. Blue carpet, matching furniture, paintings he didn't recognize on the walls, strange upright box in the corner. The bedroom was visible through an open doorway.

"What is this?" Tom asked, stepping toward the upright box. It had a square chunk of glass on one side.

"That's a television," B'Elanna told him. "You built it so you could watch old westerns and"—she paused—"and cartoons."

Tom thought he heard a small catch in her voice and wondered what to do about it. Should he offer to comfort her? He wanted to. But how? He didn't even know if B'Elanna liked to be hugged, or even touched. For all he knew, it might be against Klingon custom. So he pretended not to notice.

"Cartoons, huh?" he said instead. "Maybe if I watch a few, something might be jarred loose."

"Maybe." B'Elanna went over to the replicator. "Grilled cheese sandwiches and tomato soup. Two servings each."

The food swirled into existence, filling the room

with rich smells of cheese and tomatoes. Tom went over to the table.

"Sandwiches and soup?" he said. "Seems like an odd sort of supper for my first meal with my . . ." He trailed off, unsure how to finish the sentence. B'Elanna might be his wife, but it didn't feel right calling her that when he didn't even know her. *Spouse* had felt like a safer, more neutral word, which was why he had used it with Boleer, but in this context it seemed rude. B'Elanna, meanwhile, brought the food to the table.

"This is your favorite when you're sick," she explained. Her voice was hoarse. "I thought we might start there."

Tom gave in. "Look, B'Elanna—I'm sorry I don't remember you. I don't want to hurt you, but I just don't—"

"—love me?" she finished.

"I don't know," he said helplessly. "I don't know *you*. And it feels like everyone's pushing me." Anger swept down out of nowhere. He felt confined, hemmed in. He needed to get away. Pushing his plate and bowl abruptly to the middle of the table, Tom got up. "I have to go out."

"And do what?" B'Elanna said.

"I don't know," he snapped, heading for the door. "I don't remember."

"Holodeck, eighteen hundred," she called after him. The door shut behind him, leaving Tom alone in the hallway.

B'Elanna sat at the table and stared at the sandwich in front of her. She could almost see it growing cold and soggy. A thin skin had congealed on top of the soup. Wasted replicator energy, all of it. Usually she and Tom ate in the mess hall, but she had thought maybe they should eat alone together first so Tom wouldn't get overwhelmed. It obviously hadn't worked.

Unexpected nausea hit her stomach. B'Elanna clamped both hands over her mouth and ran for the bathroom. She barely made it, though there was little in her stomach to throw up. Mechanically she rinsed her mouth out and stared at her taut, drawn face in the mirror. Then she slammed her hand down on the washbasin. This wasn't how it was supposed to work out, dammit. Tom had been *rescued*. She had figured out a way to find him and he had been returned to the ship. There should have been a quick session in sickbay, with the Doctor grousing that he'd like to keep Tom overnight for observation and Tom maintaining it wasn't necessary. There should have been a quiet, relaxed evening at home together on the couch, followed by a noisy, not-so-relaxed night together in bed. It was now painfully obvious that none of it was going to happen.

He hadn't even thanked her.

"You're being stupid," she said to the mirror. "You've never been a weepy female, and this is no time to start. The Doctor has told you what to do, so do it. Be practical. Be the chief engineer."

She stared at her reflection for a long moment. Then she punched it.

Tom had been walking for several minutes before he almost ran into Boleer.

"It is hard to find you," she said, looking up at

him. Only a hint of the Chiar smell tinged the hallway. "Your computer gives excellent directions, but you keep moving. Have you not heard me call on your combadge?"

"I've . . . kind of been ignoring the badge," he admitted. "How have you been? I like the outfit."

"Do you?" She twitched her shoulders, and the floor-length red . . . cloak? . . . dress? . . . that covered her rippled delicately. "It was a blanket. Mr. Neelix gave me the idea, and I altered it myself. Without nanites. It was easy, and I was surprised. Mr. Neelix also arranged for me to have the run of the ship—or as much of it that would not violate security. I am fascinated at how you live without nanotechnology. You have plants in—what is the name? —*aeroponics* that grow and thrive without a single nanite in them. I was again surprised."

Tom smiled. "There's something to be said about old-fashioned gardening techniques, I suppose. Have you spoken to the Doctor?"

"About my eye and head? Not yet." Boleer ran an absent six-fingered hand over her forehead. "It is strange—now that I have the chance to change my appearance, I find I am backing away from it. I think it is perhaps that I like having the choice—once I make it, I will not have it any longer. Does that make sense to you?"

"I think so," Tom said.

"But that is not why I came to see you," Boleer continued. "I wanted to see how *you* were coping."

"Coping?"

"Without memory. Are things well with your spouse?"

"I don't remember her," he said. "I think—no, I *know* it upsets her, but I don't know what to do about it."

"You should be beside her," Boleer said. "It is your duty—and your right."

"My right?" Tom echoed, confused.

"Tom Paris," Boleer said in exasperation, "you are being stupid."

"Well, thank you."

"Whether you remember her or not, B'Elanna—that is her name, correct?—is still your spouse. I know nothing of your family customs, but if they are similar to ours in any way, you form groups to do more than couple with each other and produce children."

Groups? Tom flushed. "Yeah, I suppose."

"We Chiar form families to aid and protect each other, and through them we seek emotional attachment. It is not something done lightly. It sounds to me like you are refusing the protection and aid your spouse agreed to give you. That is why she is upset."

"How do you know?" Tom countered. "You aren't even human."

Boleer didn't look the least offended. "Our species must have much in common, or we would not be able to communicate, no matter how clever our translation programs. This, I believe, is one of those common things. And stupid is stupid, no matter what the species."

"No wonder B'Elanna likes you," Tom muttered. "You don't hold much back."

"Now that I am no longer a thrall, I see no need to." Boleer took one of his hands in hers. "And I still have not expressed sufficient gratitude for what you have done. I did not—could not—believe you when you said you would set me free. I have never been so glad to be wrong."

Tom found his throat actually thickening. "You did the same for me."

Boleer considered this. "That is true. So perhaps our debts are paid. Now come along." She kept his hand firmly in hers and towed him up the corridor with the always-surprising strength of the Chiar.

"Where are we going?"

"Back to see your spouse," Boleer replied over her shoulder, "so you can stop being stupid."

The hovercraft slid onto the beach and snuggled up to the base of a small bluff. Pek pulled a blanket from a storage area and handed it to Seven.

"Wrap this around yourself," he said. "Form a hood over your head. Satellites overhead are watching for you. The canopy and tinted windows keep you from their sight now, but such will not help you in the open."

Seven took the blanket and did as Pek said. She had considered contacting *Voyager* to let them know she was all right but had then reluctantly vetoed the idea. Captain Janeway would no doubt insist that Seven return to *Voyager* immediately, regardless of the possible information Seven might uncover. Seven knew very well that the Prime Directive forbade her to take part in the political affairs of another society, but it seemed to Seven that Janeway had already done so herself. By talking to the Goracar Alliance and dealing only with them, Janeway was tacitly, if unintentionally, saying that the Goracar Alliance was the proper ruler of Chi. She had not properly explored the Ushekti and Sherekti, and it would be difficult to do without offending the Goracar. And Pek assured her that it would not take long to show her what he wanted her to see. It would be more efficient to find out the truth now and report it to Janeway than to put the captain in a diplomatically perilous situation.

The dome popped open. Seven took a refreshing breath of fresh sea air. The overpowering smell of the Chiar in an enclosed space was difficult for even someone of her careful control to deal with. Pek sprang out. Seven and Maski followed him.

"Take care," Pek warned, and gestured toward the top of the bluff. "This is what we are imprisoned with."

Seven peered upward, careful to keep her face hidden under the soft hood made by the blanket. The bluff looked like an ordinary, windswept piece of landscape to her. Then she saw it—a subtle, shimmering curtain in the air that ran the length of the bluff and out of sight toward both horizons.

"Microwave radiation," she said. "From the Alliance satellite network."

"Indeed. Crossing it destroys nanites and causes a certain amount of personal injury."

"Then how do we cross it?"

Maski was already moving toward the base of the bluff. Pek reached up for Seven's arm, urging her to follow. His six-fingered hand was warm and dry.

"We burrow underneath it," he explained as they walked. "It is only possible in certain terrain. Goracar patrols find our tunnels and collapse them, and we dig new ones. The Goracar cannot stop the burrowing entirely, but they patrol enough to ensure that no more than a handful of us can get out at a time. Between the microwaves, the patrols, and the ocean, we Ushekti are effectively hemmed in."

Maski drew her flashlight. It flicked into an instrument that resembled a tricorder. Apparently that was what is was, because Maski examined the readout and said, "A patrol has spotted our craft. They will reach this spot in forty-five seconds."

"With swiftness, then," Pek said.

A shadow at the base of the bluff turned out to be a cleft just wide enough to allow a Chiar—or a slender human—to slip inside. Maski went first, changing the tricorder into a hand-held lamp that cast light in all directions. Seven abandoned the blanket and turned sideways to follow. Pek came after. The damp, sandy earth crumbled as her back slid over it, and a clump sifted unpleasantly down her jumpsuit. The cleft smelled of brine laced heavily with eye-watering Chiar. After a sharp turn, the only light came from Maski's lamp. Seven felt as if she were being pressed between two sandy hands, and she decided it was fortunate she didn't suffer from claustrophobia.

Once they had all three made it around the turn, Pek paused. Seven glanced at him. In the dim light from Maski's lamp, Seven saw his outer coating change from green to bright blue. The earth vibrated against her back, and for a moment panic rose. The cleft was collapsing! A moment later she realized Pek and Maski showed no concern, so she tried to calm herself. Loud rumblings mixed with the smell of wet earth from around the turn.

"My nanites have closed the entrance," Pek said. "Even if the patrol finds it, they will still have to clear the opening, and we will be gone by then."

Seven silently ordered her heart to stop beating so quickly, but it took several moments for it to comply. They continued up the tunnel, Seven still walking sideways. In the enclosed space, Pek and Maski's scents were almost as strong as they were in the boat, though Seven was becoming accustomed to it. Now that one Chiar was behind her and the other in front, Seven found she could also tell the difference between them by smell alone.

"We are passing under the microwave radiation," Maski said. "The earth shields us, so there is no need for alarm. When we resurface you will no longer need to hide your face."

Seven ran a check on her own nanoprobes anyway. They were functioning within normal parameters. She itched where the dirt had slid down her back, but there was no way to scratch. To take her mind off the problem, she kept her eyes on Maski's lamp and concentrated on moving sideways up the narrow tunnel. Eventually the floor began to slope upward. The tunnel widened, and a few steps later, Seven found herself standing on a concrete floor. Water dripped in the distance, and the only light still came from Maski's lamp.

"Old city maintenance tunnels," Pek explained. "They're useful starting points for digging."

Maski and her lamp led them along a series of darkened corridors, though Seven's Borg-enhanced senses were easily able to keep track of where they were. If she had to, she could retrace her steps right back to the original tunnel. Not, she mused, that it would do her a lot of good, since the terminus had been destroyed.

Eventually they came to a tightly wound spiral staircase. Maski started upward. It occurred to Seven that a ladder would be more efficient—easier to build and using up less room—but the centauroid Chiar were ill-equipped to climb one. Seven followed Maski with Pek again at the rear. A trapdoor at the top opened to the sky. Maski helped Seven out, and Pek joined them. Seven looked about, her features calm and cool.

"Where are we?" she asked.

"Talam-Ushek," Pek said. "Largest city on the border of Ushek. It is what I wished to show you."

The sun was setting over the remains of a street. Crumbling steep pyramids ten and fifteen stories high made spikes against the darkening sky. Tiny fires contained in low metal boxes flickered up and down the road and in the spaces between the triangular buildings. The air held a definite chill, and Chiar of varying sizes huddled around the fires. Small shacks and lean-tos cluttered much of the remaining available space on the ground. Seven's enhanced eyes easily made out color in the dimming light, and she saw that all the Chiar were wrapped in ragged clothing. None of them wore the colorful Chiar outer coating.

"Why do these people not seek shelter in the buildings?" Seven asked. "They would be more heat-efficient."

Pek reached up to take her arm in his soft, dry hand and led her forward. "Most of the buildings are not safe. A great many of them are hollow shells, the result of the war. Nanites are a powerful weapon, especially when the other side has been largely denuded of theirs."

The trio walked silently up the street. Seven noticed Pek and Maski had dimmed their outer coatings and made it look as if they wore a simple wraparound blanket. Segmented necks turned flat heads and wide eyes stared as Seven passed, though no one spoke to her. The potent Chiar smell was everywhere, but it was heavily laced with a cloying, sweetish odor Seven could only describe as sickly.

"This is my home," Pek said quietly. "This is how my people live. The war devastated our continent. Food is always scarce here. Without nanites, crops are nearly impossible to grow. We have no real access to the ocean for fishing. Medicinal programs cannot run without nanites. Diseases which we once handled with a download now run rampant because our few surviving nanites cannot handle the required complexity."

"What happened to your people's nanites?" Seven asked.

"Most of them lie about underfoot," Pek said, "rendered inert by the Goracar virus and microwave weapons. Many of us have retained a few, with limited function. I have managed to obtain a complete set of nanites for myself, my daughter Maski, and a few hundred others who work for the Movement. But it is time-consuming and difficult to arrange this. In order to cleanse a nanite system of the Goracar virus, I have to use nanite-driven tools, and all our tools were infected."

They passed a family of Chiar kneeling around a fire box. One of the smaller ones made a continual low chuffing noise. Its eyes wept a pinkish fluid, and the sickly smell Seven had noted grew stronger as they passed by. Maski looked at them as they passed.

"The sickness is advanced," she murmured quietly. "The symptoms are so visible. The child will not survive two days."

Seven looked at the child, then looked away. There was nothing she could do, so there was no point in dwelling on it. However, the image stayed with her.

"How did you manage to cleanse your nanites," Seven said, trying to get her mind off the dying child, "if all your tools were infected by the Goracar virus?"

"By stealing clean Goracar tools. Just finding a way under the microwave curtain took two years. Then I had to figure out how to get across the ocean. Maski, Hularn, and I stole a Goracar boat and managed it, but only barely. It took us another two years to get back." Pek's voice slowed. "Hularn—my spouse—did not return with us. She was caught and executed."

Maski silently ducked her head once.

Seven waited a moment, then asked, "Is this what you wanted me to see? The devastation of your people? I will report it to Captain Janeway, but I do not know what she—"

"We are not looking for Captain Janeway's help," Pek interrupted. "We are looking for yours, Seven of Nine."

Seemingly at random, Pek chose one of the pyramidal buildings. A doorway stood open and was filled with bits of small debris. With a sound of distaste Pek swept some of the debris aside with his forefeet and entered. Seven and Maski followed. A short corridor beyond showed a pair of closed doors on opposite walls.

"This is one of the few buildings that is still structurally sound," Pek explained. "I have been selfish in this small way by taking part of it for my own use."

He pounded on one of the doors, and a moment later it irised open with a stiff grinding sound. The trio entered, and Seven found herself immediately surrounded by Chiar of varying sizes. Their smell overwhelmed her, and Seven's stomach twisted with nausea. She breathed through her mouth to avoid vomiting.

The Chiar were chattering rapidly at Pek and Maski, and it took a few moments for Seven to realize that this was Pek's family. The smallest Chiar barely came up to Seven's knee, and she assumed it was an infant, though it was able to walk perfectly well. A flurry of introductions followed. Seven learned that Pek was the oldest person in his household, with two grown children besides Maski, along with their spouses, and six grandchildren. They all appeared better fed and smelled healthier than the Chiar Seven had encountered on the streets, but their surroundings clearly indicated the place was racked by poverty. The living area was low-ceilinged and poorly lit from a few wall sconces, making it gloomy as a cave. Although the apartment sported several windows, perhaps half of them were boarded up. The few floor pillows were tattered and limp. And it was definitely crowded. Seven hadn't felt so surrounded since leaving the Collective. It made a stark contrast to the two days she had spent in the bare cell.

"Enough, now. Enough," Pek said at last. "Do not

overwhelm our guest. Perhaps she would like to sit and have something to eat."

The family scattered, though the children only retreated the minimum distance that seemed required by protocol. They kept their heads high on their segmented necks and stared up at Seven with unabashed curiosity. Seven stared back. Her experience with Naomi Wildman and a few other children had taught her that they would probably find it amusing if she, an adult, mirrored their behavior. One of them blinked twice at her. Seven blinked back. The child opened its mouth wide. Seven did the same. All six children made hoarse barking sounds that Seven took for Chiar laughter.

"Enough of that now," said one of the grown Chiar. "Leave her be."

Maski, Pek, and his other two children—daughters named Rekki and Kessra—settled onto well-used floor cushions, and Pek gestured for Seven to do the same. Although she did not feel comfortable sitting down, she did so rather than appear rude. Rekki and Kessra's husbands, meanwhile, vanished into another room and reappeared with a platter of what looked like wilted lettuce. They offered the platter to Seven.

"Thank you," she said, "but I have already eaten and do not require further nutrition at this time." *Not only that,* she added silently, *but it is clearly food you cannot spare.*

The Chiar did not argue the point. In this way, Seven observed, they were unlike Neelix, who would have insisted. Instead, they all took leaves and munched on them.

"Tell us about your people," Rekki said. "We have only heard that you exist, and there are many rumors about what you are really like."

Seven gave a brief description of *Voyager* and the crew, including how the Caretaker had trapped them in the Delta Quadrant. She carefully left out the fact that she was not one of the original crew and that she had spent most of her life as a Borg drone. When she was done, questions came fast and furious, especially from the children, and Seven answered them as best she could.

"Do you truly come from outer space?"

"How do you stand up with only two legs?"

"Can you fly?"

"Do you eat people?"

"Where is your ship right now?"

"Have you come to take us out of prison?"

The last caught Seven by surprise. "That was not our intended purpose," she said carefully. "We do not interfere with the internal affairs of other planets."

"Internal affairs?" Kessra said. "Is that what you call it? Stealing our space station, destroying most of our nanites, and then walling us in like animals—all of this is a mere internal affair?"

"Kessra," Rekki said with a note of warning, "Seven of Nine is our guest. And I doubt she is responsible for the rules of her ship."

"I am not," Seven said. "I do not even have a rank."

But Kessra appeared not to have heard. "You have seen how we live. This family is more fortunate than most, and even we live in squalor because of the Goracar Alliance. They took everything we had and make us live like beasts. This building is falling down around our flanks, but we have to think of ourselves as lucky to have it. Soon it will decay completely, and we will have to find another—"

"Why do you not repair it?" Seven interrupted.

Kessra blinked bulbous eyes and hunched her head down. "Repair it?"

"Of course," Seven said. "You could scavenge materials from the buildings that are unsafe and use them to put the other buildings into better condition. You would have fewer buildings than before the war, but you would have more than you have now. They would suffice until you could build new ones."

"Just how would we repair our buildings?" Kessra said, and her scent turned sharp. "You see what I am wearing." She gestured at her back. "My outer coating is almost blank. I have so few nanites, it takes hours to make even a simple change, though Father has seen to it that I have more nanites than most. How would we make repairs on a building when we cannot even change our outer coatings?"

Seven blinked at her, truly confused. "Was every building in this city erected using nanites?"

"They were," Pek said.

"How did your ancestors make shelter in the days before the Chiar developed nanotechnology?"

"Those secrets have been lost," Rekki said softly.

"The ability to use a hammer is a secret?" Seven replied, still confused.

"What's a hammer?" asked one of the children.

"Nanites have built everything we make for hundreds of years now," Maski said, tucking her legs beneath her on the cushion. "Ancient tools and methods of construction are unknown to us. I myself do not know what a 'hammer' looks like or what it is used for, let alone how to repair something with it."

"Then you must create other tools," Seven said. "Start over from the beginning."

"We do not know how," Kessra almost snapped. "No one knows how. All we can do is watch our civilization decay, and we decay along with it."

"Seven, it is hard," Rekki said in her quiet voice. "Our people—we suffer. When we lost the war with the Goracar, we as a people lost our space station, the promise of the warp drive, and our very way of life. The Goracar took everything of promise we had. I was young, but I remember it very clearly. It is hard to start from nothing. Just surviving now takes what little energy we have, and it is hard to try to begin rebuilding."

"It is not so hard," Maski objected. "Father and I work constantly. We find the energy, and so do the members of the Freedom Movement."

"But you are an exception," Rekki pointed out. "The vast majority of the Ushekti are simply too tired to care anymore. We do not even have the tools we need to make tools. We know nothing of where to begin. I wish I did know. I would use a hammer if I knew what one was, but I do not, and I have no way to learn."

"What about books?" Seven asked. "And computer databases? They would surely be able to instruct—"

"Books and databases are electronic," Pek said, "and the Goracar wiped them out to ensure we would have access to no knowledge that would allow us to escape. My own research library was destroyed, and all my notes with it. It is very difficult to reconstruct it when I do not even have the basic tools. It all comes back to a lack of tools and resources."

"It is . . . a difficult situation," Seven said. "Is that why you brought me here? To show me this?"

"It has grown late," Pek said. "Perhaps in the morning we can discuss more of it. We should sleep now."

The children protested, but were firmly herded out of the room by their fathers. Pek, Maski, Rekki, and Kessra settled deeper into their cushions.

"Do you require another cushion?" Rekki asked. "You are larger than we, and require more room to lie down."

"I cannot sleep without my regeneration cubicle," Seven said, "but I can use the time to think. I have many things to consider."

Pek ducked his head. "At one time in my life I would have offered you a guest room, but we have none here. This apartment was meant for a family of four, and it now houses thirteen. Still, it is better than the street."

Seven glanced around the dim room as Rekki manually doused the lights. The window let in a bit of moonlight, but the room was otherwise dark and growing a bit chilly. It was a far cry from the luxurious greenhouse dining hall she had seen during the all-too-brief welcome banquet. Rekki settled on a cushion next to the one Seven occupied, then raised her head level with Seven's.

"You said you cannot sleep," she murmured.

Seven shook her head, then realized it was probably too dark for the Chiar to notice. "I require a special cubicle for regeneration. My people do sleep, as a rule. I am . . . unique in this regard."

"I do not sleep easily these days, either," Rekki said, her voice carrying no further than Seven's ear. Around them, Seven heard the breathing of the other Chiar become deeper and more even. Their smell had lessened considerably.

"What keeps you awake?" Seven asked.

"Worry. I remember when the world was bright and happy. My children do not. They were born after the war, and I worry how it will affect them."

"Why did you choose to conceive during such a time?" Seven asked, then wished she could take the question back. Most humans were touchy about their reproductive habits. Perhaps the Chiar were as well.

Rekki didn't seem to be offended. "Birth control is a nanite program," she said simply. "That is why there are so many Chiar living in this city. The children are growing up in a world without hope, and it frightens me." She paused. "I remember looking down at Trilkav, my second-born. I was only a few hours out of labor, and I was thinking how he had no way of knowing the hardships he will face, and that perhaps I should remove him from the world before he is forced to face them. I suppose I should have been horrified at such thoughts, but I was very serious. I looked at him for a long time, and even placed my hand over his nose and mouth. But I could not bring myself to do so for more than a second. Now there is no food in the house for tomorrow, and Trilkav will go hungry in the morning because I was a coward."

"It is not an act of cowardice to refrain from killing children," Seven said.

"Perhaps not." Rekki sighed. "But Trilkav and the others will go hungry in the morning just the same."

She settled down to sleep. Seven remained upright and awake. She felt glad that she had refused the family's initial offer of food. After a while, she quietly got up and went over to the window. The darkness outside was dotted with fires and huddled figures. The crumbling pyramids loomed over them like broken giants. Seven went back to her cushion and sat again. She should try to contact *Voyager,* let them know she was safe.

Except the communicator Pek had mentioned had been aboard the boat that they had abandoned back at the shore. If the Goracar patrol had indeed been on their trail—and Seven had no reason to think they had not—the patrollers would certainly have found and confiscated the boat by now. Pek had said she wasn't a prisoner, but now that she had time to consider the situation, Pek's words no longer rang completely true. Certainly she could leave the apartment. It would be child's play to slip out. But where would she go? The terminus of the tunnel she, Pek, and Maski had traversed to enter the city had been destroyed, and Seven had no means to dig another. She could not cross the microwave curtain without serious, perhaps even deadly, injury. And if the Sherekti possessed as few nanites as they claimed, finding a working communicator elsewhere would be problematic at best. How could she contact *Voyager?*

It would be best to leave that for morning, she decided. There was no point in worrying. Worrying was a human practice that she intended *not* to relearn. It was a wasteful, foolish habit that accomplished nothing.

Fatigue began plucking at Seven again, but she knew from experience that if she shut her eyes and slowed her breathing, she would not fall asleep. She would need to return to her regeneration alcove soon, within the next day or so, or she would begin to pay the consequences. Her efficiency levels would drop sharply, and she would grow sluggish. Eventually she would probably begin to hallucinate. Seven didn't know what would happen if she went longer than that. Sometimes Borg drones would be forced to work for days without regeneration. They occasionally went mad and were shut down. Seven was more human than Borg, though, and she wasn't sure how much of that would apply to her.

But she didn't want to find out.

CHAPTER

11

TOM WATCHED BOLEER'S RETREATING BACK. Her misshapen head was held high, her scarlet cloak just brushing the floor. Beside him, B'Elanna tapped the console outside the holodeck doors and consulted the Doctor's padd. Boleer had actually done very little beyond escorting Tom firmly back to his and B'Elanna's quarters and standing there while he started to stammer out an apology.

"Forget it," B'Elanna had said. "We have an appointment at the holodeck." And so they had gone.

Another stranger passed them and nodded. Tom automatically nodded back without a trace of recognition. He was getting pretty good at it.

"Do you remember what a holodeck is?" B'Elanna asked.

"Of course I do," Tom scoffed.

"What games do you play in it?"

Tom opened his mouth to answer, then shrugged. "I don't remember."

B'Elanna looked disappointed. "Let's try some of the Doctor's programs, then," she said. "Computer, run simulation Paris One."

"Simulation complete," said the computer. "You may enter."

The double-sized holodeck doors parted and Tom peered inside. Large circular room, sunken center, series of workstations around the outer perimeter. Floor-to-ceiling viewscreen, pilot's console, chairs for the captain and first officer.

"It's the bridge," Tom said.

"For what ship?" B'Elanna asked.

"Voyager. But I already saw it, remember?"

Face stony, B'Elanna led him to the pilot's chair. Tom sat. It didn't feel familiar.

"Computer, run program," B'Elanna said.

A full bridge crew appeared out of thin air, including Harry Kim at ops, the dark-skinned man with pointed ears at tactical, and Captain Janeway in the captain's chair.

"Set course, Mr. Paris," the Janeway hologram ordered. "Three eight mark one seven six. Warp four."

Tom's hands were already moving across the panel, which beeped softly. His finger hovered above the control that would engage the warp engines, and he realized he was waiting for the captain's order. He stared at the board. It didn't look familiar, but he still knew what to do.

"How did I know this?" he said, confused.

"Mr. Paris?" Janeway said.

"Computer, freeze program," B'Elanna inter-

rupted. Janeway and the other figures on the bridge
froze in place like children playing freeze tag while
B'Elanna consulted the padd. "Let's try another one.
Computer, load program Paris Two. Better stand up,
Tom."

The crew vanished. Tom scrambled to his feet just
as the bridge—and the chair beneath him—followed
suit. He caught a glimpse of a series of grids lining
the floor and ceiling before another scene appeared:
concrete floor dabbled with oil stains, high ceiling,
shelves lined with bits of machinery on the walls,
work counter with tools spread across it. In the center of the floor stood a boxy vehicle, cherry red
trimmed with gleaming chrome. The wheels were fat
and accented with a wide white stripe.

"Do you know what that is?" B'Elanna asked.

"Sure—1952 Ford Sunliner convertible. Flathead
engine, standard transmission." He reached out to ca-
ress one smooth side. "It's a beauty. Do I own one?"

"You don't recognize it?"

Tom firmed his mouth, shook his head. It was
weird. He knew exactly what the car was, when it
was built, and he had a good idea what he would see
if he popped the hood. He felt as if he *should* know
this car, but he didn't.

B'Elanna tapped the padd again. "Computer!"

An hour later they had determined that Tom,
among other things, knew how to operate a replicator, had a basic familiarity with the history of the
Federation, could perform advanced first aid, and
knew the answer to the Chaotica Conundrum, a puzzle from the *Captain Proton* holodeck game. He
could not identify his father, recognize a holographic

re-creation of his and B'Elanna's wedding, or point out the place in their quarters where he usually left his shoes. Tom's frustration grew with every scenario. He was sweaty and tired, and it felt as if B'Elanna was barraging him with images in an attempt to blast his memory back into his head.

"Computer!" he finally shouted. "End program!" The mock-up of the mess hall vanished, and Tom stomped toward the exit.

"Where are you going?" B'Elanna demanded.

"Somewhere else," he snarled, and the doors shut behind him. The memory of Boleer's voice—

You are being stupid

—rang in his head, but he ignored it. Out in the corridor, he took a deep breath, picked a random direction, and started walking. He needed to be alone for a while. It was too much, too overwhelming, too frustrating. He ignored the people who greeted him or said hello. He just walked. It was all he knew how to do.

A hand landed on his shoulder. "Hey, Tom."

Tom didn't have much choice but to turn and look. The hand belonged to Harry Kim. "Hi," he said shortly as Kim fell into step next to him.

"How's it going?" Harry asked.

Now, there was a bright question. What was he supposed to say? *Fine, except for the amnesia.* Or maybe *Fine, except for the nanites chewing on my brain.* Or perhaps just *Fine, except for the fact that I seem to be married to a woman I don't remember.*

"Fine," he said.

Harry looked concerned. "Still no memory, huh?"

"Nope." Tom didn't break his stride.

"Tom, listen, if there's anything I can do—"

Tom rounded on him. "You can leave me alone, all right? Just leave me the hell alone." Harry backed up a step and looked stricken. Tom softened. "Look, I appreciate the offer, okay? I just need to be alone for a while."

"Yeah, sure. If that's what you want." And Kim left.

Tom stared after him, then sighed and continued on his way. If he didn't even know Harry Kim, why did he feel like he had just kicked a puppy?

His stomach growled. Maybe he should go to his quarters or the mess hall and get something to eat. Except he didn't know how to get to either place. Tom Paris stood alone in the middle of the corridor, not sure if he wanted to scream or cry.

At that moment Boleer turned a corner and approached. Tom groaned silently. "What are you doing, following me?" he demanded.

"I heard what you told Harry Kim," she said, ignoring his question. "And no matter what you say, Tom Paris, I do not believe for a moment that you want to be alone."

"How would you know?" he growled.

She took his hand in an iron grip. "Because in a way I have known you longer than anyone else on this ship, and when we were at Mas—at Zedrel's house together, you did not like being alone. That was why we became friends. Now. If you do not wish to continue memory tests with your spouse, then you may come with me."

"Where?"

"Sickbay," she said. "I have made a choice."

* * *

At long last morning lightened the window. Seven stopped staring through the dirty glass and turned to look at Rekki, who awoke first and was stretching all six limbs.

"Hearty sleep?" Rekki asked.

"I did not sleep," Seven replied.

Rekki ducked her head. "Of course. This is a ritual morning question for us and saying it is habit."

"I see. Humans usually say *Good morning,*" Seven said.

"Ah! Hoping it will become true by saying so," Rekki observed. "Then I say to you, good morning, Seven."

"Good morning. Hearty sleep?"

"Yes."

The other adult Chiar began to stir and rouse themselves. Rekki, meanwhile, picked up a large basket. "I need to see if there is anything to eat at the market," she said. "Would you like to come, Seven?"

"Would my presence cause an uproar or distraction?" Seven asked.

"Probably," Rekki replied cheerfully. "It might be fun. Would you come, then?"

Seven turned to Pek, who was rubbing his neck against a doorsill to scratch it. "You said I could contact *Voyager* at any time. How can I do this when the communicator was aboard the boat you stole and no longer have?"

Pek paused in his scratching. "I had not thought of that. I do have equipment in my laboratory that we could use to create a communicator of sorts and get a signal through to your ship." He ducked his head. "Seven, I honestly did not think of this. Believe when I say it was not a trick to force you to stay. You are not a prisoner here."

"Ha!" snorted Kessra, who had awoken in time to hear the last remark. "No more a prisoner than we are, is that right?"

"Kessra, if it came to it, we could get the attention of the Goracar authorities, and they would almost certainly let Seven—"

A thudding noise came at the front door. Pek halted in midsentence and crept up to it. "Who knocks?" he demanded, standing to one side of the portal.

"Five little bed slugs sliding down the roof," chanted a voice from the other side. The words made no sense to Seven, but Pek turned a crank that opened the iris enough for him to peer through the center hole. What he saw must have satisfied him, for he cranked the door the rest of the way open. Four Chiar quickly entered with bulging saddlebags. Their smell added to the room's already rank interior, and Seven found herself backing away.

"There is no need to have fear of these people," Pek said, noticing her consternation and misreading its source. "They work for the Freedom Movement."

"These are people who tried to kidnap Lieutenant Torres," Seven said.

"Not this group," Pek replied. "I would not allow them into my home. Besides, they all committed suicide rather than risk capture. Beyond foolish."

The four Chiar gazed at Seven in awe. "This one is an alien from the great ship," one of them said. "Has it come to join the Movement? Pek, that would be—"

"I have not," Seven interrupted. "Pek and Maski

rescued me from . . . from . . ." Seven paused a moment, realizing she still didn't know exactly who had kidnapped her and Tom Paris. "From my captors," she finished lamely. "Pek brought me here. And since I am female, it is more proper to refer to me as *she*, not *it*."

The speaker ducked. "Apologies."

"What did you bring from the raid, Milpik?" Pek asked.

The four Chiar rummaged in their bags for a moment and produced various containers. "A feast, Pek," Milpik said. "Here we have a gigaquad's worth of clean nanites"—he gestured at a series of octagonal containers one of the others was unpacking—"and a stack of program disks and a dozen clean universal tools."

Pek ducked his head in disappointment. "You did not get it, then."

"Get it?" Milpik said innocently. "What *it?*"

Pek's eyes glowed. "You *did* get it. Let me see! Let me see it!"

Milpik made a chuffing sort of laugh, and from one of his saddlebags brought a fist-sized object with eight sides. It was set with a series of red blinking lights. Pek snatched it from Milpik with obvious avarice.

"What is it?" Seven asked.

"A resonance disruptor," Pek said. "It disrupts focused energy patterns within a small area and scatters them harmlessly."

"Energy patterns from an object such as a phaser," Seven observed.

"Or a microwave curtain," Pek said.

"Then you can use that to escape?" Seven asked.

"Not for more than a handful of people," Pek replied. "It uses a great deal of power, and its radius is small. Still, it will be easier to organize raids on the Goracar with this. We will no longer need to dig tunnels."

"Market," Rekki said, brandishing her basket. "Seven, are you coming?"

"Is that wise?" Milpik said. "Letting her appear in public?"

"She is no prisoner," Pek said. "If the Goracar learn of her presence—"

"—they may punish us," Kessra finished.

"Not if she tells them what happened," Rekki said. "They might even reward us for rescuing her."

Kessra laughed derisively. "You speak as if the Goracar see us as true Chiar. They do not. To them we are as animals to be kept in a cage."

More voices joined in the argument, and the Chiar smells in the room grew so strong that Seven's eyes began to water. She finally ended the discussion by snatching Rekki's basket from her and stalking through the open door. A moment later she was outside, breathing clean, fresh morning air with great relief. Rekki trotted up behind her.

"They have not yet noticed you left," she said mischievously. "Come. The market is this way."

She led Seven along the city streets. Other Chiar were up and about, and they stared unabashedly at Seven. Heads poked through doorways and windows, whispers arose on the air. Seven noticed that most of the Chiar shelters were slanted, created by leaning boards or large sheets of material against other, larger structures. Since many of the Chiar buildings were pyramidal, this was a problematic system. Seven's Borg implants allowed her to examine the shaky structures minutely even from a distance, and she noticed the Chiar had not used nails, screws, or even pegs to hold everything together. A few seemed to use some sort of adhesive, but most were simply leaning together. Seven imagined that many of them had to be rebuilt after a hard storm blew through. The smell was very strong, and it wasn't just the smell of Chiar. It was the smell of squalor, filth, and disease. Seven tried not to wrinkle her nose, but didn't entirely succeed. Rekki noticed.

"We must seem disgusting to you," she said. "But most of us do not have enough nanites to perform many everyday functions. Just ridding the body of dirt and bodily secretions takes so much time that many people do it only once or twice in ten days."

"Can you not bathe with water?" Seven blurted before realizing it might sound rude.

Rekki shook her head. "We have not had running water for a long time, without nanites to oversee the pumps. Water must be hauled instead, and it must be used more for drinking and cooking than for bathing. As I said, my family is more fortunate than most because Father has seen to it we have more nanites than most, though we take care not to flaunt this fact. Still, we can at least keep clean."

"Your people seem overly dependent on nanotechnology," Seven observed.

"There is no other way to accomplish anything," Rekki said. "Ah—the market."

The market area was a large open area of scattered trees and grass, the first greenery Seven had seen since she had arrived in the city. A dry fountain sat between pathways. With a start Seven realized the place used to be a park. Beneath the scraggly trees were tables and booths where merchant Chiar had set their wares. Markets, Seven mused, seemed to be the same on any planet. Sounds of Chiar chatter filled the place, as did the ever-present sharp smell. Conversation, however, stopped wherever Seven went, and heads turned on long, segmented necks to stare.

"The food sector is over here," Rekki said, apparently unaffected by the attention. They passed Chiar selling cloth and blankets and small devices Seven didn't recognize. Chiar continued to stare, and Seven noticed a small crowd was following her and Rekki. Seven kept a nervous eye on them, uncertain if they were hostile or merely curious.

When they arrived at the food sector, a two-story vehicle with six wheels had pulled up to the edge of the market, and a large group of Chiar were clustering around it.

"Praise to the moon!" Rekki exclaimed. "The farmer has arrived a day early."

"The farmer?" Seven repeated. "You have only one?"

Rekki cocked her head negatively. "We have two. The other comes to town on a different day."

"You have two farmers to feed an entire city?" Seven said incredulously.

"We are a large city and require that many," Rekki said a bit defensively. "Both our farmers have complete sets of nanites, thanks to Father, and they use them to grow food for us. It is never quite enough.

With any luck, Father can cleanse more nanites for someone else so we can have a third farmer and half again the food supply, but I imagine another sector will lay claim first."

"I see," Seven said faintly.

Rekki, meanwhile, rummaged around in her saddlebags and came up with a set of plastic chits. "These are ration markers, and they will let us have a certain amount of food today. We also use them as money, sometimes. Father could see to it that we got more rations than anyone else, but he does not. I suppose I can see the fairness in it, but when the rations run out and Trilkav and the other children go hungry, I wish he would try to be less fair."

Behind them, the little crowd grew larger.

"You should grow food without nanites," Seven said.

"No one knows how," Rekki said, then paused. "Actually, this is not quite true. We know if you put seeds into soil, crops may grow. Some have tried it. Farming is much more intricate than we first believed. At what time do you plant? How much fertilizer do you use? How do you make fertilizer? How do you know when something is ripe enough to harvest? How do you preserve enough food to last until the next growing cycle? And then there are insects, storms, droughts, disease—it is amazing our ancestors were able to grow food at all."

A pungent smell Seven recognized as the Chiar anger scent wafted by. Seven turned and saw over her shoulder that the crowd of Chiar following them was now even larger, with perhaps thirty or forty members.

"The people behind us are hostile," Seven told Rekki quietly.

Rekki glanced at them. "They look peaceful to me," she said. "Perhaps a bit restless. What makes you think they are angry? They may be only curious."

"Several of them have a hostile scent," Seven said. "You can tell how they feel by their—"

"Filthy alien!" one of the crowd shouted. "Goracar collaborator!"

"It is a spy!"

"Collaborator!"

A stone flew through the air. Seven ducked and it whizzed overhead.

"Stop it!" Rekki shouted. "My father Pek rescued her from the people who captured her. She isn't here to hurt us. Father thinks she can help us."

Another stone flashed through the air, though it went wide of its mark. The Chiar who were shopping or merchanting at the market stared, heads raised high on their segmented necks, but none of them spoke in Seven's or Rekki's defense. Sticks and more stones appeared in the crowd's hands, and the anger smell intensified. Abruptly Seven felt as if she was back on the holographic playground with Mel trying to knock her flat. Her own anger flared, and she wanted to fight. But though the Chiar were short, they were stronger than they looked, and they far outnumbered Seven and Rekki. The crowd shifted and shuffled in place, none of them quite ready to charge yet, though Seven was sure it was only a matter of time.

"We should leave," Seven urged. "Now."

"Filthy alien!"

Rekki ducked her head. "It was foolish to bring you. This way—through the market. Do not move too quickly. They may take it as cowardice and begin an attack."

As one they turned to head deeper into the market and almost immediately ran into another group of a dozen Chiar. These carried sticks, and also clubs. A small part of Seven's mind wondered why she hadn't smelled them coming. Perhaps it was because there was already so much of the anger smell around. Seven's heart pounded and her mouth went dry. Tension rode the air.

"Where are you going with this collaborator, Rekki?" one of the Chiar asked.

"Let us pass, Nikku," Rekki ordered, though her voice was shaky. "Father would be unhappy if she were harmed."

The Chiar raised his club. "I care nothing about Pek."

"If the people on board my ship learn that you have damaged me," Seven spoke up, "they will descend with weapons that make the Goracar look like primitive creatures from the Stone Age. You will learn true misery then."

The leader of the second crowd glared at Seven for a moment, then lowered his club. "Why are you here? You have already helped the Goracar finish the warp drive they stole from us. I suppose you wish to see how we live in filth and poverty so you can sneer and laugh."

The crowd stirred with an ugly noise. Rekki shuddered once and clutched her basket.

"I know nothing of a theft," Seven replied evenly.

"But I can inform my captain of your plight and let her decide what to do—unless you do me harm."

Silence fell across the market. Seven was acutely aware of hundreds of Chiar eyes on her and on Rekki. Chiar scents assailed her, and most powerful of them all was still the pungent smell of anger.

"Come, Seven," Rekki said in her soft voice. "This way."

The other Chiar didn't move as Rekki led Seven away from the market, though not one of them stopped staring until Seven turned a corner and left their sight. The moment they were alone, Rekki dropped the basket with a low warbling sound Seven had never heard a Chiar make before.

"They would have killed us," she said hoarsely. "I was such a fool. I thought the attention might be pleasant, a diversion. Instead, we almost died."

Seven didn't know what to say to this, so she picked up Rekki's basket and put a hand on her flank. Rekki was shivering.

"I have never been so frightened," Rekki whispered. "Never in my life, not even when I lost my nanites to the Goracar virus."

"We should return to your home," Seven said.

"There is no food," Rekki pointed out, gesturing at the empty basket.

"Then someone else will have to go to the market later," Seven said firmly. "We, however, should not remain near this place."

Rekki ducked her head in acknowledgment, took back the basket, and trotted swiftly away. Seven had to hurry to keep up with her. Rekki kept to the side streets and alleys, speaking little. As they walked,

Seven's anger, far from dissipating, began to grow. Who were these creatures? They stole, they lied, they kidnapped, they terrorized, and they threatened. They treated their own kind with casual indifference, even cruelty, and outsiders worse. Every time Seven thought there might be something favorable about the Chiar, something else happened to destroy that thought. Seven had been kidnapped and tortured. Then she had been rescued, but her rescuers had turned out to be self-serving—though Pek had still not told her exactly how he thought she could help— and now the people Pek thought she could help had turned on her just for showing her face in a public market. And what had Seven done to the Chiar? Nothing. Not one thing. The anger grew until it was all Seven could do to keep it from showing.

They arrived back at the apartment without further incident, though Seven was acutely aware that she hadn't eaten since the boat ride yesterday afternoon. Hunger pangs twinged through her stomach, and she felt a bit unstable. Rekki explained what had happened at the market in a low, shaky voice while Seven stood near the doorway trying to calm her raging emotional state. The children had been sent to another room.

"Seven, please," Pek said when Rekki had finished speaking. "Please do not judge us on the actions of these few. We have been reduced to this state by terrible circumstances. We are a fine, compassionate people. This is not how we usually react to new situations."

"Is it not?" Seven said neutrally.

"You are too optimistic, Father," Kessra put in

with a cynical twist in her voice. "You always want to believe the good in people."

"They would not act this way if their lives were not so desperate," Pek said firmly.

Kessra chuffed in derision. Pek looked ready to carry the argument forward, but Seven interrupted.

"You said you thought I could help you, but you have yet to explain how," she said. "Please explain. I am growing weary."

Pek ducked his head. "Of course. You must be hungry, too. Apologies that we could not give proper food to a guest."

"Or our children," Kessra muttered.

"My laboratory is upstairs," Pek continued as if she hadn't spoken. "Come, and I will show you."

Seven let Pek take her up several flights of rickety-looking stairs. Maski trailed behind them. The smell of Chiar was fainter in the hallway, but still omnipresent. As they passed other floors, Seven heard other Chiar voices, some raised in argument.

"How many families occupy this building?" Seven asked.

"Four or five per floor," Maski replied. "This is one of the few sound buildings in the city, so it is crowded."

At last they reached the top floor, which sported a single door. Pek hurried forward to press his six-fingered hand to it. The door irised open with a clank. Seven strolled toward it, refusing to hurry. Pek crossed the threshold, then seemed to realize that Seven was no longer directly behind him. He pressed his palm to the threshold, holding the iris open, until she caught up to him. Maski came behind.

"Apologies," Pek said. "I have not been here in several months, and I was rude to rush ahead in this way."

Seven acknowledged Pek's apology with a nod and stepped through the door. The well-lit room inside made a stark contrast between itself and the squalor she had seen elsewhere in the city. It was a gleaming, shiny laboratory. Several workstations, sized for Chiar height, were scattered about the room, and a great deal of equipment Seven didn't immediately recognize occupied the shelf and counter spaces. At first it all appeared state-of-the-art, but Seven's keen vision quickly picked out the fact that the equipment was secondhand. Repair seams marked most of it, and several units were clearly nonfunctional. Seven was blinking at it all when her nanoprobes sensed the presence of foreign nanites on her body. She tensed, but the intruders did nothing but observe before disengaging contact.

"My laboratory," Pek said. "I have ordered the security system to accept you rather than attack or sound the alarm. This place is better equipped than anyplace else on the continent, but you can doubtless see that my equipment is not as fine as it once was."

"What did you mean when you said you wanted my help?" asked Seven, who was growing tired of asking the question. "You said you would show me, and I am growing impatient."

Maski bustled about the room, switching on some machines, checking the operation of others. The lab was amazingly spotless for a place that had not been used in several months, as Pek claimed. Seven assumed that nanites kept the place free of dust and grime.

"This lab," Pek said, "is one of the few places that has a level of nanite use approaching what we had before the war. It took for me several years to assemble it. Twice it has caught the Goracar virus and I had to start over. Removing the virus from a set of nanites is slow and painstaking. It would take decades just to cleanse the nanites from the people living in this block of buildings."

A suspicion grew. Seven said nothing, though her posture clearly showed her impatience. Her jumpsuit, still filthy after two days of capture and a trip through a dirty tunnel, clung unpleasantly to her skin.

"I was hoping," Pek continued casually, "that you and your nanoprobes could help us with this problem."

Again, Seven did not respond, this time because she was thinking of the best way to formulate a reply. She was still dependent on Pek. Seven was certain it would be difficult to contact *Voyager* from inside the microwave prison, and she needed his resources. She didn't want to upset him, but the news she had for him would not be good.

"What is it exactly you are hoping I can do?" she stalled.

Maski came over and stood quietly behind her father. Seven realized she could see a resemblance in their faces and expressions. Their wide mouths were the same shape, their bodies had the same stance, their eyes had the same look of hope.

"Your nanoprobes are more sophisticated than our nanites," Pek said. His outer coating gleamed pink with excitement, and Seven noticed a musty overlay to his strong scent. "You—we—could program them to cleanse our downed nanites—clear them of the virus and start them working again. It would be easy. We would be free of the Goracar's crushing fist and live like ourselves again."

Janeway would have bitten her lip. Torres would have rolled her eyes. Seven of Nine did neither of these things, but now she understood the human impulse to do so. Pek had not thought clearly, or he had not fully understood the nature of her nanoprobes. Seven was also tired and hungry.

"I could do all these things," Seven admitted, and Pek's outer coating gleamed brighter still. Maski joined in, though her glow was more cautious. "But it would not have the effect you are hoping for."

Pek's outer coating dimmed a little. "What do you mean?"

"Borg nanoprobes are designed to assimilate other technology," Seven explained. "Mine would do exactly what you say—cleanse your nanites of the virus and start them running again. But they would also assimilate them and make them into Borg nanoprobes. They would no longer be Chiar nanites. They would spread over your entire continent and assimilate your technology—"

"—such as it is," Maski muttered.

"—until it was all Borg," Seven finished. "The change would be permanent. Eventually the nanoprobes would assimilate not only your technology, but your people. The Chiar would become Borg drones."

She paused. For a moment she could hear the billion-fold voice of the Borg Collective. Seven was back in her tertiary adjunct. The Collective's voice hummed in her head, almost drowning out the screams of the female on the table in front of her and those of the other aliens around her. Conduits snaked everywhere and data screens covered the walls. The light had a subdued, green-brown cast. Seven of Nine, Tertiary Adjunct of Unimatrix Zero One, extended her fist, and two tubules shot out. They pierced the neck of the struggling female on the table. The female stiffened. Borg implants burst through her skin. Seven waited until the implants were more secure, then calmly pushed an optical implant into the female's eye. The growing Borg technology merged seamlessly with it as two other Borg efficiently fitted her with a cybernetic arm that would allow her to recalibrate a transwarp sensor array. A male cried and begged on the table behind Seven of Nine, but she took no notice. The female, no longer screaming, sat up, and Seven felt an almost infinitesimal shift in the voices as the female joined the Collective as Twelve of Twelve, Secondary Adjunct of Unimatrix Zero Four. The new Borg drone moved stiffly off the table, and two more drones replaced it with the struggling, kicking male.

"Borg drones?" Pek said. "What is a Borg drone?"

Seven blinked at him. A dreadful, heavy feeling she had only recently begun to know as guilt pressed down on her. It didn't matter that she had not been in control of her actions. The fact remained: she had been responsible for the destruction of thousands of people. She would not do it again.

"The Borg are a collective race," she said, and gave a brief explanation. "If I were to infect your nanites with my nanoprobes, it would destroy your people."

"My father is a world-level authority on nanites,"

Maski spoke up. "Your nanoprobes could not be too foreign for him to work with."

"Impossible," said Seven. "The Borg have encountered many races that use nanotechnology, several of them more advanced than yours. None of them was able to overcome Borg nanoprobes."

"There is a way," Pek insisted. "What if we alter the subroutine that affects the assimilation process? If we erase that routine, your probes will start up our nanites but stop short of assimilating them."

Seven shook her head. "That would fail. My nanoprobes have extensive backup protocols. Nanoprobes damaged in such a way would have new subroutines downloaded to them from the others."

"Then perhaps we could take a set from your body and reprogram all of them at once," Pek said. "That way there would be no subroutine to upload."

"They would contact the probes that remained within my implants and download the missing subroutines from them," Seven countered. "They all share a subspace link."

Pek set his features and continued with more questions and possibilities. Seven calmly refuted each one. Pek and Maski's outer coatings grew dark with dismay and frustration.

"It is not that I do not wish to help you," Seven said, "but that there is no way to do so. The fact is that any nanites that interact with my nanoprobes in the manner you desire will be assimilated into the Borg Collective. That is nothing you want to be part of."

"Seven, please," Maski said. "Our people are in a desperate situation. You have seen how we live. How much longer can we as a race survive in this prison?"

"Perhaps you should try harder," Seven said bluntly. "You do not attempt to better your situation. Rekki said you tried conventional farming but gave it up when it became difficult. You say you cannot use a tool as simple as a hammer, but how hard have you tried to make one?"

"What is the point of trying when there is no hope?" Maski said in a pained voice. "Our brothers and sisters are thralls to the Goracar. Our greatest achievements were stolen from us. There is no hope, no reason to continue, especially now that you withhold your gifts."

Seven found herself softening slightly. Maski showed true concern for her people. The Chiar were not all bullies like Mel. Maski and Pek, she reminded herself, were obviously working very hard to better the Ushekti.

"I am not a . . . a god who gives or withholds gifts on a whim, Maski," she said. "I am telling you the truth. I am truly sorry, but if you removed the security protocols from my nanoprobes and made them interact with your nanites, my probes would only assimilate them and you. There is nothing I can do. I wish I could help you." And even as she said it, she knew it to be true.

Pek chuffed twice and shifted on all four feet. "Perhaps you are right." Then his face grew thoughtful. "But perhaps you can help us after all." He produced a universal tool and tapped it once on his chest. It shifted.

"What do you mean by—" Seven began, but got no further. Pek fired the energy weapon he had created, and Seven fell motionless to the floor.

CHAPTER

12

CORRIDORS. Kilometer after kilometer of corridors. Tom Paris was sure he'd wandered most of them by now. Problem was, there wasn't a whole lot else to do. He had no duties aboard *Voyager,* of course—officially he was on "long-term medical leave"—and with no memory of who his friends were or what he might like to do with them, he found himself at loose ends. So he walked. Endless blue and gray corridors flowed steadily past him. Every so often he met one of the crew, but he avoided eye contact, and they learned quickly enough that Tom Paris wouldn't answer even the simplest of greetings. Today they all treated him as if he were invisible. Tom pretended that this suited him just fine, but he knew very well that it didn't. He was lonely, but didn't know how to talk to anyone.

After escorting Boleer to sickbay to confer with the Doctor, Tom had gone back to wandering aimlessly around *Voyager.* Eventually exhaustion had driven him back to B'Elanna's quarters. That was how he thought of them—as B'Elanna's, not his. B'Elanna was already in bed, and he had spent the night on the couch. When he woke up in the morning, she had been gone. Tom had passed a fair amount of time watching cartoons on the television—they hadn't brought back any memories—and now he was back to pacing the hallways again.

Eventually Tom's feet took him past the doors to one of the holodecks. Part of the display caught his eye, and he looked closer. The doors hadn't been secured. Odd—most people locked the doors during holodeck use so that they wouldn't be disturbed. Curious, Tom tapped the console.

"Computer," he said, "who's using this holodeck?"

"Lieutenant B'Elanna Torres is using holodeck one," replied the computer.

Tom didn't know why he did it—he just did. He stepped toward the double doors, and they parted with a faint metallic sound. The moment he entered, they closed behind him and vanished. Tom found himself in a rough stone tunnel with a sandy floor. The ceiling was low, forcing him to duck slightly. Torches provided the only illumination. Ahead of him up the tunnel, he heard the heavy thud of fist meeting flesh and a grunt of pain.

"Warning," the computer said. "Safety interlocks for this program have been disengaged."

Uh-oh, Tom thought. He didn't know exactly what that meant, but he knew it was dangerous. Slowly he crept up the tunnel, dodging the occasional stalactite, until it opened into a vast cavern. The floor and ceiling were several meters above and below the floor and ceiling of the tunnel, so Tom found himself looking down at the bottom of the cavern. More thuds and thumps, accompanied by little shouts and grunts. In the sandy pit below, Tom saw B'Elanna Torres. She was fighting a Cardassian, and Tom was surprised that he recognized the race. Both B'Elanna and her opponent were dressed in black. The Cardassian's yellow face and spoonlike forehead ridges were twisted into an angry rictus as it swung a roundhouse punch straight for B'Elanna's face. With a smooth agility Tom couldn't help but admire, she ducked beneath the punch and swept the Cardassian's legs out from under him. He fell flat on his back and lay still.

B'Elanna paused only to wipe the sweat from her face. "Computer," she barked, "increase difficulty to level five!"

The Cardassian sprang to his feet with impossible agility. The heel of his hand rammed B'Elanna in the forehead, driving her backward and eliciting a surprised cry of pain. Before she could recover, the Cardassian rushed forward and wrapped her in a bear hug. B'Elanna screamed in either rage or in pain, Tom couldn't tell. She struggled to free herself, but remained trapped. Tom was already moving. He dropped to the floor of the pit, stumbled, recovered. In four strides he covered the distance between them. With his fists laced together, he smashed the back of the Cardassian's head. The Cardassian stiffened, then dropped B'Elanna—she fell to the ground—and spun to face Tom. With impossible speed the Cardassian's foot whipped out and caught

Tom in the stomach. Every scrap of air burst from his lungs. He flew backward and landed hard on his butt in the sand. The Cardassian flung himself toward Tom, who managed to roll aside, and the Cardassian landed in a cloud of sand. In an impossible maneuver, the alien turned the crash landing into a somersault and was on his feet in an instant. Still gasping, Tom tried to get to his feet, but the Cardassian was faster. He swung his leg, intending to catch the side of Tom's head in a vicious kick. Tom braced himself for the impact—

—that never came. B'Elanna was there. She caught the Cardassian's shin, twisted his leg, and brought her elbow down hard on the side of his knee. There was a wet popping sound. The Cardassian screamed and collapsed, writhing, to the cave floor.

"Computer," B'Elanna panted, "freeze program."

The Cardassian froze in mid-yell.

"Nice save," Tom said.

B'Elanna put the back of one hand to her mouth. It came away dark and sticky. "What the hell are you doing here? This was my private program."

"If it was so private, why didn't you lock the door?" Tom countered. "And speaking of 'what the hell,' what were *you* trying to do? Kill yourself?"

"That's none of your concern," B'Elanna snapped. "You had no right to come barging in here like Kahless himself. I didn't need your help."

"If you say so," Tom grunted. He got to his feet. Landing on even the soft sand had jarred him from tailbone to neck. He rolled his head around, trying to loosen the already-stiffening muscles. "Geez, level five? What is that? Kill you five times instead of just four?"

"What do you care?" B'Elanna wiped the blood on her jumpsuit. "I thought you didn't care about anyone on this ship."

"I don't remember anyone!" Tom shouted. "Is that so hard to figure out?"

"How can I forget?" she yelled back. "You remind me three or four times an hour."

"Hey, it's not *my* fault," he snarled. "You think it's fun knowing there are these little things inside my head that won't let me remember anything about my past or my friends? I'm supposed to be married to you, but I have to think to remember your name."

"You think it's any easier for me?" B'Elanna's voice echoed off the stony cavern walls. "I look at you and think of what you mean to me, but you won't let me touch you. The only time I see you is when you do something stupid like swoop into the middle of my holodeck time."

"What was I supposed to do? Let that Cardassian crush you to death?"

"Would it matter to you if he did?"

"Ye—no—I don't know!"

"Fine." B'Elanna's voice dropped into a low, steady tone. "When you figure it out, give me a call. Computer, end program."

The cavern vanished, leaving gridded walls behind. B'Elanna stomped toward the doors. They hummed open to let her exit. Tom Paris stared after her, a lump in his throat, wondering why the room felt so horribly empty now that she was gone.

"You are still being stupid, Tom," Boleer said. Her

head came around the open doorway and poked itself into the holodeck.

"When I want your help, I'll yank your tail," Tom snapped.

"The Chiar have no tails. And you are acting just like Nylo."

"What are you, insane? I'm nothing like that bastard."

"Nylo can actually be rather nice," Boleer said, "when he is not feeling angry or threatened. And it is obvious you are angry, just as Nylo was. I told you Nylo was not angry at you, just as you are not angry at me, or even at your spouse B'Elanna. You are angry at Zedrel, just as Nylo was, and you are angry at the people who kidnapped you, just as B'Elanna is. Unfortunately none of those people are here, so you both show your anger to those who *are* here, however undeserving those people might be."

"You know who's deserving?" Tom snarled. "Someone who literally pokes her head in where it doesn't—" He broke off and stared.

"Yes?" Boleer cocked her head. "Please continue, Tom Paris."

"Your eye," he said. "You have it back. I don't even have my teeth back yet."

Boleer blinked both eyes rapidly at him, then came fully around the corner of the doorsill. Her scarlet cloak rippled as she did so, and Tom noticed an elaborate wire clasp now held it in place around the base of her long neck.

"The Doctor was most gracious and polite. Unlike some," Boleer said, wandering in to peer about the gridded holodeck with two good eyes. The door whined shut behind her. "He anticipated that you would complain about this very thing and explained to me that soft eye tissue grows faster than hard dental material. Your teeth will be ready tomorrow morning."

Caught off-guard, Tom wasn't sure what to say next. "You . . . that is . . . the new eye looks good. Uh, what about your head? Is he going to fix that, too?"

"I haven't decided yet," Boleer replied. "Do you like my new clasp?"

"It's nice. Where did you get it?"

She tilted the object with one hand so it gleamed in the light. "I made it. It is nothing but a bit of extra wire that I was playing with while the Doctor grew my eye. I have found I enjoy making things with my own hands. It is . . . liberating. Neelix has already gotten permission from the captain to let me read about hand tools and basic craft techniques. It is even more interesting and satisfying than the weaving I did in Zedrel's household, especially now that I make everything for myself. You are lucky to live in such a place as this, Tom Paris."

"What place?" Tom said, not sure how much of this strange conversation he was able to follow.

"A place where you can work with your own hands or with tools or even with *replicators*"—she gave the foreign word a strange accent—"that create what you wish out of thin air. So many options where my people have only had one for so long."

"Right now I don't feel very fortunate," Tom said miserably. He sank to the holodeck floor. "I want my memories back, Boleer. I want my *life* back. I want . . ." He trailed off, and Boleer laid a gentle hand on his shoulder.

"You want B'Elanna back," she said. "Even though you don't remember her."

"Yeah." Tom felt his throat thickening up, and he swallowed hard. "I don't even know *why.* How did I—my old self, I mean—fall in love with her? She's bossy and loud and stubborn."

Boleer laughed and bent her neck to rub her cheek against his. Her face, like her hands, felt like suede leather. The gesture felt oddly comforting. "She would need to be so, Tom Paris. I have only known you for a few days, but I can see that loving someone like you would take a great deal of strength."

"What's that supposed to mean?" he demanded.

"She is bossy, but you are impulsive. She is loud, but you do not listen. She is stubborn, but you move quickly from one thing to the next. Do not be so hard on her, Tom. She is hard on you because you need her to be."

A stab went through Tom's stomach, and in that instant he knew that Boleer was right. Still, he couldn't keep himself from saying, "What's with you, anyway? Trying to become a prophet or something?"

Boleer winked at him with her new eye. "Perhaps I am. We can only wait and see."

Seven of Nine slowly came awake. The first thing she noticed was the cloying, overpowering smell of Chiar. She opened her eyes. It was the cell again, the same one she had occupied before, or one with a similar design. She wondered muzzily if the hole in the rear wall had been repaired but couldn't turn her head to look. Her head hurt. How had she come here? The last thing she remembered was—

Memory returned in a rush. Pek's lab. Her nanoprobes. The flash of an energy weapon. Anger surged through Seven. Again and again the Chiar abused her, flung her around like a toy, tortured her, made her go hungry, shot her. Was there nothing but treachery in them?

A Chiar was standing over her. It said something to her—a question? Seven couldn't tell. It leaned down and put a hand on her shoulder. The moment it touched her, it began to scream. It was a high-pitched sound that drove straight through Seven's aching head. She bolted upright and clapped both hands over her ears. The Chiar's scream continued, and a moment later half a dozen more Chiar galloped into the cell. When they crossed the threshold, they too began to scream. Their outer coatings swirled into black, and odd protuberances grew out of them. A horrible smell flooded the chamber, and Seven could only assume it was the Chiar smell of fear or pain. Seven scrambled to her feet, catching a fleeting glimpse of a still-open tunnel opposite the cell door.

More Chiar arrived, and their screams were added to the din. Their coatings also turned black, but Seven didn't stop long enough to look closely at any of them. With her hands still over her ears, Seven ran for the door. The howling Chiar made no attempt to stop her, and Seven made no attempt to understand what was going on. She simply fled.

The twisting, turning corridors with their riots of color and design confused her. Seven chose turns at random. Twice she ran into Chiar, and both times they collapsed to the floor, howling in some kind of pain. Seven didn't stop—her first priority was escape. But as she hurried breathlessly down yet another hallway filled with clashing colors, she couldn't help but try to analyze what was going on. The last thing she remembered before waking up in the Chiar cell was Pek aiming an energy pistol at her. He must have stunned her, then perhaps sedated her? In any case, he had arranged for her to be put back in the cell where he had found her, probably even used the stolen resonance disruptor to get her through the microwave curtain. But why? Was he angry at her for saying she couldn't help him? Had he realized that she was telling the truth and therefore decided to return her to her original captors? But what would be the point? Pek had seemed a compassionate person to Seven, someone who truly cared about his people and about the injustice done to them. Why would he visit injustice on Seven by attacking her and returning her to the people who had kidnapped her in the first place? It made no sense.

No, she thought as she ran, *that is not true. The Chiar are treacherous and deceptive. It makes perfect sense.*

But why did the Chiar now scream when they saw her? The only thing Seven could think of was that something was wrong with her nanoprobes. At the moment, however, she didn't want to take the time to examine them.

Seven chose another corridor and found that it ended in a large irised doorway. It remained stubbornly shut when she approached. Seven pried at the center opening and managed to widen it with aching slowness. Beyond was a sandy area beneath a balcony overhang. Footprints and scuffle marks were everywhere, and Seven saw several prints that could only have been made by Starfleet-issue boots. Pek had been right about that, then. A team from *Voyager* had indeed come to get her out. Except if an away team had tracked her to this place, why was anyone still here? Shouldn't all the Chiar have been arrested for kidnapping her?

Beyond the overhang was a tall cavern wall that shimmered slightly in the dim light. The shimmer was clearly a force field—the generators were in plain sight—but why would anyone put a force field in front of a cave wall?

Because the wall is not real, she thought. A quick glance showed she was right. One of the force-field generators was equipped with a holographic emitter. Lights flickered across the surface. Seven trotted over. The generator was clearly a replacement—a pile of slag stood nearby, indicated the previous one had failed rather spectacularly or been destroyed. She placed a hand on the generator to see if she could figure out how it worked. The moment she touched it, however, a shower of sparks erupted. Seven leaped backward and the unit sparked again. It shuddered once, and the lights went out. With a short, electric sound, the force field came down and the cave wall vanished. A rocky desert landscape greeted her with a long, sighing wind.

A flicker of movement caught Seven's eye. The generator had turned black just as the Chiar had, and now that she wasn't running, she saw tubules grow out of it like snakes. Before her startled gaze, the little machine became a piece of Borg technology. Seven stared. Her touch was doing this, and that meant the problem had to lie within her nanoprobes. A pang stabbed her stomach. Her nanoprobes were also responsible for the screaming Chiar.

Seven closed her eyes and ran an internal diagnostic. Without a tricorder or other sensing equipment, her ability to judge her own nanoprobes was limited, but she could still get a certain amount of information. What she saw sent an icicle of fear down her spine. It was easily apparent that the security protocols that prevented her nanoprobes from interacting with anything but her own cybernetic implants had been severely damaged, as were the safety interlocks that stopped them from assimilating everything they found into the Borg Collective. Seven pursed her lips as she realized what had happened. Pek, a world-class expert in nanotechnology, had done the damage while she was unconscious.

Her nanoprobes were reasserting their Borg programming.

"No!" she shouted aloud. "No! I will not do this again!"

A Chiar rushed out of the fortress behind her. Seven heard its claws beating the sandy ground, smelled its musky scent long before she turned to see it. Fear combined with determination on its face as it rushed toward her.

"You will die for this!" it screamed at her. "You will suffer hurt!"

"Stay back!" Seven said. "Don't—"

The Chiar gathered its legs and leaped. Seven

backpedaled, but the Chiar landed squarely on her. The moment it touched her, its outer coating went black and rigid. Borg tubules sprouted, implants sprouted like growing spiders. Seven was bowled over backward, and she landed hard with the unmoving Chiar lying atop her. Desperately she scrambled out from under it, leaving the alien lying on its side like a quivering statue. She pushed herself away in horror. Memories of the thousands of people she had assimilated as a Borg drone rushed at her. It was too much. The only sound was the cries of the Chiar, now looking small and sad in its Borg armor. Seven got to her feet, her face an expressionless mask, and looked down at the trembling, mewling Chiar. Without a hint of emotion she nudged it with her foot as if it were a piece of garbage.

"Good," she said. "You deserve it."

"Captain, we are receiving a communication from Secretary Nashi," Tuvok said. "She claims it is an emergency."

Janeway looked up from her captain's chair. "On screen, then."

Nashi blinked onto the viewscreen. Her outer coating was swirling with agitation. Other Chiar rushed back and forth behind her, some of them pausing to converse in hurried whispers or gesticulate frantically. Their heads bobbed like frightened birds.

"*Captain,*" Nashi said. "*We are in the midst of a dreadful emergency and desperately need your help.*"

"I'll do what I can," Janeway said cautiously. "What's the nature of the emergency?"

"A virus," Nashi replied. *"It rips through our systems, taking over nanites everywhere. The entire world is being affected, Captain, and we can't seem to stop it."*

"Confirmed, Captain," Tuvok said from his station. "A virus is spreading through the Chiar communication systems and affecting nanites on the entire planet. Correction—*almost* the entire planet."

"Almost?" Janeway echoed.

"The Ushekti continent remains unaffected, presumably due to the microwave pulse."

"Can it affect *Voyager?"* Chakotay asked.

"I sincerely doubt it, Commander," Tuvok told him. "The virus seems limited to nanites, and *Voyager* does not use them. However, I will take precautions."

"Can you help us?" Nashi said.

"Captain," said Harry Kim, "I'm getting some strange readings, here."

"Report, Mr. Kim."

"The way the virus is spreading and the way it seems to be working reminds me of . . . of Borg assimilation."

"Really?" Janeway turned to Secretary Nashi. "Are your people being affected, Secretary, or just your nanites?"

"Just the nanites," Nashi replied in a bewildered voice. *"People and other technology are left alone, but so much of our equipment depends on nanites that it is as if we ourselves are also being attacked. Computer systems all over the world are going down. Vehicular travel is paralyzed. Hospitals have lost the ability to treat patients. And we can't stop any of it."*

Janeway's mind raced. That the nanite virus must have come from Seven of Nine was obvious, but what had persuaded Seven to unleash it? Had she actually done so? Or had the Chiar killed her and stolen her nanoprobes? A knot tightened in Janeway's stomach. On impulse, she spoke aloud.

"We can help you, Secretary," she said, "but only if you return Seven of Nine to us immediately."

Chakotay raised an eyebrow, making the tattoos on the side of his forehead bunch up, but he said nothing.

"Captain?" Nashi said, head rising high.

"Come now, Secretary. We know you have her," Janeway said, and as she spoke, several ideas crystallized in her mind. The puzzle came together with a click, and Janeway experienced the rush of exhilaration she always got whenever she found the solution to a complex problem. She leaned forward. "You arranged all this from the start, Secretary."

"Captain, I—"

"You—the Goracar Alliance—wanted Seven of Nine for her nanoprobes. Perhaps you thought they would help you perfect Zedrel's warp drive, or perhaps you wanted them because they were more advanced than your nanites and you wanted the technology. In any case, you decided to kidnap Seven. You arranged for that cloud of nanites—released from your own station, no doubt—to drift over my ship so some of them could slip aboard during the test of Zedrel's warp drive. Your nanites took a long look at our transporters and built a transmitter to send you information on how to build one so you could beam aboard and grab Seven. Tom happened to be in the wrong place at the wrong time. Any competent transporter technician would have been able to beam out only Seven and her kidnappers, but the technology is new to your people, so he was taken by mistake."

"Captain, I don't—"

"You took advantage of the Freedom Movement's attempt to capture Lieutenant Torres and blamed Seven's kidnapping on them. Then you decided to collect a little extra money by disrupting Tom's memory and putting him up for sale, especially because you knew Zedrel would be fascinated enough to buy him. If someone made a mistake and got caught, Zedrel would make the perfect scapegoat." Janeway shook her head. "I should have known you were behind it all the moment you let me interrogate Zedrel. He had been arrested barely half an hour earlier, but somehow he made it up to your space station in that time. How? Your shuttles aren't anywhere near that fast. He must have been transported there—with the transporter technology you stole, Secretary. Did you program his nanites to keep him silent about this fact?"

Nashi remained silent. Panicked Chiar continued to scurry about behind her. The Chiar station lights flickered, went out, came back on again. Chakotay gave Janeway a look of admiration.

"We almost blew your entire plan out of the water when we discovered where Seven was being held," Janeway said. "You must have been relieved that your investigators arrived before my people could figure out who owned the installation—because the place was run by you and your people. That was why you insisted on 'investigating' the place yourself. Did the Chiar you arrested actually commit suicide, Secretary? Or did someone arrange a convenient accident?"

"They did not die," Nashi said. *"I just needed—"* She stopped.

"I see. I do take it that Pek's breaking into Seven's cell and spiriting her away wasn't part of your plan. I just don't see you and Pek working in collusion. He simply outsmarted you—and me and my people. Am I right?"

Silence.

"Secretary," Janeway said softly, "if you want our help, you must return Seven of Nine. Not only is it a condition of my aid, it is a requirement of circumstances. It's clear her nanoprobes are causing the disaster, and we need to find out from her exactly what's happening." Janeway paused. "Your answer, Secretary?"

Nashi's head bobbed from side to side and her outer coating darkened with dismay. Janeway kept her gaze steady. Finally Nashi said, *"Yes, Captain. I am transmitting the coordinates of the place where she is being held. We repaired the force field but—"*

"I have the coordinates," Tuvok announced. "It is the same place we . . . explored earlier. I am reading no force field, however."

"One human lifesign," Kim said. "Now that I know where to look, it's easy to find her."

"Can you bring her aboard?" Janeway said, ignoring the restless, uncertain Secretary on the monitor.

"The residual ion radiation is still within safe levels," Kim replied. "I'm alerting transporter room one."

"Have them beam her directly to sickbay," Chakotay ordered.

"Yes, Commander," Kim said.

"Seven of Nine is on board," Tuvok said a moment later. "The Doctor is examining her now."

Relief flooded the captain. "Janeway to sickbay," she said. "Is Seven of Nine injured?"

"Not as far as I can tell," the Doctor replied over the comlink, *"but I've only been able to examine her for a few—"*

"If she isn't in any immediate medical danger, Doctor, I need her on the bridge. Now!"

"Yes, Captain."

"Captain," Nashi pleaded, *"are you going to help us?"*

Janeway faced her, arms folded. "There are a few things we need to discuss, Secretary. First I need the complete destruction of the transporter technology you stole."

"Already done, Captain," Nashi said. She looked regretful. *"The infected nanites have already wiped the portion of our computer system that held the information."*

"I'll send a team over to have a little look," Janeway said with a tight smile. "Just to be sure. After all, we also need to destroy your transporter. Second, I need to have a Chiar doctor who specializes in memory suppression examine Tom Paris—under the strict supervision of our Doctor, of course—in order to restore his memory."

"Captain, I agree to whatever conditions you may set," Nashi said desperately. *"Only stop this. I do not—"*

Nashi's outer coating changed. It went white, then black. Tubules and cybernetic implants sprouted from it. Nashi stiffened, then cried out. Janeway stared. Tubes and spiky protuberances crawled over Nashi's entire body until she was encased in a suit of Borg armor, though Nashi herself seemed unaffected. The other Chiar visible on the screen scrambled over themselves to stampede away, then froze themselves and watched in terror as tubes and implants sprouted from their own coats.

Nashi let out a long wail. *"Captain, help me!"*

"She appears to be uninjured," Tuvok said in a calm voice from his station. "But the nanites that make up her coating have been assimilated into the Borg."

The turbolift doors parted with a hiss, and Seven of Nine strode onto the bridge. Her hair was pulled back in a rough ponytail and her gray eyes were hard as stone. Her blue jumpsuit was torn and dirty, but she showed no evidence of injury.

"Seven," Chakotay said, rising.

"Welcome back, Seven," the captain said. "I trust you're all right?"

"I am uninjured," Seven replied, "though my nanoprobes have been damaged. It will take time to repair them."

"Can you stop the assimilation?" Janeway said. "I assume you know about it."

"I cannot stop it," Seven said stonily. "The process is irreversible. A pity."

Nashi let out another long wail. The Borg armor held her stiffly in place, though she struggled mightily against it. Janeway wondered how many Chiar on the planet were similarly afflicted.

"You said you can repair your own nanoprobes," Janeway said. "Why can't you help—"

"My nanoprobes started this process, yes," Seven interrupted. Her voice was even more dispassionate than usual. "But they cannot stop it. Eventually they will assimilate all the nanites on the planet, and then they will move to take any nanite-drive technology. In the Chiar's case, that is nearly everything. It is in some ways fortunate that Pek only programmed my nanoprobes to begin by taking over nanites. Otherwise the Chiar themselves would be assimilated. I am sorry, Captain."

She didn't look in the least bit sorry. Janeway was about to say something when Nashi interrupted.

"Please, Seven of Nine," she said. *"This is affecting more than only me. It affects innocent people and children. They did nothing wrong."*

"You are their chosen leader," Seven told her, "and now they must live with their choices. The Goracar also benefit from the resources you drain from the Sherekti. Have any of your people protested about that?"

"Seven," Chakotay said.

"Once enough nanites on your planet have been assimilated," Seven continued as if Chakotay hadn't spoken, "they will band together to send a subspace signal to the Borg. The Borg will send several cubes via transwarp corridor. Once they arrive, they will finish the assimilation process. I am sure they will find the planet . . . intriguing. The Chiar's knowledge of organic nanotechnology will be a formidable addition to their own."

"Captain, please!" Nashi cried. *"You have to help us. People die as we speak."*

"Who did this to you, Seven?" Janeway asked urgently.

"An Ushekti Chiar named Pek," Seven replied. "He damaged the security protocols of my nanoprobes so they would begin assimilating the next nanites they came across. Once they gained access to enough nanites, the assimilated ones began transmitting a virus through subspace. The Goracar nanites will assimilate each other while Pek's people remain safe behind the microwave pulse, at least until the arrival of the Borg. It would seem that Pek is more skilled with nanites than I gave him credit for."

Janeway put a hand on Seven's arm. "You have to stop this, Seven. Secretary Nashi is correct—no matter how you feel about the Chiar for kidnapping you, you can't—"

"They used me, Captain," Seven said in a voice that shook with—what? Anger? Pain? Both? Janeway couldn't tell. "Both sides used me like a piece of equipment to be reprogrammed at their leisure. I was left in that cell without food or water, and then when someone rescued me, it turned out he only wanted to use me as well. The Chiar are like bullies on a playground taking advantage of someone else's weakness."

Chakotay got up. "Seven," he said gently. "Anger is a perfectly normal response to what happened to you. You have every right to it. But you're punishing innocent people."

"Please, Honored Seven of Nine!" Nashi cried from the viewscreen.

"I am punishing no one," Seven said. "The Chiar have done it to themselves."

Janeway was on the verge of ordering Seven to help, then bit back the response. She only *suspected* Seven could help Chiar. Certainly Janeway could give an order, but she suspected nothing could make Seven find a solution if she honestly didn't want to.

"Lieutenant Torres and Lieutenant Paris to the bridge," she said instead.

"Acknowledged," Torres's voice responded.

"On my way," said Paris.

"Why do you need Tom?" Chakotay asked.

"He's spent more time with the Chiar than anyone but Seven," Janeway said. "He might be able to offer insight, amnesia or not."

"Captain," Kim interrupted. "The assimilation virus has reached the Chiar satellite system—including the microwave generators. Power levels are fluctuating all over the—uh-oh." He looked up from his console. "The microwave generators have gone off-line."

Janeway stiffened. "Was this whole thing an attempt to shut off the generators so the Ushekti could attack the Goracar Alliance?"

"Doubtful, Captain," Seven said. "The Ushekti are desperately poor and could not muster the resources for war. It is merely that rebels and agitants often fail to foresee all the consequences of their actions. Their plan was imperfect from the start. I suspect that what few nanites Pek has managed to bring back on-line will be assimilated, now that the microwave pulse is nonfunctional and the Ushekti nanites are no longer isolated." The corners of Seven's mouth turned up in a tiny, grim smile. "Perhaps this will be for their greater good. The Chiar will be one people now, and their conflicts will end."

Nashi trembled with the effort of trying to move within her assimilated outer coating. *"Captain, my people will go mad. And those who do not will die of thirst or exposure."*

"Riots are breaking out on the planet," Tuvok reported. "I am reading several frantic broadcasts from both private and public media. They are—" He fell silent.

Janeway turned to him. "They are what, Commander?" she demanded.

"Captain, I am reading strange fluctuations in rhometric radiation from the planet."

Janeway spun to face Nashi again. "You said those weapons were harmless."

"They—we couldn't—"

"If even one of those things go off by accident," Harry Kim said, "it'll wipe out the population of maybe a third of a continent."

"How many rhometric weapons are you detecting, Mr. Kim?" Janeway asked.

"Several dozen."

The turbolift doors parted. B'Elanna came onto the bridge followed by Tom Paris and Boleer in her long red cloak. The little Chiar had been turning up all over the ship—usually in the vicinity of Mr. Paris—and although Janeway rather liked her, she didn't think it was best to have her on the bridge at this moment. She was about to say so when Nashi made a high-pitched kind of gasp.

"Boleer," she said, clearly shocked.

"Nashi," Boleer replied with an ironic duck of her head.

"You two know each other?" Chakotay said.

"She is my sister," Boleer said.

"The *secretary?*" Tom blurted. "You said your sister was a powerful politician. You didn't say she was the secretary!"

"She is my half sister," Nashi said quickly, still struggling against her immobile Borg armor. *"My mother was Goracar, and yours was—"*

"Filthy Ushekti," Boleer finished. "Yes, you have said such before. But which of us is free now, Secretary Nashi?"

"This is a fine family reunion," B'Elanna said, "but I still don't understand what's going on."

"We need your expertise." Janeway spoke rapidly, explaining the situation.

"Please, Lieutenant Torres," Nashi said. *"We will give you all the dilithium in our stores if you can help us."*

B'Elanna shook her head. "I don't know, Captain. I mean, I'm good with nanites, but this is way out of my league. Seven should be able to—"

"I cannot," Seven repeated. "The process is irreversible."

"Why not give the nanites amnesia?" said Tom Paris.

The bridge went silent, and everyone's gaze turned to him, including Janeway's and Nashi's.

"Would you care to explain, Mr. Paris?" the captain said.

Paris looked a bit uncomfortable, but spoke steadily. "The Doc said that the nanites in my brain are programmed to disrupt memory. It's probably a basic program . . . I *was* their only human subject. Can't you take take their program and adapt it so that it disrupts the memories of other nanites? They would forget what they're supposed to be doing and stop the assimilation. And if you put the amnesia program into a virus it would combine with the Borg assimilation process and spread really fast. Even the nanites that have already been assimilated would be affected because Borg nanoprobes are in constant contact with each other, right?"

"B'Elanna loves an intelligent man," Boleer murmured loud enough for all to hear.

Tom flushed and B'Elanna shot him a quick glance.

"I do not understand," Seven said. "Lieutenant Paris is infected with nanites that are interfering with his mnemonic processes?"

"If that's your way of asking if I have amnesia," Tom said, "then yes."

"Yet another crime of the Chiar," Seven said.

"The buildup of rhometric radiation is increasing," Tuvok said. "As are the riots and casualty reports."

"Captain!" Nashi all but shouted. *"We won't be able to—"* The viewscreen went blank.

"The virus has assimilated the nanites in the Chiar communication system," Kim said. "I'm also reading power fluctuations on the Chiar space station. Life support, gravity, and anti-ionic shields are all in danger."

"B'Elanna, how fast can you develop something like Tom's suggesting?" Janeway said.

B'Elanna shook her head. "We're talking a couple weeks for that kind of delicate work. Look, I'm a crack engineer, but they don't teach you a whole lot about nanites at Starfleet Academy or in the Maquis. Seven knows ten times what I do. Why don't you ask her?"

"Seven," Chakotay said, "listen to me. These people need your help. Isn't it possible to do what Tom is saying and more quickly than B'Elanna can?"

Seven's steel-gray eyes met Chakotay's brown ones. Janeway held her breath.

"It may be," Seven finally admitted in a grudging tone. "But I would have to scan the nanites that have already been assimilated and compare them with Lieutenant Paris's. Since we cannot risk bringing nanites aboard *Voyager*, Lieutenant Paris and I would have to beam down to the planet together. I see no reason to endanger myself or the lieutenant in the process, especially since the Chiar brought assimilation upon themselves even after my repeated warnings."

"Captain!" Harry Kim started. "I'm reading a weak Borg signal from the planet."

"Enough nanites have been assimilated to begin that process," Seven said. She didn't sound particularly concerned.

Janeway bit her lower lip. This was unlike Seven. The younger woman had learned a great deal about compassion and being human in the last several years. Right now she showed little concern for anything but efficiency. Why was she acting this way?

Because Seven still feels guilty about the people she assimilated into the Borg, even though it wasn't her fault, Janeway thought in a flash of understanding, *and she feels guilty about what her nanoprobes are doing to the Chiar, even though that wasn't her fault, either. If she thinks of them as a deserving enemy, she doesn't need to feel guilty.*

So what was Janeway supposed to do about it?

"The Borg signal is growing stronger," Harry warned.

Inspiration struck. Janeway unceremoniously pushed a startled Harry Kim away from his console and started tapping furiously at the sensors. Tom and Seven were just reaching the turbolift when Janeway's call stopped them both.

"Seven, I want you to look at this," Janeway said, and she punched the boards without waiting for a reply. Seven turned. On the viewscreen appeared a scene in a Chiar city. Some of the buildings were in flames. Small groups of Chiar rioted in the streets, creating a tangle of legs, segmented necks, and flat-shaped heads. Broken glass lay shattered on the streets, and great numbers of Chiar, paralyzed by their own assimilated outer coatings, stood like statues. Many had been knocked over by their panicking fellows, whose nanites had also been quickly assimilated. Janeway's dancing fingers brought the focus in tighter, until the viewscreen was filled with a small Chiar, obviously a child, huddling against a wall. The child was mewing piteously. Next to it stood the paralyzed form of another Chiar, presumably the child's father or mother. As the crew watched, the child gave a shriek of terror. Cybernetic implants sprouted along its body and its outer coating took on the look of Borg armor. The child cried out and tried to reach for its parent, but at the last moment it was paralyzed into immobility. Seven stared at the image.

"This child is just like you were, Annika," Janeway murmured, using Seven's birth name. "She's alone and terrified and there are thousands just like her. Just like you."

The bridge fell dead quiet. Seven of Nine continued to stare at the viewscreen.

"You don't need to feel guilty, Seven," Janeway said. "The Chiar did some terrible things to you, and the results of it are spreading over the planet, but it's not your fault. *You* aren't assimilating them. You don't need to demonize them to make yourself feel right about what happened."

"You can be better than the bullies, Seven," Chakotay said. "Will you do that?"

But Seven didn't move.

"Seven of Nine," Boleer said unexpectedly. "Please listen to me. The Goracar destroyed my people and stole their advances for themselves. They threw me into slavery, crushed my head, and put out my eye. My own sister would not help me. When the captain said your nanoprobes were assimilating the nanites of the Goracar, my first thought was *Good! They deserve it!* and no one has more right to think that than I. But the more I look at these images, the less I see Goracar or Ushekti. I see a child. And a child is a child, no matter what the species. Please, Seven of Nine. You have the power to help us. Will you use it?"

Something in Seven's posture broke. She turned away, toward the turbolift, but Janeway thought she caught a brief flicker of brightness in the other woman's eyes.

"I will do my best," Seven said quietly. "Mr. Paris, you need to accompany me."

They headed for the turbolift together. Janeway returned to her chair with a tiny sigh of relief and caught B'Elanna Torres looking at Tom with an anxious expression on her face. Seven entered the lift with Tom right behind her. Boleer stayed where she was as the doors hissed shut.

"Thank you, Boleer," Chakotay said. "I think your words moved her more than any of ours."

Boleer ducked her head.

"Please be careful, Tom," B'Elanna whispered in a voice that only Janeway heard. Janeway wanted to reassure her, but other matters were more pressing.

"What's the status of the rhometric weapons arsenal, Mr. Tuvok?" Janeway asked.

"Radiation levels are still increasing," Tuvok said. "I estimate ten minutes before one of the weapons discharges. This will set off a chain reaction and ignite every other rhometric weapon on the planet."

"And the Borg signal is gaining strength," Kim put in.

"If we don't get those weapons off-line, there won't be much for the Borg to assimilate once they arrive," Janeway said, "and there's no way Seven will be able to shut down the assimilated nanites in ten minutes. I need options, people."

"I had considered the idea of somehow modifying *Voyager*'s shields to encompass the endangered area," Tuvok said, "but there are a great many residences in the immediate vicinity. Encompassing the weapon site would also encompass several houses, leaving them in the blast zone."

"Along with *Voyager*," Janeway pointed out.

"Can we destroy the weapons?" Chakotay said. "Or beam them into space?"

"Rhometric radiation interferes with transporter locks," Tuvok said. "And firing on the weapons with phasers would only set them off."

"Microwaves," B'Elanna said suddenly.

"Lieutenant?" Janeway said.

B'Elanna's hands were already moving swiftly across the bridge's engineering console. "Microwaves. The reason the weapons have been activated is because the nanites overseeing the systems have been assimilated, and they're setting off the weapons as an accidental side effect. If we flood the weapons with microwaves, the nanites will be destroyed and the weapons should shut down. Too bad we can't do the same thing to the Chiar without hurting them— I'd flood the whole planet."

"Microwave weapons were used to destroy nanites on a large scale during our war," Boleer said.

"But the weapons silos are underground," Tuvok pointed out. "And earth is an effective shield against microwaves."

"Then you'll just have to make a hole with the phasers," B'Elanna said. "You up for it?"

"It will require a high degree of accuracy," Tuvok said with a trace of doubt in his voice.

"Four minutes to detonation," Kim said.

"Do it," Janeway said, and only she noticed the way Tuvok pursed his lips as he reached for the weapons board.

CHAPTER

13

SEVEN OF NINE BLINKED as the transporter room faded away and was replaced by the stone walls of a narrow alley. The Chiar stench was strong enough to turn her stomach over. Tom Paris stood beside her, his face working hard. The shouts and screams of a thousand Chiar in utter panic assailed Seven's ears, though there were no Chiar in the alley. Seven opened a tricorder. It showed several thousand Chiar lifesigns, but none of them were moving.

Paris took a couple of deep breaths. "God," he muttered. "I thought I'd gotten used to the stink."

"I am getting a strange reading," Seven told him, deciding to also ignore the smell as irrelevant despite the strong memories—

—standing for hours and hours so tired and hungry and thirsty while nanites crawled over her skin

testing probing searching while she desperately spun defenses that were constantly under siege from—

—it invoked. The captain had been correct. It was unfair to demonize an entire race for the actions of a few. The cries and shouts of the distant Chiar continued. Seven tried to think of them as innocents who were paying for the mistakes of someone else, but some of her anger remained despite the pitiful screams, and the anger mixed with a terrible certainty that, no matter what the captain said, it was all Seven's fault.

"What's going on?" Paris peered over her shoulder. "Weird. They aren't moving. Not one of them. How come they—oh. *Oh!*"

"I believe you are correct." Seven shut the tricorder and headed for the mouth of the alley, her mouth set in a grim line. Paris followed. She emerged onto a street and stopped to stare. Paris's mouth fell open. The Chiar screaming burst into full volume around them. Horror stole over Seven, but she couldn't look away.

Scattered up and down the street were thousands of Chiar of all ages and sizes. Some stood upright, others knelt or even reared up on their hind legs. Some lay on their sides, legs poking out like stiff sticks. A few were contorted into strange positions. Every single one of them was encompassed, neck to claws, in a black suit of Borg armor, and every single one of them was screaming. They tried to move, but the armor held them frozen in place. Thousands of bulging eyes darted frantically, though others were covered over. Seven swallowed. Thousands of living statues trapped in their own horror. None of them were free.

"Holy—" Paris muttered.

Seven didn't reply. She opened her tricorder again and moved among them. The stench of Chiar fear swept over her, and she opened her mouth to breathe. Paris followed like a dazed puppy. The eyes of every Chiar fell on them, but the screaming didn't stop. Seven wanted to clap her hands over her ears. She could make out individual words and phrases in the noise. Adult Chiar were howling for help, children were crying for parents, others were screaming in rage. Some of the rage was directed at Seven. She did her best to ignore it.

"Their nanites have all been assimilated!" Seven shouted above the din.

"You think?" Paris shouted back. "So what do I need to do?"

"Hold still," Seven replied. Paris did so, and Seven laid her fist on his shoulder. Two black probes flicked out from the back of her hand and pierced his neck.

"Ow!" Paris yelped, but he didn't pull away.

Seven sent several hundred nanoprobes into Paris's bloodstream. They swam through the plasma, dodging the white blood cells that attempted to latch on to them and destroy them as intruders. Half a dozen failed and were crushed or dissolved. Most, however, made it into Paris's brain, where they encountered the Chiar nanites snuggled in among the cells. The Chiar nanites outnumbered Seven's probes by ten to one or more, but that was unimportant. Seven's nanoprobes each attached to a nanite and, with Borg ruthlessness and efficiency, assimilated it. Instantly everything the nanite "knew" was integrated into the nanoprobe's database, including the amnesia program. Seven next ordered the probes to destroy their respective nanites, and they obeyed. The loss of a few hundred neural cells would have no impact on Paris's brain. Just as one last probe was about to destroy its Chiar counterpart, a white blood cell engulfed it. The probe struggled, but was crushed and dissolved. The single Chiar nanite, now also a Borg nanoprobe, sat among its Chiar compatriots, quietly ignored by an immune system that had grown used to its presence.

Seven collected the rest of her nanoprobes, and the tubules slid back into her fist. Then she turned and let them flick out to touch the closest Chiar so she could steal a few of its assimilated nanites and make comparisons. The anger was still there, just not as intense. The captain's words, along with those of Boleer and Chakotay, had had an impact on her thoughts, but hadn't changed them entirely. While she couldn't condemn them to death or Borg assimilation, Seven still wanted to punish the Chiar, continue to think of them as demons. Seven forced the thoughts aside to check her tricorder and her nanoprobes.

A bit of data caught her eye. Seven stared at it, then suppressed a smile. So that was the solution. A simple projection, something that no one, including her, had considered. A weakness in Tom Paris's solution, and one she had no choice but to implement. Perhaps both anger and guilt could be satisfied.

"Now what?" Paris demanded, breaking into her thoughts. Seven blinked at him, bemused, then turned back to her tricorder.

"Now," she said, "I work and you wait."

Around them the Chiar continued to scream.

* * *

"One minute to weapons overload," Harry Kim announced.

"Mr. Tuvok," Janeway said, "fire."

Janeway watched the view on the screen as red beams lanced down to the ground, her face betraying none of her tension. Indeed, her face said that she had perfect confidence in her officer's abilities, that she wasn't in the least worried that he might make a mistake and set off a chain reaction that would destroy half the population of an alien continent. Not at all. A glance at Chakotay showed his expression full of certain, perfect confidence as well.

She bit down hard on the inside of her cheek.

The beams lanced down again, and again, and again as Tuvok's hands moved coolly over the panels before him. "The rhometric weapons systems are exposed," he said. Janeway tensed, waiting for word from Harry Kim.

"Thirty seconds to overload" was all Kim said. No mention of rhometric discharge. Janeway never thought she'd be pleased to hear a half-minute countdown to destruction.

All a matter of perspective, she decided.

"Activating microwave pulse," B'Elanna said.

Janeway watched the screen again. The invisible microwaves did not appear on the viewer, but Janeway thought she detected a slight ripple in the atmosphere.

"I'm still reading a steady increase in rhometric buildup," Kim said. "Fifteen seconds to discharge."

"Increase power, B'Elanna," Janeway said. She realized she was standing up but didn't remember rising.

B'Elanna didn't reply but adjusted her controls.

The atmospheric ripple below the ship grew more noticeable.

"Eight seconds," Kim said. "Seven . . . six . . ."

"I don't understand," B'Elanna muttered. Her fingers danced with increasing rapidity over the console. "It should be working."

"Three . . . two . . . wait." Kim checked his boards. "Rhometric radiation is decreasing . . . decreasing . . . we've achieved safe levels, Captain."

B'Elanna gave a heavy sigh and shut down the pulse. Chakotay, looking greatly relieved, tapped his combadge.

"Voyager to away team," he said. "The rhometric weapons are off-line."

"Acknowledged" came Paris's voice.

Janeway turned to B'Elanna, eyebrow raised. "What happened, Lieutenant? The deactivation should have been instantaneous."

"I'm not sure, Captain." B'Elanna checked half a dozen readings. Her eyes narrowed, then widened. A small laugh escaped her.

"What?" Chakotay said from his chair.

"The initial pulse did destroy the nanites," B'Elanna said with a rueful shake of her head. "It just took a while for the weapons systems to shut down."

"So all the suspense was for nothing?" Chakotay demanded.

"Well, it used up my adrenaline quotient for the month," B'Elanna replied, "so I wouldn't say it was for nothing."

"Any sign of activity from Tom and Seven?" Janeway asked.

"Not yet," Kim said.

"Damn," she muttered. "What could they be doing down there?"

Tom Paris peered over Seven's shoulder. "What are you doing in there?"

"I am reprogramming my nanoprobes to convert the amnesia program into a virus which I must then integrate into the assimilation protocols." Seven's fingers moved rapidly over her tricorder. "It is not as simple a task as you may have supposed. And it takes a certain amount of concentration. I would appreciate fewer distractions."

"Yeah, fine." Tom looked around the alley for something to do. They had moved back to their original beam-in location. Tom found the sight and sound of paralyzed, screaming Chiar unnerving. It didn't seem to bother Seven in the slightest, but Tom noticed she readily agreed that the alley would be a better place to work. The cloying smell of Chiar still invaded Tom's every breath, and the screams were still all too audible. He also had nothing to do but watch Seven work, a boring prospect at best.

And he couldn't keep thoughts of B'Elanna Torres out of his mind. The way she moved, the way she spoke. The firm decisiveness which combined with an odd impulsiveness and sometimes got her into trouble. And him, for that matter. There was a certain amount of physical risk being involved with a Klingon, even a half-Klingon. Like that morning he had decided to surprise her with breakfast in bed. Tom had startled B'Elanna awake, and she had lashed out and knocked him flat, dumping food all over his bare chest and stomach. She *did* apologize, of course, and then went on to make it up to him. Tom smiled at the memory. The bruise had been tricky to explain to—

Tom froze. A memory! He was *remembering* something. But the moment he realized this, it all began to slip away. Tom lunged for it, but it slid away from him like a trout in a river or a song from a dream. The harder he concentrated, the less he remembered. Frustration clenched his chest, and he had to force himself to relax. Maybe he was trying too hard. Maybe a more . . . Vulcan approach would work.

A sideways glance at Seven told him she was still busy at work. He sat carefully on the hard alley ground. Eyes closed, he tried to empty his mind.

And the Doctor would say, "That shouldn't be too hard for you, Mr. Paris," he thought. Was that a memory, too? Or had he just spent so much time in sickbay lately that he had gotten to know how the the Doctor would respond?

Don't think, he admonished himself. *Just let it come.*

B'Elanna. *Voyager.* Captain Janeway. Harry Kim. Black hair. Black and white world. Captain Proton. Whatsername, the blond secretary who screamed all the time. Queen Arachnia. Walking down a corridor explaining to Captain Janeway who Arachnia was and exactly why only Janeway could play her. It was the voice, really, though Tom would never have said so. No one else on board had the voice to pull off such a hilariously trite and campy role. Janeway hadn't ever admitted it, but Tom knew she had enjoyed slinking around Chaotica's laboratory, making silly goo-goo eyes at him and plotting his downfall all the—

It was another memory. Tom gasped, and his realization popped the whole thing like a soap bubble. Tom ground his teeth and tried again to empty his mind. B'Elanna. He wanted to remember more about B'Elanna. Sitting on the couch. The smell of popcorn. His arm around her. A western on the flat screen of the television. The tinny crack and pop of gunfire. Her hand toying with his hair. Dropping downward to stroke his neck, then his chest. Turning to—

"Lieutenant Paris," she said. "I have finished the programming."

Tom's eyes popped open. Seven of Nine was staring coolly down at him. "Your timing is less than perfect," he groused.

Seven raised an eyebrow but made no comment as Tom got to his feet. Her normally impassive face held a strange expression that Tom couldn't identify. Perhaps if he had his memory back, he'd be able to place it. Was it pride? A grim satisfaction? Tom couldn't tell. They strode quickly for the mouth of the alley. The skin-crawling screams of the paralyzed Chiar burst into full volume, and Tom found himself with his hands halfway up to ear level. Without fanfare, Seven approached the closest Chiar—a quivering, whimpering child—and extended her fist. The two tubules shot out, touched the Borg armor, and flicked back in.

"Now what?" Tom yelled over the noise.

Seven tapped her combadge. "Seven of Nine to *Voyager.* Our task is complete. Two to beam up."

The blue light and strange tingle started to surround them. The last thing Tom saw before the transporter pad appeared around him was the child's Borg armor. It split into a dozen pieces and fell away just as Tom and Seven disappeared.

"Seven of Nine and Lieutenant Paris are back on board," Chakotay said from his chair.

"Did it work, then?" Boleer asked in a hushed voice.

"What's the status down there, Mr. Kim?" Janeway asked.

Kim's fingers worked the board with grace and speed. "Seven's virus is spreading fast," he reported. "Tom was right. The Borg program keeps the nanites in constant subspace contact with each other. They're transmitting the amnesia virus to one another, and the assimilation process is actually helping to speed up the—what the hell?"

Janeway threw him a startled glance. Harry Kim wasn't one to swear, even mildly. "What is it, Mr. Kim?"

"One moment," Kim said unhelpfully. "Still a moment."

"Mr. Kim," Janeway warned.

"The nanites on Chi," Kim said. "They're not reverting to normal."

Boleer's head rose high above her cloak, and she made a slight hissing sound. A tiny spasm of tension ran up Janeway's spine. "Explain."

"He means the virus was successful," said Seven of Nine as she emerged from the turbolift with Tom Paris in tow.

"Nice to see you back in one piece, Seven," Chakotay said.

"Tom!" Boleer said. He smiled at her and crossed the bridge to touch her flank. "I am glad you are unharmed."

"So am I," he said.

"I'm still waiting for an explanation, Seven," Janeway said in a carefully neutral voice.

"It would be easier to show you than tell you, Captain," Seven replied, and Janeway got the sense she was quoting someone. Seven touched a panel and the main screen lit up with a view of Chi. As Seven worked the controls, the view swooped closer to the planet. One of the northern continents seemed to rush toward the ship. Janeway felt like she was skydiving. Finally the rushing picture resolved itself into a sky-high view of a city. Seven brought the focus in closer until Janeway could see streets and individual Chiar on them. Bits of Borg armor lay scattered up and down the street like the remnants of some massive vehicular collision. The Chiar themselves looked dazed and . . . different. It took Janeway a moment to realize they were all the same color—a pale, smooth brown. Was that their real skin? Or was it perhaps fur? Janeway shot Boleer a glance, trying and failing to remember what she had looked like without her cloak. The Chiar, meanwhile, wandered aimlessly along the streets and sidewalks looking like survivors of some sort of natural disaster.

"The results of the virus," Seven announced.

Janeway narrowed her eyes. Coming from anyone else, the comment would have sounded snide. "Seven," she said. "Explanation. Now."

"The virus caused amnesia, as requested," Seven

said. "That means all the Chiar nanites have, in essence, had their memories destroyed. It was the only way to stop the assimilation. All programs, including the Borg assimilation process, have been wiped."

Boleer gasped in understanding. "Oh. Oh dear me."

"In other words, they can't assimilate anything," Chakotay put in, voice hushed, "but they can't do anything else, either."

"Correct, Commander."

"That'll destroy their civilization," Kim said, obviously shocked.

"On the contrary," Tuvok said. "The Chiar nanites were used primarily for maintenance and upkeep, not storage. Computer data has not been destroyed, merely rendered difficult to access."

"Difficult to access," Boleer murmured. "Mr. Tuvok, you have a powerful gift for understatement."

"Commander Tuvok is correct," Seven put in. "The virus did not destroy the Chiar nanites. They can be salvaged and reprogrammed." At that, Janeway thought maybe she did detect some trace of regret in Seven's voice, but Seven moved forward. "It will only take time and cooperation, especially between the Goracar Alliance and the Ushek-Sherekti."

Boleer's head snapped around. "What?"

"How do you mean, Seven?" Chakotay asked.

"An Ushekti named Pek is, as far as I know, the most skilled Chiar at restarting deprogrammed nanites. He has only lacked resources. The Goracar Alliance has resources but lacks the skill. Perhaps this event will bring the two sides together."

Janeway stared at the viewscreen and the Chiar on

it. Already some of them had recovered from their daze and were moving to help some of the others. A vehicle moved jerkily up the street, as if the driver weren't quite sure what he was doing. A strange barking noise came from the part of the bridge where Tom and Boleer were standing. After a moment Janeway realized Boleer was laughing.

"They have become just like me," she chuffed. "Oh, what a day! And perhaps this will be our opportunity."

"Opportunity?" Tom said.

"Indeed, Tom Paris." Boleer held up her hands. "Do you know that most Chiar have never touched anything that did not contain nanites? Or built something without using nanites?"

"I have a certain idea," Seven said.

"I gave up my nanites to come on board this ship," Boleer said. "And at first it was frightening. Even when I was a thrall, I at least had my nanites with me. Here I was alone and naked, and do you know what happened to me? Nothing! I was perfectly fine. And I learned how to make a garment and how to make a clasp for it, and even more, I learned I find satisfaction in doing such things. Great satisfaction! I wonder how many other Chiar will feel the same way once they have the chance."

"I am surprised that more of the Ushekti do not feel as you do," Seven said.

"I am not at all surprised," Boleer said bluntly. "The Ushekti and Sherekti were prisoners with no hope and no good reason to try to better their lives because we did not believe they *could* be better. Now, without nanites, there is no way to enforce slavery, no way to keep an entire race in prison. We are all equal and we have hope once again."

Janeway smiled at her. "I think someone will need to show them this hope."

"I think so as well," Boleer said thoughtfully. "And politics has been part of my family for a long time."

"You said you might become a prophet," Tom said.

"Captain, we are being hailed," Tuvok said. "It is Secretary Nashi."

"Speaking of politics," Kim muttered.

"On screen."

Nashi appeared on the viewer. A long blue cloth covered her like a combination cloak and horse blanket. The transmission was full of static.

"Captain," Nashi said.

"Secretary," Janeway replied.

"Sister," Boleer said.

A moment of uncomfortable silence stretched across the bridge. Janeway looked at Secretary Nashi, the person who had stolen *Voyager* technology, kidnapped one of the crew, tortured her, and lied about it every step of the way. Janeway understood why she had done it, but that didn't make Janeway feel any better toward Nashi about any of it.

Finally, Nashi spoke. *"I am unsure whether to thank you or not, Captain,"* she said. *"I am assuming you and your crew are behind what has happened here. The strange virus is gone, but our nanites are no longer functional. Our machines work, but we must adjust them manually, and no one seems to know how to restart our nanites to aid us. If you wanted revenge, Captain, you have achieved it beautifully."*

Janeway hadn't wanted revenge, but something in Nashi's tone made a red anger rise. "The assimilation virus was the fault of your own people, Secretary," Janeway said through clenched teeth. "If you hadn't kidnapped Seven in the first place—"

"As you say," Nashi interrupted. *"I just wanted the chance to bid you goodbye."* She turned to Boleer. *"And I see you have allied yourself with the people who have destroyed us."*

"They have destroyed nothing, Nashi, and you fully are aware of this," Boleer said. "Our friends from the Federation Starship *Voyager* have liberated us instead."

"Liberated?" Nashi sputtered. *"How can you say—"*

"We have become so dependent on tiny machines that we have forgotten how to do things for ourselves," Boleer said. "This is a grand opportunity to learn again. It will take time, but we can make our nanites function again—the Ushekti Pek knows how—and in the meantime, there is much for us to relearn. I intend to see to that we learn it."

"We have little choice," Nashi admitted.

"Then we bid you goodbye, Secretary," Janeway said. "And good luck."

The screen went blank. Janeway took up her chair.

Boleer gave a heavy sigh, and her head drooped. "Do you think we can do it?" she said. "Can we work together?"

Janeway inclined her head with a small grin. "Work together? I expect to see you in the Alpha Quadrant. And speaking of which." She raised her voice. "Helm, set course for home. We'll drop off our guest with those books Mr. Neelix promised her and then on be on our way."

Tom looked up at Boleer, who was standing on the transporter with a small stack of computer padds. Crewman Marija was at her regular station behind the console, running diagnostics and otherwise trying to look busy and completely deaf while Tom and Boleer said their goodbyes.

"I'm glad we met," Tom was saying.

Boleer tossed her head back. "You cannot be—the only reason we met was because you had been sold into slavery."

"That's true"—Tom laughed—"but if I had to be enslaved, I'm glad you were in the household. And I have to tell you—your advice about B'Elanna was dead on."

"Then you are not so stupid as I thought, Tom Paris." She dipped her misshapen head down to rub her cheek against his. "I will miss you. I hope you and your spouse find your happiness again."

Tom grinned at her. "I suspect we will." He hesitated. "Boleer, I was wondering—"

"Why I didn't have the doctor fix my head?" She ducked once. "Because someone once told me that I was not ugly—I am merely unique. And looking unique is a good thing for someone who intends to lead her people along a new path. They will remember me more easily." Boleer brandished the pile of padds. "It is also a good way for a teacher to hold her students' attention."

"Then I wish you more luck." Tom stepped back and gestured at Marija. He waved as Boleer and her scarlet cloak vanished into blue light, then he nodded absently at Marija and left the transporter room.

There was one more thing he had to take care of.

The children laughed and shrieked and chased each other across the playground. Seven, in a clean jumpsuit and with her hair sternly forced back into its habitual blond helmet, watched them with keen gray eyes. After a moment the main doors whined open and shut behind her, though she didn't turn around.

"I thought I might find you here," Chakotay said.

Seven continued to watch the children. They were playing freeze tag again. "Because you feel you know me or because you checked with the computer?"

"Let's leave that a mystery," he said, and smiled.

In silence they watched the children play. After a while Seven felt the quiet was growing uncomfortable, and she was a little surprised she felt this way. She had never needed to fill a silence with inefficient, undesired chatter, though she recognized why other people did; it was a need to be social, a sense that silence indicated a lack of attention. Now she was feeling that very thing herself. Perhaps Chakotay would break the quiet. The silence grew heavier and harder to bear, and Chakotay failed to speak. All at once Seven found herself saying, "I don't know if Secretary Nashi was correct or not."

Chakotay arched an eyebrow. "If she was correct?"

"In her estimation that Captain Janeway—or rather I—deliberately destroyed the Chiar way of life."

Tenna tagged Mel, who froze in place. The minute none of the other children was looking, he unfroze and reentered the game, though no one had freed him. Seven pursed her lips.

"Do you think that's the case?" Chakotay asked.

"I do not know," Seven said. "I simply do not know. I have thought about it. I have had numerous conversations with the Doctor about human psychology, and although he has proven . . . less than effective in the past as a therapist, many of his views concur with the material I have read."

"And what have you read, Seven?"

The game continued. A girl tripped, staggered, and was instantly tagged. She froze awkwardly, tottering like a half-felled tree. A boy darted in to free her, but the child who was It tagged him as well. The halfway girl lost her balance and collapsed.

"Sometimes," Seven said, "sometimes the human subconscious moves in subtle ways. It wants something done, and it manipulates the conscious mind into doing it, perhaps by making a particular course of action seem like the only possibility."

"And you think that happened to you?"

"I do not know." More silence. Seven struggled not to fill it, but her mouth carried on without her. "I am wondering if there were other alternatives to the program I ran, other possibilities that I overlooked because I was angry at the Chiar who . . . bullied me and because part of me wanted to see them punished, even though my conscious mind knew the vast majority of the Chiar were undeserving of such treatment."

"You're feeling guilty, then," Chakotay observed.

"Perhaps."

Chakotay thought for a moment, then sat down on a nearby bench. "Seven, please sit down."

She was about to refuse when she noticed her legs were feeling shaky. Obeying would be a good way to cover this disconcerting development, and she did so.

"You remember when you first came on board *Voyager*," Chakotay said. It wasn't a question, but Seven nodded an affirmative anyway. "Did you know that I was dead set against having this crew work with the Borg in any capacity?"

Seven shook her head, wondering where this was leading.

"I definitely was," Chakotay said. "At one point when the captain was unconscious in sickbay and I was in command, I started to dissolve the alliance she had built with the Borg. I hated the idea of having an entire shuttlebay assimilated by the Borg, and I definitely didn't want you to be any part of this crew—definitely not as a speaker for the Collective."

Seven found Chakotay's words upsetting. Her stomach clenched and her heartbeat changed. "I was unaware that my presence makes you so uncomfortable," she said, beginning to rise. "Perhaps I should—"

Chakotay's hand flashed out and snagged her elbow. "That was a long time ago," he said. "And my feelings toward you have changed. Completely reversed, actually. You are a valued member of this crew. You've saved our bacon more than a few times. And you've become my friend."

Seven allowed him to pull her back down on the bench. She noticed that his hand lingered on her arm longer than was strictly necessary.

"I didn't tell you this to upset you," Chakotay continued. "I told you so you could understand something else. When the captain told me she wanted to pursue a Borg alliance, I tried as hard as I could to persuade her not to do it. I told her a story about a scorpion that stung a fox to death, even though that very act meant the scorpion, too, would die. The scorpion stung the fox because stinging was its nature."

"And you believed the Borg are—I am—like the scorpion," Seven said.

"I believe that *everyone* is like the scorpion, Seven. None of us can go against our nature. And that is the reason I told you all this." Chakotay looked her straight in the eye, and Seven found she couldn't look away. She didn't want to. "It would be against your nature to hurt an entire race, Seven. A scorpion has to sting, but you are not a scorpion. You are a good and fine person *by nature,* no matter what a bunch of bullies might do to you."

Something snapped inside Seven. Out of nowhere her eyes teared up and her vision blurred. She turned her head so Chakotay wouldn't see. In the distance she heard the ever-present shrieks and laughs of the holographic children. Some emotion gathered inside her and thickened her throat. The uncertainty she had been feeling melted away, leaving relief in its place.

"Seven?" Chakotay put a tentative hand on her shoulder. "Are you all right?"

"I am fine," Seven said. "I just—" She swallowed hard to regain control. "Your words meant more to me than I anticipated."

"You're welcome, then," he said, and stood up. "I'm supposed to be inspecting the warp core, so I guess I'd better actually show up. See you in the mess hall later?"

Abruptly Seven was both starving and exhausted, and she remembered she had neither eaten a full meal nor spent a full regeneration cycle since the Chiar had kidnapped her. "I need to regenerate," she said, "and then I definitely should eat. So yes—you will see me in the mess hall later."

Chakotay nodded goodbye and left the holodeck. Seven stood up and took another look around the playground. Exploring the pursuits and problems of childhood no longer held any appeal for her. Perhaps it was time to concentrate on adult behavior. And perhaps Chakotay would be willing to help her with that as well.

At that, Seven paused. What if he said no? Certainly he had said they were friends, and she found that more than pleasing. But what if he thought Seven harbored more . . . personal intentions toward him?

Did she?

Seven stared at a tree without really seeing it. Her feelings were confused. She liked Chakotay a great deal, and she looked forward to the possibility that they might be able to spend more time together. Was that what romantic feeling was about? Seven wasn't quite sure.

And what if she had feelings for him, but he didn't have them for her? That scenario held potential for great social discomfort, she knew. Or what if he *did* have romantic feelings for her? How was she supposed to show him she felt the same way? She had no real experience with such things, and she had learned the hard way that imitating someone else in these matters invariably led to disaster.

For a long moment Seven looked around the playground she had created, then she said, "Computer, end program and erase."

"Please confirm deletion."

"Confirmed."

The playground vanished, replaced by a blank hologrid. Seven thought for a moment. Then another wave of fatigue swept over her. She shook her head. "Computer, exit."

The holodeck doors whined open to let her leave.

Seven nodded and left. She would regenerate, and then consider an efficient plan for action.

Lieutenant B'Elanna Torres poked moodily at the stew on her mess hall food tray. She hated eating alone, had at one time been used to sharing meals with the other ex-Maquis on the ship. And after she and Tom had started dating and then been married, they had always eaten together. Now Tom refused to have anything to do with her, and the crewmen she used to eat with were either on different shifts or had simply fallen out of the habit of inviting the chief engineer to eat with them. So she ate alone.

And dammit, she was lonely for Tom. The anger she had felt toward him had lately passed into depression. She missed his merry blue eyes and gentle voice and even his smart-aleck remarks.

She speared an unidentifiable chunk of . . . meat? Vegetable? B'Elanna didn't care. Maybe it would be easier just to make a clean break of it—move into separate quarters again and dissolve their marriage. It would hurt like hell, but it'd be easier than being strung along day after day after day. Or would it? She would be in constant contact with him on *Voyager.* No way to avoid it on such a small ship. How would it feel, seeing him, working with him, knowing that he had loved her once, would still love her if not for—

A shadow fell across the table. B'Elanna looked up, expecting to see Neelix bent on trying to cheer her up. A sharp dismissal died on her tongue when she saw it was Tom. He was holding a food tray.

"Mind if I sit down?" he asked.

Staring, B'Elanna gestured mutely at the chair across the table from her. Tom slid into it. His metal tray scraped across the tabletop. B'Elanna realized her heart was pounding.

"I'm sorry I've been so rough on you lately," he said. "Even if I don't remember you, I could still have been—"

"It's all right," she said. "It's not your fault. Look, I've been thinking maybe we should"—her mouth went dry and her tongue felt as if it were coated with sawdust, but she forced herself to speak—"maybe we should get separate quarters or something until all this is sorted out."

Tom sat up straighter. "Is that what you want?"

"It's what's best for the situation," she said, firmly keeping the lump in her throat from cracking her voice.

"Well, if that's how you feel," he said.

B'Elanna looked down at her stew again and saw only a blurry mess. It took her a moment to realize it was because tears were gathering in her eyes.

"But," Tom continued, "I don't really want to move.

I mean, you're an . . . attractive woman, B'Elanna. I'm starting to see that now."

Her head snapped up. "What?"

"Boleer told me I was being stupid for avoiding you and taking out my anger on you. It took me a while to see how right she was. I'm really going to miss her."

"Uh . . ."

"Besides, the more I look at you, the more attractive you get." Tom reached across the table and touched the back of her hand. "Maybe I could learn to like brow ridges."

"Tom," she said, flustered, "I—"

"There you are, Lieutenant! You must be just bursting with the—ah!"

B'Elanna looked up sharply. Neelix, dressed in a bright hodgepodge of a tunic, was clapping Tom on the shoulder.

"Neelix," Tom said, "this isn't the time for—"

Neelix quickly took his hand back. "Of course. Pardon me. I'm just glad that it's all worked out."

"What are you talking about?" B'Elanna demanded.

"Tom's memory," Neelix said, still perplexed. "Seven said she had neutralized that Chiar program as well . . . on the planet . . ." He faltered. "Didn't she?"

B'Elanna snatched her hand away from Tom, who wore a weak, uncertain grin.

"Surprise?" he said.

"It was a *trick?*" she yelled. "This whole thing was a *trick?*"

"I just wanted to see if you—" Tom began, but B'Elanna reached across the table and shoved him hard. With a grunt of surprise, Tom went over backward and landed flat on his back. B'Elanna pounced on him and grabbed his face between both hands, heedless of the stares she garnered from the other crewmen. Neelix gaped.

"You're going to pay for that, Tommy-boy," she hissed.

"B'Elanna," Tom gasped, "B'Elanna, it was just—"

Then she kissed him. Hard.

Look for STAR TREK fiction from Pocket Books

Star Trek®

Star Trek: Deep Space Nine®

Star Trek: Voyager®

Star Trek®: Stargazer

Star Trek®: Starfleet Corps of Engineers (eBooks)

Star Trek®: Invasion!

Star Trek®: Dark Passions

#1 • Susan Wright
#2 • Susan Wright

Star Trek® Omnibus Editions

Invasion! Omnibus • various
Day of Honor Omnibus • various
The Captain's Table Omnibus • various
Star Trek: Odyssey • William Shatner with Judith and Garfield Reeves-
 Stevens
Millennium Omnibus • Judith and Garfield Reeves-Stevens
Starfleet: Year One • Michael Jan Friedman

Other Star Trek® Fiction

Legends of the Ferengi • Ira Steven Behr & Robert Hewitt Wolfe
Strange New Worlds, vol. I, II, III, IV, and V • Dean Wesley Smith, ed.
Adventures in Time and Space • Mary P. Taylor, ed.
Captain Proton: Defender of the Earth • D.W. "Prof" Smith
New Worlds, New Civilizations • Michael Jan Friedman
The Lives of Dax • Marco Palmieri, ed.
The Klingon Hamlet • Wil'yam Shex'pir
Enterprise Logs • Carol Greenburg, ed.
Amazing Stories Anthology • various